Praise for TWO CITIES

"Masterly . . . sex, violence, the rage against injustice, and the vicissitudes of love, these elements alone would make a good novel. But *Two Cities* goes beyond the conventions of a simple love story . . . it is as enjoyable as it is important . . . capturing images of everyday surroundings to reveal the crimes and passions of our world."
— **Walter Mosley,** *New York Times Book Review*

"His sentences are rapid-fire meteor showers of language, history, and urban landscape." — *Los Angeles Times*

"A writer who shows you things you would never have seen without him; his prose at once bears the weight of a brutal, complex legacy and exults in a sort of weightlessness." — *The New Yorker*

"Captivating . . . In its masterful pages, the two-time PEN/Faulkner Award winner explores the inner and outer selves of three characters caught between rage and redemption." — *Philadelphia Inquirer*

"A mix of gritty realism and dreamlike fantasy to explore the saving graces of love and hope." — *People*

"One of the most original, and accomplished, of modern American novelists." — *Kirkus Reviews*

"A heart-wringing story, masterfully told, and Exhibit A of the certainty that John Wideman is a worthy successor of the giants — Richard Wright, Ralph Ellison, and others — upon whose shoulders he stands."
— *Cleveland Plain Dealer*

"A top-flight effort. *Two Cities* is a good place to visit."
— *Chicago Sun-Times*

"Wideman always brings his startling intellect to the table, his voluminous vocabulary, his lyrical language." — *Atlanta Journal-Constitution*

"The book has an unrelenting power that comes from its savvy exploration of love, loss, forgiveness." — *Essence*

"Wideman is unquestionably one of our finest novelists . . . Wideman's success depends equally on his sensitivity to language and his understanding of the valuable dislocations created by his unique approach to fiction-making." — **Clarence Major, *Washington Post***

"A series of searing and moving scenes framed by a narrative of love's risks . . . What it does is point to the necessary and continuing efforts at small acts of vigilant caring." — ***Chicago Tribune***

"This dreamlike blend of unsparing realism and charged fantasy carries the reader along a climaxed vision of cathartic force and clarity." — ***Publishers Weekly***

"A layered and complex love affair that defies the conventional notions of time and space." — ***Philadelphia Weekly***

"Searing . . . eloquent." — ***Pittsburgh Post-Gazette***

"A writer of an especially musical quality whose prose is a harmonic blending of high and low, of the music of the streets and the music of the spheres." — ***New York Times***

"Two beautiful love stories in one novel . . . a masterpiece of verve and feeling . . . His writing, like Toni Morrison's, is so pure and convincing that he can break the rules of classical storytelling, even invent some new ones." — ***Boston Sunday Globe***

"When the last page is turned, there is more than a sense of plot, there is a sense of intimacy with the characters. Wise and beautiful." — ***Rocky Mountain News***

"Powerful, poetic . . . Wideman mirrors communities and individuals in crisis, offering them a respite from their sorrows in the realm of peaceful and compassionate reflection." — ***San Francisco Chronicle***

TWO CITIES

Books by John Edgar Wideman

TWO CITIES

John Edgar Wideman

A Mariner Book

HOUGHTON MIFFLIN COMPANY

BOSTON • NEW YORK

First Mariner Books edition 1999

Copyright © 1998 by John Edgar Wideman
ALL RIGHTS RESERVED

*For information about permission to reproduce selections from
this book, write to Permissions, Houghton Mifflin Company,
215 Park Avenue South, New York, New York 10003.*

Library of Congress Cataloging-in-Publication Data
Wideman, John Edgar.
  Two cities / John Edgar Wideman.
    p.   cm.
  ISBN 0-395-85730-9
  ISBN 0-618-00185-9 *(pbk)*
  1. Afro-Americans—Pennsylvania—Pittsburgh—
Fiction. 2. Afro-Americans—Pennsylvania—
Philadelphia—Fiction. I. Title.
PS3573.I26T9 1998
813'.54—dc21 98-22915 CIP

Printed in the United States of America

Book design by Robert Overholtzer

QUM 10 9 8 7 6 5 4 3 2 1

OMAR WIDEMAN
1971–1992

———

In Memoriam

We didn't try hard enough.

CONTENTS

MISSING JOHN AFRICA

H E READ the definition again: 1. A *small park or an institution in which living animals are kept and usually exhibited to the public. Also called zoological garden.* 2. *Slang* — A *place or situation marked by confusion or disorder. The bus station is a zoo on Fridays.* Sipped the definition. Let the taste and smell of it seep slowly inside him, like coffee after the first hot gulp in the morning at the diner. Uh-huh. The words tell him what he supposed they would. Not too many words. Not too few. Uh-huh. He liked it like that. When words led him into a familiar place, as if they'd shared all along the secret of what he was looking for and had waited patiently for him to find them. A place in his mind matching a place the words helped him enter. Zoo was stink, roars, steel cages, walls of glass, the kept, keepers, the watchers. Many times and places and things, too many to hold in his mind but also always zoo, what the words of the definition claimed, and it was nice to find zoo waiting, available in these pages, his and not his, this other place black and white where words and meaning are clean as a baby's behind even when the diaper's messy.

Before they built the high-rise dormitories for the tech college you could walk north from Powelton Village to the zoo or east to the art museum and not be bothered. No scared, bundled-up white kids in winter or half-naked white kids in summer, swarming, blocking your way, stealing your attention, ignoring you. The ones who look like they want to shoot you or the ones who want to follow you home. Ones who look at you with their mouths open like they can't make up their minds whether you are walking past or not, whether they love you or hate you or just wasting their precious young time acting dumb and foolish about a ghost not really there, a black man walking through that hive of buildings where students live, a black man with no business except passing through where he's not supposed to be anyway. Ones who turn away quickly like they're seeing the nasty evidence of something wrong they did the night before and don't hardly need to be reminded of it first thing on a new morning.

Best to go through there in packs like the young boys. Harder to hassle more than one. John Africa his partner in the early evening and early morning strolling through the students' turf. *Taint* time, when daylight's rising or falling, the half-light of dawn or dusk. Taint day and taint night, John Africa said. You know, like that honey spot down there between a woman's thighs, taint pussy and taint asshole, it's just taint, he said. Ummmm. Ummmm. You a taint man, my friend. Dog for it myself. Once upon a time when I was more dog than man. Dog for that sweet, sweet taint. Know what I'm saying. When the sun's coming up and when the sun's going down. Taint one time nor tother. It's taint.

Before the new dorms and squall of eyes, when he had walked with John Africa to the zoo or the museum, the row houses of the neighborhood stopped and then there had been a whole bunch of nothing at the edges of the Village. Vacant lots, abandoned warehouses, long, low sheds like airplane hangars, barbed-wire-topped

Cyclone fences guarding acres of rusting junk. A no-man's-land shortcut to cross the river into center city by way of the Spring Garden Street Bridge. Lots of trucks, occasional cars bumping through a maze of dead, dead-ending streets and alleys. He'd always wondered what cargo the trucks hauled. Everything hidden in containers, square corners so they stacked and fit the square corners of the trailer trucks. Boxes inside of boxes inside of boxes. Trailers without cabs, hitchhiking on flatcars that pass on the railroad tracks beneath them when he used to stand with John Africa on the Spring Garden Street Bridge at taint time.

After the high-sided trestle section of the bridge whose steel walls schoolkids will decorate years later with hot-colored paintings of a city where the kids wished they lived, he and John Africa would stop, lean on the railing, and the river'd be there silent below them. You could depend on it. River running. Depend on it sliding silently under the bridge. Wouldn't be a bridge, would it, without something under it that needed to be crossed over. You check to make sure, anyway. A quick glance as you lean on the railing. Behind you the bridge sounds like it's coming apart. A truck strikes the steel plates the city lays instead of fixing the bridge the way they should fix it once and for all. Patch. Patch. Patches on the patches like everything else in the Village. Shake, rattle, and roll. Shake, rattle, and roll. Then the rhyming line about can't do nothing to save your soul, your doggone soul.

John Africa gone but not yet. Stay a while longer, my friend, while I check to make sure the Schuylkill's still under us. Sky spreads dull morning gray or the gray of smoggy nightfall. Behind me an unseen trailer-truck-size chunk of sky breaks away, slams into a steel plate all sixteen wheels spinning. An invisible world up there in the sky, shaky as this one, and huge pieces of it can rip loose and fall and buckle your world and race away before you know what's hit you. You don't need to turn around to believe the hole in the sky, the groaning steel. You see in the gray churning above your head how such a thing could happen.

Elbows on the rail, John Africa next to you, close enough to touch, his back against the railing so you're facing him but his face a blur, a hooded shadow in a mirror in a dark room and you know he's tired, know he's had enough of this world, but you say, Stay a while, I need to talk to you a while this morning, old partner — elbows holding you up as you gaze into the grayness, thick in the air surrounding you, the air from which John Africa's features refuse to detach themselves and become his face again.

Anything could be in the grayness. Truck-size swimming through it happy as a whale till it crashes through a rotten spot and lands rattling and rolling behind you. The bridge shivers. Ice-cube-cold water she sprays on your hot skin when she dashes from the lake and shakes her snakes of black hair dry. Don't know whether to holler or smile. Know it makes you want to do something back to her so she'll holler and laugh and want to do something worth hollering and smiling about back to you.

Anything could break loose from the sky, everything's up there, this city and all the cities it can't be, beyond the layers of gray, of blue, all the colors of sunset and sunrise, all the black tunnels, the plunging, spinning, giddy wheels of light.

Sometimes, without any reason either of you could say, you'd stop with John Africa at the middle of the bridge, pinned there till something gets you moving again. Sets you free. A train rumbling below on the tracks. A plane so high and quiet you wonder what causes you to gaze up and find the twin white wakes you expected. A cop car scoping you out. Don't need to turn around to see it's a cop car. When it slows down, the weight of its hesitation sucks away the ground on which you're standing. Weight of what the cops are thinking as they decide to hassle you or not nearly buckles the bridge. If they say you are in the wrong place, you're in the wrong place. Doesn't matter how old and harmless you are, if they want to teach a lesson you'll never forget, the ground opens up, people fall through and keep on falling and who knows where you'll land.

Wings. Pages 2078 and 2079 of the dictionary spread before him like wings. Two wings to hide your face. Can't keep his eyes from wandering. *Zone, zombie, zodiac* in the first column. *Zoroaster, zucchini* across the way. *Zoogeography* — he ought to know the meaning of this strange-looking word printed in bold black letters at the top of 2079. He separates zoogeography into two parts and each part is familiar. Zoo. Geography. He understands both words pushed together in this new word, but *zoogeography* puzzles him unless he breaks it down into two parts and then he's back where he started so he reads the definition. *The biological study of the geographic distribution of animals, especially the causes and effects of such distribution.*

Every word a story and he could waste more time than he could afford chasing after each one. Was it curiosity or exhaustion killed the cat. John Africa would know. Wink. Flash the cat's smile that says, Whatever took me away from here, my friend, satisfaction's gonna bring me back.

The last word on the open pages of the dictionary, *Zugunruhe.* Just peek at it. Quick peek at this odd word and no more, he promises himself. A noun — *the migratory drive. . .*

Instead of turning the page to undress more of the story, he flops the big book closed. What he needs this morning's not in the dictionary. He's trying to recall a particular incident, a specific sky, the two of them halting on the bridge, a cop car behind his back, slowing down. Recall the river exactly as it was that day, that moment like no other before or since. If he concentrates, will he see John Africa's face, hear his voice. Is there some magic phrase *alakazam, Open Sesame* that would bring back the moment or is he groping in a bin in the Salvation Army secondhand store, rummaging through cast-off rags good for nothing for anybody anymore.

> *Chinaman, Chinaman*
> *Sitting on a fence*
> *Trying to make a dollar*
> *Out of fifteen cents.*

What had John Africa said that day on the bridge. Were his words, whatever they might have been, getting him ready for this moment, this morning. John Africa gone, words spoken a year ago on a bridge gone with him. Words lost in a space he thought was behind him, finished, except now, in the space opening before him, he needs John Africa's voice to return. If the memory creeps back, could the dead rise. John Africa's dead, the dead of the gray, dying city.

Sometimes things seem crystal clear as long as he studies each part, makes his peace with it. Another story altogether when he tries to string parts together. Doesn't matter how familiar this moment or that moment might be. He is lost, lost trying to figure out the space where they are supposed to connect. Strange but true. He's lived long enough to gather plenty of pieces of the puzzle, long enough to know he'll never find a way to fit them together.

Everything connects; nothing connects. Two simple truths and each made perfect sense on its own but together they mystified him. Once upon a time he'd stood on the Spring Garden Street Bridge with John Africa. Today he's in another city, alone in a room on Cassina Way. Then and now. Two cities. He thinks he understands each in its turn, but now. Now. No words for what separates and connects these moments. He couldn't understand, could only witness. And the arc of his witness explained nothing, brought him no closer to solving the puzzle, the truth of a moment lived then, truth of another moment lived now, and him always muddling somewhere in between, becoming a stranger to himself, a taint man sure enough.

Poor John Africa dead. They say the cops never found his head. Morning after the fire, and cinders still hot, smoke still stinging the air and city workers clearing away the mess of 6221 Osage Avenue with bulldozers and cranes they say scooping up big heaps of burned trash to haul to the dump and the arm of a crane they say swinging through the air with a hand or leg or something dangling out the steel claw and the operator slowed the machine they say cranked down the bucket and found enough body parts mixed up in the ashes to say it was a dead man. Say it was John Africa.

His walking and talking buddy dead, and still John Africa the one this morning, just like he was the one the day the news hit the radio, John Africa the one he needed to ask what happened. What did you do, my friend. Why'd they do what they did to you.

What kind of world is this, John Africa? Homes bombed. Women and children roasted alive. A man shot, burned, chopped to pieces, swinging through the air in a bucket.

John Africa would understand. John Africa would have something to say about it. Something sensible to help get past it or make sure it didn't happen again. Didn't matter John Africa was the one crumpled up in the steel fist. John Africa would understand and say what we had to do next.

Motherfuckers never found my head, did they. Bucket of bones and cracklings. Coulda been anybody. Coulda been Kentucky Fried Chicken. Viva Zapata, motherfuckers. You remember that movie, Mr. Mallory. The one with Marlon Brando on his pretty white stallion and the soldiers thought they shot the shit out of him, *rat-tat-tat-boom*, but that horse rears up Hi-ho Silver and Zapata gallops off to the mountains. The gingerbread man. Catch me if you can, motherfuckers. Hi-ho Silver.

They stand on the bridge discussing the terrible fire. John Africa and his Move family, men, women, and children incinerated, their ashes shoveled up, bagged, trucked to the dump, tossed in the trash. He's staring into a gray sky waiting to hear what else John Africa thinks about it all. This is the time he wants back. Why can't they go back, stop the massacre before it starts. Warn John Africa. Prepare him. For what hasn't happened yet. And has. He wants John Africa's help. Words to make sense of no sense. Remembers the surprise of a train all yellow diesel locomotives back to back, passing on the tracks below them. A tattoo of soot from the bridge on his fingers, soot red as blood he tried to wipe off on the railing where it came from. You move on, you have to move on. Living your life. *Move*. Finding space for it, space for the things you believe you understand and space for what you'll never understand. Space like this gray sky with room for everything.

On the bridge the sky wasn't only up. It loomed behind him, beside him, stealing John Africa's space. Sky spread in front of him, a dirty curtain you peer through, monkey in the zoo, at the tall buildings downtown. Sky under your feet, on your shirt, between your toes. Sky in the river below dyed sky gray. Everywhere and nowhere. You poke a finger through it. It pokes its finger through you. Bulldozers and cranes and dump trucks, the scorched, gouged earth could rumble out of the grayness, crush you, bury you, grind your bones to ash under clanking steel treads.

He's searching for John Africa's soothing voice, his good sense. A moment of clarity that perhaps never happened, not then, not now, but he needs it, aches for it, and since he's not a god and can't make his wishes come true, he must believe the moment happened yesterday or years ago or soon in the sweet by-and-by. Somewhere in his life running like the gray Schuylkill always runs there had to be a moment shaped as it would need to be shaped to fit what he's looking for.

Dogman. He was never quite comfortable calling John Africa Dogman. Dogman a name for some half-and-half Hollywood werewolf creature or a sorry soul so hound-dog ugly the only way you can get past the ugliness is to go ahead and say it out loud. Admit the truth of what you see, say what you both can't help thinking when you bump into him on the street, say it so it's out of the way, give the ugliness a name, *Dogman*, and maybe that's that, we don't need to bother with it anymore.

Dogman's not my name, Mr. Mallory. It's what I do. People call me Dogman because they see me walking dogs every day. Whole army of dogs. So people say, Here comes the Dogman. Be a whole nother dog of a different color if they said, Here comes Africa. Here comes me. Nobody ain't ready to say that so it's Dogman. Here come the Dogman.

Must have been how everybody once upon a time got names. You know. People see what you do and say it and it sticks. Carpenter. Painter. Shoemaker. Hunter. Taylor. Walker. See you handling something or around something that has to do with your work.

Stone. Wood. Gold. Or see you following around behind your daddy. There goes John's son. Jack's son.

People give me a little change to walk their dogs. Do more running than walking. Poor animals locked up most the time. Penned up in the house or on a chain in the yard. They forget what running is. I help them remember. Ain't work for me, really. Be running our dogs every morning anyway. Just do a couple extra shifts. Keeps me in good shape. Keeps the dogs from whining and fretting all day. Somebody ought to come by the Village and run some these folks. Know what I mean. Let em romp loose in the park a couple hours every day. Guarantee you it be a lot nicer around here.

All us in the Movement trains hard. Men, women, and kids. We put in hard time training. Be in the park early while most everybody else asleep. Crack of dawn we're stretching and running, doing our yoga and hand-to-hand combat. We getting ready for the struggle. Ready for whatever it takes. Pregnant women. Babies. Everybody exercises. Everybody up and out at first light, rain or shine.

He watches John Africa fade into the grayness, the grayness give up John Africa again. When you burn hard, strong bodies, does the smoke smell sweeter than flabby bodies smoking.

He remembers being a kid and spitting in a rain river rushing along the curb. Throwing a popsicle stick in and wondering where it goes. Part of him goes with it, rides and rides. Another part stands there wondering where things end up, wondering how long it takes and what you'd see along the way.

He snatches Dogman, who's light as a feather now, from the walkway of the bridge. Tosses him over the bloody rail and Dogman hits without a splash, laid out gentle in the water on his back with almost a smile on his face the way they would have fixed him in a funeral parlor if they'd found his head and tucked the satin winding sheet up under his chin like they did that poor boy Emmett Till so it looked like his head was still attached to the rest of him when you pass by the casket. Old Dogman looks good, a mourner whispers. Yes he does, another answers. Looks just like he's sleeping. Uh-huh. Napping peaceful as a baby when he lands in the water light as a feather and starts floating with the current, the slow pull of the river leaving here, going somewhere else who knows where.

You call after him. Yelling a name after him that's different because you never did like Dogman even though everybody called him that and he didn't seem to mind. You had a different name for him you never said aloud. Not John Africa. A secret, private name for the man you're missing this morning and you shout it now in the thought you are thinking of him being carried away by the Schuylkill, the thought that ends with you saying to yourself it doesn't matter, it's too late now, he can't hear me and even if he could I can't go where he's going even if I jumped in the river after him. Your secret name for him will always be an unspoken name, the name you never said aloud can't catch Dogman either.

Not the gray sky of a rainy day. It's everyday gray that may or may not lighten, may or may not break up and lift. This gray ain't weather. City don't have weather, John Africa said. City just does shit to you. Pisses on you. Or flash-freezes your nuts. Or microwaves your behind. City gray's like walking around with cotton balls stuck up in your ears, eyes, nose. Sooner or later they'll drop out and city pours in and then you're gone.

People miss weather, John Africa said. Running to the suburbs to find it, but weather ain't out there neither. Got to get far away to the real country. Open country. No houses, no people. Where you got sky and ground, running water, trees and seasons. Weather ain't a hophead mugger out there.

They're coming more often. These strange, dizzy pauses in the middle of what he's supposed to be doing, brushing his teeth, strolling across a bridge. Maybe he doesn't have to lose his friend after all. Maybe these pauses a chance for John Africa to slide beside him again, real as the memory. A choice, an offer. Just take one teensy giant step over to John Africa's side. You're dizzy because you're in two places at once or too many places and maybe it's your own fault you're stuck here where you are and he isn't. The work your body does, putting one foot in front of the other, locating a safe spot to plant the raised foot, the simple business of not bumping into a chair when you cross a room, or going through the openness of a door without bramming your shoulder, all that easy work you usually manage without a conscious thought bogs down, becomes hard, confused, treacherous. The map in your head, your hands, the million pictures your eyes snap to guide your feet and ears and lungs are blurred. Ten maps at once or no map. One shoe sinks into the ooze of a swamp, the other skids on ice. In your face a hot desert wind shrieks. Don't know whether you're running or standing still.

When you hear him, feel him behind you, beside you, when you remember how simple it would be for things to be different, you see a world flowing on, flowing on with him in it and you in it, no fire, no clanking machines ladling the dead from one pit into another, when you realize how easy it would be, how hungry you are to speak with him in another world which could be this one except it isn't, you lose your bearings, twist like a fish on the end of a hook.

Your hands shake, you lose your balance, you're short of breath. Two cities, two places at once. Is the bridge coming apart. Will this wave of dizziness pass. Maybe dizziness and helplessness are not momentary failures of your body. Maybe truth's riding you. Truth's sudden weight, sudden absence. You pause because trouble's not only inside your body, it's outside. No up, no down. No near, no far. Your body failing you not because it's getting things wrong. At last, at last it's beginning to get things right. Say yes to it. Say yes. Let go.

At one end of the bridge, where 34th Street curves into Spring Garden, the crumbling, potholed asphalt is reinforced with steel plates. A bread van in a hurry explodes the morning stillness, its wheels jackhammers jigging across metal patches. He stares at the wake of silence that spreads behind the vanishing truck.

Will silence repair the bridge, restore the spot about two thirds of the way across where solid steel sides end and the railing you lean on with John Africa to see over begins. If the river stopped, if it became still and clear as a rain puddle, could you throw in a pebble, would the mirror shatter, would ripples skim across the surface of the water, ending one scene, forming another, one circle climbing out from another, chasing the other, chasing itself.

DANCING AT EDGAR'S

INSIDE HER DOOR, standing aside to let her slide by and lead, ducking his head at the entrance as if he's in a bumpy-roofed cave, not somebody's home, he finds himself in a house he might have lived in once, a house of stories told before he was born, his mother's mother's house where he was dead, then a baby spoiled in women's soft arms, then a kid wild with fear of the dark after his grandfather had joined the drooly dead and lurked in the shadows with them. She is whispering, making noise so he won't make noise, shushing him as if she thinks he might have something to say to this familiar, easeless darkness closing around him, the stale smells trapped inside old walls, trapped since he was a boy because he recognizes them, could name them, claim them. Has anything changed in all the years since the last time he woke up here in the dark, his little brother asleep beside him in the bed snoring, pliffing sneaky farts that walk the air like serial killers knife in hand looking for somebody to stab. She nudges him up steps. His hand finds the rail that's been waiting since the last time, forty years holding a familiar shape his fingers close around.

He's trying to recall the arrangement of rooms, who slept where, what went on in each closet-sized space. You used to be able to see the icebox at the far end of the house when you came in the front door, its square, bare white shoulders and the edge of the bandy-legged stove, oven side white too, glowing in the darkness, though he couldn't remember dark thick as this, this pitch-black box in which someone besides her must be living if a bar of yellow under the bottom of a door is a sign of life, and snoring, and her shushing him.

He thinks his eyes are beginning to adjust to the darkness of the upstairs hallway, picking out shapes, darker against the darkness, a map he trusts because he's been here before, or in a place very much like this, but forms shift, he slips through what seemed to be a solid black wall blocking his path. Things he used to bump into or stumble over wouldn't still be here, would they. None of his toys on the floor, no wobbly rack downstairs piled with coats, no chest where his grandmother stored sheets, towels, and blankets in mothballs. No cardboard cartons of comic books. No boots at the bottom of the hallway steps where his grandfather sat each evening and pulled them off on his way to the kitchen. Workboots crusty and untied, waiting untouched, waiting because his grandmother said they must be there when his grandfather returns from the dead to lace them on again.

The city had probably gutted and remodeled the row houses on Cassina a long time ago. Nothing the way it once was. He swallows a biley belch. An edge of her flames, catching light leaking under a closed door. The old days gutted and skinned and nothing left but ghosts who were never here anyway except in the mind of the silly kid he used to be.

Honey, you're getting to be too big a boy to need a light. Light just keeps you awake. Why don't you try falling to sleep without it tonight.

Is some other scaredy-cat boy hiding in this lighted room at the end of the hall. His body stiff in a corner of the bed, light dragged like a blanket over his head.

What was he thinking then. And what the fuck's he doing here now, too drunk, dick too hard to care. Grown man jittery as a scaredy-cat boy. Creeping in some strange woman's house young enough to be his daughter.

Ought to be ashamed of yourself. When you going to grow up, boy. Wake your little brother one more time and that darned flashlight's coming out of here.

When she opens the door he's blinded, then sees why he's been tripping over himself, knocking good sense the hell out the way to get here. A smallish woman in a very short green dress. Skinny almost, neat, slim shoulders but that bubble-butt and something plumping out the dress's plain front. Around eleven when she'd cruised into Edgar's, sat on a stool at the bar, crossed those fine, skinny legs. One hour thinking about it, drinking about it, peeking, holding his ground, not looking away when she'd finally caught his eyes resting on her and then he got up and planted his elbow on the bar, close enough to her stool to smell her perfume, the bourbon she'd been knocking back. Smooth brown skin under the crisscross straps of the dress's cut-out back. A high collar in front so her smallish, pretty head a flower on a stem.

Jones. Robert Jones, miss.

And what do your friends call you, Mr. Jones. Robert. Bobby. Rob.

Her name only halfway heard above the perfume, those eyes. Enough to know it's a different-sounding name and he hopes she'll say it again soon and he'll get it straight next time and never, never forget.

Then she says, Yes. Why not. Sure I'd like to dance. And they danced three times to the same slow drag last jam of the night Edgar let somebody keep on playing past closing time. On the weekends a deejay but it's Thursday so quarters if you want music and somebody did and Edgar must be in a good mood he lets a fellow pump in another coin. Edgar's old-timey jukebox with mostly old-timey jams. *Edgar where you find that ancient shit.* Edgar his age plus or minus a few years. Kept his box loaded with stuff from back in the day when they were teenagers running the streets, Dells, Spaniels, Imperials, Five Royales, Five Satins, Louis Berry, the Diablos.

Edgar, my man, why don't you leave them dusty disks alone, man. Cop you some new tunes. Pull some foxy young girls in this antique motherfucker for a change.

And just what would you do, brother, if pretty young things started flocking round.

Same thing he do now with all us pretty women already in here. Buy nobody but his own sorry self a drink. Drink it. Lay his bald head on the bar and nod off.

Edgar had let the slow song go again. Then one last time. And she's sleepier in his arms each play. A small bundle of bones barely moving, the surprising fullness of her bosom snuggled hot against his belly, his arms draped over her shoulders, hugging her closer and closer, his wrists crossed, dangling so her hips as they sway to the music brush his fingertips.

Newish song. Old doo-wop a capella style. Big hit by a big new group out of Philly. He knew that, you couldn't help knowing it if you watched TV, listened to the radio. If he'd ever known the song's name, he'd forgotten it. Didn't need to know its name to know he'd hear it again, be humming it to himself a long time, caught in the warm, soft melt of it if he followed her into the bright room off the hall she'd turned into.

Oh baby. Oh. Oh. Wasn't a matter of her saying yes or no. Show was over the second time the song started up and they hadn't let go after the first time.

A small cut-glass lamp with a pleated shade on a night table beside her bed had painted the yellow stripe on the floor at the end of the upstairs hall, had blinded him when she opened the door. The bed empty. No scared boy hiding under the covers. She tilts the lampshade and light arcs backward on the wall behind the bed, lifting shadows, clearing space for the dark to press in with him as he enters.

Shut it, baby. He turns for the door. His fist closes around the knob. He pushes, twists to seal the door quietly in its frame. The click of the lock engaging, click of the lamp she turns off are one sound. Where she'd been standing, smiling, pretty woman in a little girl's green dress, he could see nothing. His heart stops. He doesn't move till he hears a zipper, the scuffle of shimmery green dress riding up her body, over her head, the weightless sigh of it landing at her feet.

Somebody wakes up first. Maybe him needing to pee out all the booze. He doesn't want to move, counts shots of V.O., Iron City nips, groans inside when he loses track. Too many is how many, fool, his bladder squeals. Or maybe it's her awake first, rolling over, hip bumping his, wanting him gone or wanting that syrupy number to play again. Both awake when she pops up. Whoa, he thinks. Anybody moving that fast first thing in the morning hurts his bones just to think about it. Her bare feet pittapat across the bare floor. A long, sizzling piss. Toilet flushing and run, runs. She hits the bed again like somebody had jacked her up and tossed her. His stomach bounces. Damn, girl. What's wrong, baby. Where's the bathroom. You'll see it. Left the door open and light on. Knew you wouldn't be far behind me. How you know all that. Heard you gritting your teeth over there. Had to go bad, but I didn't want to wake you up. Thank you, sir. I like a considerate man. Bathroom's all yours now. Go on. Don't want you considerating all in my bed.

He could just about touch the bathroom's four walls from where he stood over the toilet bowl. A little lean and stretch for the furthest wall on the far side of the tub. No shelves or counters. A plastic brush, comb, and hand mirror crowd the toilet back. Plastic shower curtain with sailboats. Plastic bottles lined up on the tub's end. One rack with a yellow towel draped over it. Matching washcloth plastered stiff to the tub's lip. No signs she didn't live here alone, but no room for nothing of nobody else's if she didn't. In the corner behind his shoulder a waist-high straw hamper overflowing with dirty clothes he didn't notice till he turns to leave. Dirty clothes and he hadn't thought about walking around naked in a stranger's house till he saw them and none of them his.

Funny thing is how you spot a woman and that pussy meter starts to beeping, beep-beep-beep a mile a minute and she looks so good you'd pimp your grandma's booty just to peek at what this woman's got under her clothes. Next thing you know she's lying in the bed butt-naked next to you and you crawl out to take a piss and don't even look back over your shoulder. Everything in the world you thought you wanted and there she is all her glory spread out beside you and not only don't you reach out and touch her, you don't even so much as take a look. Matter of fact some other woman crosses your mind on the way to the toilet and your dick got the nerve to start thinking about getting hard behind the one you ain't with.

No big thing, bro. Nothing worth worrying your mind about anyway cause nothing you can do. It's the dog in you. All men got the dog. Women know. Men mize well go on and fess up.

Guess you some kind of expert on this shit, huh. You the Dogman ain't you.

Hey, they call me that cause I walk dogs, not cause I act like one. Ima tell you the truth now. There was a time I trotted around here on all fours like you guys, sniffing every behind let me sniff. Lifting my leg and pissing on every tree, bush, fireplug didn't have sense enough to scoot out my way. That was then, but it ain't me now. No. No. Gots to respect the sisters. Thing in your pants ain't no orchestra baton. Ain't no whipping stick, neither. Nor a licorice stick. Nor a Billy the Kid goat pistol you got to keep notching. No no no no. Procreation, brothers. Respect. Life give you the holy power to make life.

Fuck procreation. What about recreation.

Recreation's a holy gift too. When you save it for the one you love.

Right. Right. Trouble is some us love all the ladies.

And that's why you a dog. Giving in to that dog nature.

Woof. Woof. Woof. If I gotta be a dog, mize well be the Big Dog. Bow-wow and woof. Arf-arf.

Shut up youall. Trying to watch my stories down here. Hush. What's wrong with youall, barking and carrying on already this afternoon.

Yo. Sweet Emmalee. Leave them dumb whitefolks on TV alone, girl. C'mon down here and sit on my lap. Got a real nice story for you. Story about a snake with one eye.

Fuck you, Ricardo.
What I'm talking about, sweets. Yeah. Arf-arf. Bow-wow.

She's sitting up in bed. Lamp's on. Sheet tucked to her chin.

Feeling better, baby.

Oh yeah. Feeling better all the time looking at you sitting there like a princess on her throne.

Don't start lying already this morning. I don't need no bullshit. You feeling good cause you just emptied your bladder. Cause you scored some pussy. Your head probably aching bad as mine this morning behind too much of Edgar's nasty whiskey. What you seeing this morning's got nothing to do with last night. You did me in the dark, sugar. You would have fucked me last night if I had a hump, snaggle teeth, and a beard. You just happened to luck out, mister. That's what you see this morning. A lucky shot in the dark. I know what I got and know it ain't half bad. Don't need to hear no lies this morning, trifling as I feel and look.

Whooa . . . hold on. Gimme a break. I just . . .

You already got the biggest break I'm ever going to give you. Something for nothing. Cause I was in the mood for it, just like you. A free ride. Going to cost you a bundle from this moment on. Every inch, every scrap.

And damn if it didn't. I'm standing beside the bed limp-dicked and tongue-tied and she twists around so she's facing me. Lets go the sheet she's so busy talking trash with her hands. Looks like no woman I ever saw before. Hands moving, eyes flashing, eyes on her titties, eyes on her belly and shoulders because all of her, every fine brown inch I couldn't help staring at was staring back, staring me down. A whole civic arena full of eyes and I'm buck naked on the foul line and the crowd hopped up like they gonna come out the stands and whip my ass if I don't sink both ends of a one-and-one.

Stood there and don't know if I'm melting or turning to stone. Felt like both. Loose as a puddle. A man chained up so tight I can't blink.

Started that way and stayed that way. Her ninety-nine yards ahead running full steam and me stumbling along behind, trying to catch up one gimpy step at a time. And loving every minute of it, too.

One thing I'll always remember from the first day after the first night is how we never really got out of bed once she let me back in bed. Another thing I won't forget is her on my lap and I'm rocking her and she's all cuddled up and clinging and I'm thinking there ain't nothing to her, this woman's small as a child. I'm holding on to her, resting my back on a pillow propped against the wall behind the bed, rocking this child and singing, singing to this stranger who couldn't be a stranger could she because we'd been naked together two or three lifetimes and I was a different person, a new singing person I'd never been in no other life and here she was curled in my arms starting a new lifetime too, a baby, and a lullaby my mother used to sing to me kind of sneaked out my mouth before I knew I was singing or humming, me just trying to make a nice peaceful noise that's all it was, and she's warm and rising and swelling in my arms like new baked bread brother till I can't sing anymore, or do whatever it was I called myself doing anymore, because her tongue's halfway down my throat and she ain't little no more, she's huge as the sky, big and warm and soft and light as summer air. The two of us. Just the two of us. Then there's one. Singing together, not missing a note.

There was one other thing I won't forget. Mize well give it up too. Crying. Wetting her chest like a baby. A beat-up fifty-year-old man so happy and sad because it took me every one of those years to find her and feel good as I did.

The more I tell the more I remember and truth is every minute of the first day we stayed together is stored inside me and the only reason I don't let myself think back over all of it, tell you or tell myself the whole story, minute by minute, is cause the day ain't over and I sure don't want it over so I'm still there in the bed wondering what's going to happen next. Know what I mean. Couldn't forget if I tried. And believe me my friend I have tried. Needed to forget her and get on with my life, but that's another story. That day would come. And something else after it. But what I started telling you about was the crying. Part of me like the singing part I'd forgot I owned till that day in her bed. Like all the sudden a banquet's set down in front of me. Fancy food I'd never seen before, didn't even know the names of, didn't know I knew how to eat. But there it was and I'm steady greasing. Seems like I could eat forever and more and better on the way when a voice, one of those creaky Inner Sanctum, Shadow knows voices used to be on the radio, you know, this voice says, Boy, when you stop, boy, you're going to die.

I'm in the middle of a feast and here comes this voice stopping up my throat, putting the idea in my head of me locked in a death row cell and this meal tastes so good is my last meal on earth and the warden and guards checking their watches, counting down to the finish line when this good food turns to shit and piss and throw-up they got to hose off me when the meat wagon comes.

Voice said its piece, went on about its evil business, left its nasty taste in my mouth. But I didn't cry over none of that. Everything turning to shit's something I've worried about my whole life. Worrying's in my nature, the way I am. Worry about living. Worry about dying. But I know that's the way life goes so I didn't cry over none of that sour old spilt milk.

My head in her lap. Eyes googled up to the top of my head so I can see her eyes and what I see in her eyes is she's like me, like all us out here with good reason to worry, damned good reason to expect we're going to be hurt bad. Her eyes say she knows about the hurt, knows how hard things can get. Knows this goodness going down between her and me, knows nothing could be better, but really it don't mean a thing. You know. Here while it's here. Then gone. Poof. Into thin air. Nothing.

Then I don't want the world to be the way it is. Okay for me and my hard-leg self to live in a world works the way it does. I could handle it. Have to handle. And little as she is, I had a feeling from those eyes maybe she could handle it too. But it's not okay for her. She's all bones. Light little bones. Soft places for me to lay my head, tuck my hands. Places for me to get lost, sweet hollering lost in, but she's delicate bones and velvet skin and I'm sorry my big thick head weighs so much. I reach up and hold her. Feel like I'm dangling upside down, hanging on with nothing but my toenails and it feels good, feels like there ain't no place I'd rather be but I better hold on tight. Not too tight. Squeeze her gently. Finger her ribs. Let my hands slide down past the narrowest part of her and rest on the firm meat of her slim hips. I think she deserves a world better than this one we're stuck in. I ask myself why anybody'd want to make the kind of world that would crush these bones and breath floating in my hands.

Thump of her heart just above my ear. Little jumps and gurgles inside her. I started missing her there and then. Missed the quick way she popped out her side of the bed. Started feeling scared. Lost it. Tried to hide my face in her chest, like if she couldn't see me, she wouldn't know I was losing it. Started shaking and tearing up and my eyes wetting her chest.

Yes indeed, it was some night and quite a day too and everything that happened comes back when I let it come back but I'll only tell you bits and pieces. Turning it all loose would wear me out. Couldn't stop it coming. Story catch me before I got to the end, swallow me in one bite.

Stepping with her into the dark hallway of a house on Cassina Way was like stepping back in time, a time he'd thought he'd forgotten. His car parked across and up the avenue from Edgar's. When they'd left the bar she'd tucked her arm into his and every couple steps or so let her body sink into him, a lean, a sway as if they were still slow dancing and him believing he was still leading till he started towards the curb, towards his car and she tugged him back.

C'mon, baby. Not far to my house. We can walk.

That's me over there. We can ride.

Let's walk. I need to walk.

And the night air felt good to him too. Took some of the shamble out of his legs, his brain. Straighten up and fly right, fella. Don't blow this. Wherever, however this fine woman on his arm wanted to go just fine with him. Long as they wound up alone, together.

Avenue empty. If a car passed, he missed it. They were backtracking one of the routes he used to walk on his way to elementary school. His grandmother would go with him as far as Hamilton Avenue some mornings. Tell him tales about the people who once lived on the little side streets and alleys along this way. The Spite Lady, who burned down a brand-new Seventh-Day Adventist church because they stole her property and tore down her house to make room for their building. Mr. Samuels the junkman, who kept a horse in his back yard. Clyde Hollinger, his mother's uncle, who was a barber and machine-gunned a hundred of the kaiser's spike-headed soldiers before they killed him so his name's on a plaque in front of the Homewood Library.

Gradually, as he got older, he'd hang with his little crew on the trek back and forth to school. One by one the other boys would drop off at their doors and he'd wonder if the kids who lived in the houses his grandmother talked about had heard the stories he learned from her. Wondered what this woman beside him who seemed not much more than a girl knew about these streets, the houses, the people who had lived and died in them. Did she know his family had stayed on Cassina Way before she was born. Before he was born. When she steered him down Cassina did she feel his arm tense, a tension that was also surrender and disbelief, a quick pinch of fear he might not be alive yet, only a ghost who would rise and float away if she let go. Cassina Way. A place buried so deep in his memory he'd forgotten it was also real. These skimpy bricks and boards. Never thought of Cassina Way unless somebody else brought it up. Even then the name of the street reminded him how much he'd forgotten, how far away he'd traveled. A narrow, cobblestoned alley of back fences and back yards and back lots and back doors. Some of the back doors also front doors for the row houses that lined two blocks of Cassina, skinny two-story houses sharing a spine like Siamese twins so one family's dwelling opened onto a street, the other into the alley. Cassina Way had been sitting here all this time and he had ignored it, aging and falling apart like the rest of the neighborhood. Like him. Cassina Way a skin he'd shed and discarded. How could he step into it again.

They were a block and a half down the alley before he missed the cobblestones. Were they under this river of asphalt that reflected light from the streetlamps, spreading it, dulling it, a damp sheen underfoot, banked by shadows. At the beginning of the second block, row houses that had formed one wall of the narrow corridor he remembered as Cassina Way were gone. Now, from the cement steps of 7215 where he used to sit and daydream, staring at the butt end of houses on Tioga Street, making up lives for the people who never seemed to come out their back doors, you could see straight through to Tioga's far side and beyond. Few houses on Tioga Street remained intact, most of them gone now just like the ones once forming a wall that had made Tioga's far side invisible when he was a kid on his steps. Tioga's houses boarded up or shells or bulldozed into vacant lots, craters, mounds of rubble. The row of six or seven houses standing on one side of Cassina the last stale slice of a cake somebody had gobbled up a long time ago.

She dug for her keys in a tiny, fish-scaled bag he hadn't noticed till she started digging. No cobblestones. No sheltering walls. Was this really Cassina Way. Maybe the sign at the corner was wrong. No number visible on the house they were about to enter. Might be 7215 or might not. Too much had changed. Newish siding. No cobblestones. Whole blocks he remembered had been flattened. Intersections erased. Same again, same again low-rises on the horizon. Where were the houses with porches. Not two stone steps like lips poked out of the shacks back in Cassina but cement porches with iron rails, wooden porches with columns, brick porches with green striped aluminum awnings, porches where people could sit and not have to dangle their feet in some nasty alley belongs to nobody. Porches that made strolling down Tioga or walking up Susquehanna like being downtown and window shopping, each house different, the life in them different, as far from Cassina's identical, barefaced doorways as the moon, even though you just had to go around the corner and turn up the block to find houses with porches.

No secrets in Cassina now. No place to hide. Who's out there, straggling around in the night with nothing better to do than spy on him. Old wolf creeping in the henhouse. Are the eyes he feels checking him out his own eyes watching himself do something he knows he shouldn't be doing. One-night stand. A girl half his age he knows nothing about except she's got his joint hard and he's riding it boing, boing, bop like a blind man on a pogo stick.

Words forming already for the story he'll tell the fellas about the night. Don't know how I let myself get in that mess. Shaking his head, disgusted but bragging some too about being the same kind of fool at fifty he was at fifteen. Fine. Woman was fine as wine. Said to myself you know she's too young. You know good and well how messy things bound to turn before it's over. Going to get your feelings hurt or hurt hers. Little kids somewhere in the picture, no doubt. Rent money she's behind on. Some jealous hard-leg ex-husband or one of those dick-shriveling, dry-you-up-and-choke-you-to-death diseases. Or drugs. Junky boyfriend hiding in the closet with a gun will stick you up when your pants down around your ankles. Pistol-whip my ass just for good measure. Shit happens daily. Especially to old think-they-slick fools chasing young pussy. But man, if you'd been in my shoes, I swear, good as she looked strutting in Edgar's in that little green dress, you wouldn't have turned it down neither.

Dog nature, Dogman said.
   Bow-wow chorus from the guys seated at the bar.

The beginning of June, right around my birthday, when I met her. Heat wave the week before. August dog-day hot for a whole week. Then a rainy day cooled things off. Another day after of clouds moving fast. I remember looking up and thinking those clouds sure in a hurry. High, fast, long white clouds but mostly miles and miles of blue after the rainy day. Not like a furnace anymore but warm enough at night you didn't need the jacket you carried out of habit anyway since it was still early June and nights could turn cool again. Best kind of weather, really. Summer but you don't go round wringing wet. Kind of weather right at the edge of sweaty summer heat and you can't help thinking of what used to come next, playing ball all day, sun on the court crisping you like bacon in a frying pan. Mize well be barefoot the way the asphalt burns through your All-Stars. Didn't matter, felt good in a way. Nothing could stop you. Summer when you could run ball till the sun went down then cruise out and party all night. Full of juice. Of that young power. No reason to believe things would ever be different, that you might wake up on another June morning and wish, wish you could have just one of those long hot days back, that juice back, that lift and rise with your legs strong under you, flying, running all day and never ever dreamed about shit changing, about being a different man and having the best part of your day be memories of a day that ain't coming again. Know what I mean.

Met her on a night after a weather-perfect June day like that. Day full of little jolts, little teases of Shit yeah. I'm ready. Let's roll on up to the court and get it on. Find us a run and yeah, the jumpers a little rusty, legs a little dusty but watch me put those young boys in a trick. Uh-huh. Uh-huh. Count it. Sorry, youngblood. Take a seat. Who's next. Who got winners. Yeah. An evening after a June day like so and I'm minding my own business, cooling out, having a nightcap or two in Edgar's when *boom*. Up pops the devil with a green dress on.

I was stone wrong. Right, too. How it always is, isn't it.

In the narrow house on Cassina before he'd dreamed of fucking women, before a little brother came along looking for a corner of his kingdom, there were women making him feel better than all the humping all the years after ever would. His mother, his grandmother, one or another of his pretty young aunts in and out as they changed jobs or lovers or husbands or came home to help out in an emergency or be helped. Spoiled for life by these women spoiling him, first male child, only male except for his grandfather in a houseful of women, spoiling any chance one woman could do for him what his mother, her sisters, their mother did. A world of women who seemed to be at his beck and call. Bringing him treats back from the A & P, toys from Murphy's Five and Dime on Homewood Avenue, sitting him on their laps, resting his head on their bosoms to read him a story or sing him a song. Women who fought over whose turn it was to earn his smile.

He is sitting on the steps of 7215. His grandfather in the kitchen cleaning chitlins. Chitlins the one thing his grandfather brings home his grandmother won't clean. She'll clean the whiskered catfish he catches, gut and cut up the birds, rabbits, possums, and coons he shoots. Whatever his grandfather pulls from the sagging, bloody pockets of his hunting vest, she'll take and turn into something smells good frying or baking, but chitlins, No. Not putting my hands in pig nastiness. No. You want to eat pig guts, mister, you clean them and cook them and clean up my kitchen when you're done. Warn me before you start, too, because I don't intend to be in the same house with those stinky things.

Chitlin smell didn't get real bad till they began boiling. Bad enough before they boiled to draw tears to his eyes if he stood in the kitchen doorway watching his grandfather scrape and chop and run water over them and scrape some more then drop them into a pot to soak. Same speckled blue pot they'd soaked in overnight after his grandfather carried them home from the butcher's wrapped in brown paper. Same black-bottomed blue pot they'd boil in. Pot for his pig guts not fit to cook anything else huh-uh no no not in my kitchen she'd say. Don't care how long you scrub it just stick it back down under the sink, way under there, way in the back. Don't want it close to touching nothing else I use in my kitchen.

Whiter and whiter after each soaking and scraping and finally the boiling that sicced the air so bad you had to leave the house and sit on the steps, hoping your grandfather won't smell too much like chitlins when he's finished inside and comes out to take you on his shoulders for a ride around the block.

He was twenty something at somebody's house, maybe Elaine and Harold's, for New Year's Day, hungover but also a little bit high again, watching football games, on his second or third cold beer and bowl games blurring into one another on a TV that every few minutes lost its grip so the picture rolled off the screen and when it rolled back he wondered if he was seeing the same game or different fields and players flipping past, before he was ready to taste chitlins. Gonna try some of my chitlins, huh. Or maybe I should say *chitterlings* and maybe they taste better to a been-to-Howard-one-year negro like you. A smidgen cut off somebody else's plateful, little wrinkly wedge he still couldn't help but think of pig foreskin and puckery meat around pig asshole so he waited till he couldn't feel anybody watching him and smothered that first chitlin morsel about to pass his lips in a forkful of black-eyed peas and greens and sprinkled on Louisiana Red Devil hot sauce. Little nougat-colored soft center in a heaping mound of the kind of food he loves so much if somebody said a roach just sprinted across it he'd blow off the tracks and scoff it down anyway. Still, he didn't chew. Popped the entire forkful down his throat and didn't taste much of anything except familiar flavors and salt and the red burn of cayenne. Tried again — maybe later that afternoon or another New Year's party. By then his tongue and his nose sniffing right behind it (where else it going to be) had sampled every nook and cranny of women's bodies and learned how some of those places he once ignored or sidestepped were as close to home, to the house on Cassina Way where he was a child in a paradise of women's hands and eyes, their warm skin and scents and musical voices, as he was ever going to get again. The ravioli-sized curls of chitlin dotted with a spot of hot sauce he bit into and chewed were not the pigsty, eye-flinching rankness of the house when his grandfather boiled hog maws but the tease of something new baking in the oven and when you open the oven door to see what's been cooking you know it's something somebody who cares has fixed so your nose wide open and you breathe in deep and let it talk to you, teach you. New smells, old smells, blending, without losing what's good about each one, changing each other, changing you.

She said, Things a whole lot different since you used to live in this house. If you ever did. I don't know whether to believe you or not. Sure, it could be true. People probably been living in this raggedy shack since Noah. It's just weird thinking of you here once upon a time. Bet you were a cute little boy. Bet you were bad. Bet they did spoil you rotten. Well, I'm not exactly sitting here believing you and I'm not exactly saying you're lying. Don't matter, does it. This is a different place now. No houseful of women. Just me. Everybody else who stayed here since I been here male people, men and boys. My two sons, my husband. Mr. Mallory boarding in the downstairs front room. I could have used some female company around here. Just me and Mr. Mallory left now. After my Marcus gone, Kwami, my oldest, moved out. Don't know where he was sleeping. Once in a while he'd come by. Mealtimes, you know. That boy always could eat. Loved creamed tuna fish on toast. Any time of day or night. With the other one, Marcus, when he was little, it was rolled oats. Drove me crazy demanding rolled oats. I'd fix a nice dinner and he'd turn his nose up. Rolled oats, Mom. A bowl of rolled oats with a teaspoon of milk and a pound of sugar. Lived on rolled oats.

Just boys and men the whole time I been in this house. Men who act like boys, boys trying to be men. One run-ragged woman trying to teach them the difference between man and boy. As if I knew. As if they ever had a chance. As if trying to work out the difference wouldn't tear me up. Wouldn't break my heart, like it broke theirs.

This half-a-house on Cassina Way lost all its men, like a whole lot of houses round here. Bunch of babies and women now.

Funny, ain't it. Many times as I've heard of women living together raising kids, I can't think of a situation of men getting together and taking care of kids. Not in any of these hangdog half-a-houses on Cassina Way. Huh-uh. Plenty of mothers and sisters and grandmothers and great-grans and aunts and mothers-in-law scuffling to make a decent life for a pack of ungrateful, hard-head boys, but you tell me if you ever heard of a household of men raising girls. Don't think I'd want to look too close at something like that if something like that ever happened. What kind of strange woman would come out of a mess like that. You know sooner or later one of them be pestering her. Men breathing down a poor girl's neck all day. And what goes down at night when the lights go out. Don't know which be worse, men leaving her alone at night when they go out to do their dirt in the street or men staying home, pestering her. Drive the poor thing crazy if they didn't kill her.

Bluussh, she says. Says I'm in bed one night halfway reading a magazine to put myself to sleep when *bluussh* the toilet flushed. My back arches up off the bed and all my hairs standing on end like that silly cat in the cartoon struck by lightning. Heart's beating a mile a minute. I'm afraid to move a muscle but my eyes jumping around the room because far as I know nobody's in the house but me and Mr. Mallory who never comes out his room at night. And even if it's him he got his own little commode downstairs and what flushed was mine, right next to my head, so who the fuck's up here using my toilet in the middle of the night. *Excuse me,* I hollered.

Those very words, believe it or not. *Excuse me,* to some rapist or robber or doped-up woogie got the nerve to use my toilet and flush it before he jumps in my bed after me. *Excuse me.* Like if I'm nice maybe the murderer get it over quick and not hurt me too much. More squeak than holler first time I was so scared but when I yell again it's loud enough to be heard down at the Number Five police station, loud enough to wake Mr. Mallory from the dead.

When nobody answered, I sat and shook a minute, watched my whole life fly past, and my life wasn't no great show, a mess really, reason why I couldn't fall asleep that night, but it was mine, the only one I was going to get, so I grabbed the butcher knife I keep under my bed. Shit. Time to get it on. Whatever. Maybe whoever's out there will answer to a rusty, saw-toothed butcher knife since *Excuse me* don't get his attention.

Open the door and nobody. Not another sound except the toilet running the way it acts dumb after a flush till it decides to stop. Not a living soul but me in the hall as far as I could tell and I'm shivering scared. Realized I don't have a stitch of clothes on my body. Grabbed my robe. Then I whipped open the bathroom door, jabbing anybody in my way with the butcher knife before I reached for the light. Nothing. And thank Jesus nowhere for nobody to hide neither. Checked the other rooms. Turned on every light in the house. Stopped a minute at Mr. Mallory's door listening. Had to laugh at myself. What if the poor man peeked out and saw me standing there shaking like a leaf with a butcher knife in my hand. Not a sound though, just him snoring and wheezing inside his room.

I never figured out what happened that night. Either a ghost flushing ghost shit or the silly toilet flushed its own self. You know. Like people say a pile of rags can set itself on fire and burn up somebody while they're sleeping. If something can set its own self on fire, no matches, no help, just bust out in flames, then I guess a toilet can flush itself. Don't you laugh at me, man. You got a better story. Why can't a toilet or anything else for that matter just get all pent up, get tired of waiting on somebody to come along so it goes on and does what it got to do.

Haven't heard it flush itself since. Toilet will burp and run and tinkle, you know, but ain't never flushed on its own again. Scared the pee out of me that night it did. And I sure did hear it. Wasn't dreaming. Not making nothing up neither, and you better stop grinning. If it was a ghost, why would it need to flush. I mean you couldn't see ghost shit, could you. No more than you can see a ghost if the ghost don't want to be seen. So why a ghost bother to flush. Maybe you can't see ghost shit but maybe it's stinky. Why you grinning. You think I'm crazy, don't you.

Go on. Shake your head. I don't blame you if you think I'm out my mind. Men drove me crazy when they lived here. Now I'm getting even nuttier with no men around.

Maybe I wasn't raised in this very house but one like it. One just like this one was back then. I was scared of the dark. My mama always left a light on for me. I thought of that when we came up the steps and I saw a light burning under a door. Wondered if there was a little scaredy-cat boy like me still living here.

My light. I leave it on for me. With toilets flushing and all the evil stuff you hear daily on the news done to women I keep a light on when I go out at night. Hardly ever go out anymore. Don't know who be pestering you. Who might follow you home. Not a whole lot better with a light on but it helps a little. Once old Mr. Mallory's asleep he mize well be dead. Expect the poor soul to pass any day. Every morning and night, like I said, I listen to make sure he's still breathing. So he's no help, really. More like living with a spook than having another person around here. But he's a veteran, gets that disability check every month. Like clockwork. They wire money straight from his bank account to mine. Clickety-click. Rent's paid.

A blue room. Project babyblue like the other wannabe bright and cheery project colors, pink, green, yellow, colors you can see through, paint slapped on in a hurry by somebody never coming back. Everything the same skimpy washed-out blue. Walls, ceilings, doors. A room once you put in a double bed hardly any space left for furniture. In one corner a vanity table with little wee drawers and a mirror, and a no-backed stool tucked under it. A chest two drawers high just inside the door with her stereo and one of those mini-mini-TVs stacked on top. By the dresser a closet too stuffed to shut and more clothes humped outside on the closet door so it looks like the hunchbacked coatrack in the front hall of the old house on Cassina that could be this house, gutted, drywalled, water-thin paint skimmed on end to end. If you punched the wall behind her bed, your fist wind up in somebody else's bedroom. Bet you could smell food like he used to cooking in the ass end of the house butting the ass end of this one. No side windows even though 7215 the last one of the row. One sooty square of glass upstairs and down in the airshaft between houses, then blank wall front to back just like everybody else.

Nothing's exactly the same but everything familiar. Crowded, empty little rooms like when he was growing up here. Empty because all the clutter (clothes not fitting anyone now, but maybe next year), all the junk that didn't work and never was going to be fixed, the stuff for living day to day crammed everywhere wasn't enough. Far from enough of what you needed to get by. Never enough so you could eat and sleep and cover yourself and wash yourself and piss and shit in peace. No room for those needful things. Just cluttered emptiness with no room to breathe. Not enough space for the less than enough you owned, so where are you supposed to put extra if you ever lucked up on something extra and needed to find a place for it.

He'd sit on the front step and daydream all the nice extra things he wanted, beg for them sometimes even though he knew there was no room in the house on Cassina, and even if God or the devil handed him what he asked for, he'd have to give it back before he went inside, wouldn't he.

No room inside the house for the emptiness he needed to fill. And here he was again, grown man in a flimsy bed in a tacky room he could tear apart with his bare hands in a minute. Kick down the walls. Let light in.

She does her best to keep the blue room clean and neat. Her perfume and toiletries scent the air. Colored bottles and tubes doubled in the vanity mirror the way there seems to be booze backing up booze, glasses backing up glasses, enough so Edgar will never run out, in the big, gold-edged mirror behind the bar. She takes time to lay out colorful, African-looking cloths. In front of the TV, under the lamp on the table beside the bed. A white, lacy-edged liner for a shelf under the night table where she keeps a Bible. Cramped as he is, cheated as he feels in the see-through skimpiness of the room, he's reminded of his mother's hand, the hand of his grandmother and aunts in the details, the little extras that change nothing, add more clutter to the clutter, but also add space, space blessed because it's touched by something of them, from them. Space the women open. Space beckoning him, saved for him, space for his daydreams to fill when he squats on the steps staring at the bricks and boards across Cassina Way.

Hey Spoonboy. What you thinking about, Mr. Spoon. Better watch your toes, boy. Something might jump out from under those cobblestones and grab you.

His grandfather called him Spoon or Spoonhead or Spooner or Spoony or Spoonboy or some other no sense string of noise, all the sounds rhyming with Spoon, like Spoon-doon-ooney-roon. Said you the baldest big head niggerbabyboy I ever seen. Bald as a spoon. That's why you always Spoon to me.

This boy has a name, your mother be fussing, hand on her narrow hip like I better stop calling you out the Christian name she gib you. Told her, say, Spoon's a spoon, little darling girl. Ain't nothing gone change that. He's Spoonhead just like you always be my Sweetpea, Miss Grown-up-with-a-baby-already Elizabeth Alfreeda Jones.

My grandfather said China under the cobblestones. And fish so big they swallow a minnow like you in one bite. Some so big swallow 7215. Swallow all of Cassina Way. Drop a hook down in there don't know what you liable to catch. What might catch you.

Sitting on the top step so his feet solid on the bottom step and not on wobbly cobblestones subject to gobble your toes, he taught himself to brew a load of spit, roll it around in his jaw, and skeet it through the gap in his front teeth almost as far as his grandfather shot tobacco juice. His grandfather's spit left dark stains on the cobbles. Bull's-eyes he'd aim his spit at. His wet white spit piggyback on his grandfather's marks, riding like he rode on his grandfather's shoulders down Cassina, through a vacant lot, up Susquehanna or Tioga, to houses with porches.

After the stroke, his grandfather needed to lean on somebody to get through the door and out on the steps to chew the Prince Albert tobacco he wasn't supposed to chew and hawk it in the alley, even though the women begged him not to spit because it was ignorant and niggerish, begged and fussed at him as if they weren't the very ones helping him to the steps, as if they didn't know why he fought pain to stagger outdoors, as if they didn't know exactly what he'd do, dig the pouch of Prince Albert from the breast pocket of his shirt first thing after he slumped his behind on the steps. The last summer of his grandfather's life, blood mixed in with the gobs of tobacco juice he spit, blood draining, blood coughed up, spatters of pure bright red. He was afraid one huge cough would shake his grandfather and he'd tumble down off the steps, splash like those spit bombs splashed. His grandfather sinking down through the cobblestones where giant, dagger-toothed fish circle and wait.

His back's against a pillow and with one glance he takes in the blue room, the whole invisible house, familiar and unfamiliar, how everything changed, nothing changed. An old man, a scared little boy. Where the fuck was he. Why is he shaking inside, heart rattling in its cage like his grandfather's heart must have rattled and jiggled just before it broke. The booze. The young woman's body saying yes yes yes, and his body answering, moving with her again and again as if his arms and legs and mouth and dick and heart didn't belong to the old head knew better than to fly so fast, so hard, so close to the edge, over the goddamn edge. No. You know you shouldn't but hot damn, you're doing it, ain't you. Yes. Up half the night boozing and wrassling with her, talking, crying, singing, and now his heart flutters, flinches, says I told you so fool or is it just gas or is he scared again, worried she won't come back through the blue door and say yes again. Yes. Yes.

I'm the eldest, four years older than the brother comes next after me. The others born two years apart so we're all on our even years or odd years together. Don't see my brothers or sister much. Truth is we've lost touch if there ever was much touch after we left the house and went our separate ways, but I think of them when I think of my age, feel closer to them when I count my years and figure theirs, which I've been doing more lately.

Four years of being the only child, a male child in a family of women enough to spoil me for life. Thought I was always going to be the only child. Didn't like it much when other kids started butting in. Loved them and always will the way you love your blood but I don't think I really liked any of my brothers or my sister till I was grown and out the house. I could like them better when we weren't all pressed together, crowding up one another. By then we were in different places, never saw too much of each other. Now when I do the counting down, put years on each one, I miss them. If I could, I'd go back and be a different way with them. Course, I'd try and change a lot of things if I could go back.

I'm the oldest too. Two younger sisters. Chantal, Yolanda. Two sad stories you don't want to hear and I surely don't want to think about this morning. Is it still morning. If it ain't, it might as well be, huh. Us still lazing here in bed.

And I was happy when a little sister came along. Wanted more sisters. And a little boy baby doll to play with and take care of, too. Me and my sisters real close in age. Mama a sure enough baby machine. What she seemed like for a while anyway. Just drop in your quarters, out slides another cute Coke-bottle baby. Till number four popped out too soon after the three of us, popped out dead and took my mother away with him or her, nobody never told us kids which it was, a boy or a girl. Born dead so I guess it don't matter, does it. Girl or boy. Couldn't ask Mama. She's gone too. Couldn't ask the daddy because nobody told us who he was. Wasn't none of our daddies. Me and Chantal probably got the same one and Yolanda a different one and we hardly knew who they was but seems like we'd of heard if it was one of them this last time when Mama died having some man's baby. More sad stories I didn't mean to get into this morning. Point I'm trying to make is girls is different. Born different. Nothing I liked better than being a little mother to my baby sisters. Just a baby myself but I helped raise them. Not only play raise but doing stuff for them nobody else had time to do or cared about doing because we didn't really belong nowhere, belong to nobody, specially after Mama died. Looking back now, I guess maybe Mama, bless her soul, wasn't around that much neither, even when she was around. With her gone for good, people took us in, relatives sometimes, sometimes not, some out the goodness of their hearts, some because those foster care checks follow us around.

Loved my baby sisters. Gave them baths. Dressed them, combed their hair, fed them, wiped their nasty butts when some grownup ought to have been doing all that kind of do for me. Just about killed me when the welfare split us up. Whew. Can't get away from sad stories this morning. Or whatever damned time of day it is.

Come on over here, old man. Wasn't acting like no old man

last night, was you. You got some sugar left for me this morning. Hold me tight, baby. Whisper something that ain't sad in my ear.

Maybe I sang to her then. Then again, maybe not. On second thought the singing must have been later. Yes, much later. Longest, sweetest day of my life, but it passed in a minute. A short, hot minute.

I'd nod off and wake up and be half asleep, half dreaming, I couldn't tell if a second or hours passed. Didn't care. Thought it was getting dark outside but hard to be sure with no windows in the room and the whole house dark anyway. Even in daytime. Could have been the ending of a day or the beginning of one for all I knew.

Got out the bed sometime because we ate a hot meal so somebody had to fix it. And I remember soaping up her bony back while she sat in the tub. Can hear her now splashing and giggling behind me while I fiddled with the handle and innards of the toilet as if my total ignorance of how toilets worked couldn't stop me from solving the mystery flush. Fussed at it, cursed it, put a mojo on the sucker, dared it to scare her again.

We snacked in bed and drank wine and played checkers in bed. Sat up butt-naked in bed so she could trim my toenails then I trimmed hers. Believe it or not, she read to me from her Bible in bed. Not exactly a believer she said but when she was down and just about out the words helped her think, helped her handle what she didn't believe she could handle, she said. Bible words like music sometimes. Better than turning on the radio, she said. She had always liked to read. Always enjoyed a book in her hands. But nobody ever told her the Bible just a book. She'd thought it was part of church and she didn't like church nor church people. Said she hated being scrubbed till her skin hurt then dragged to church like church people would do her.

Church the place where I felt most alone, where me and my sisters belonged to nobody. Just three black, skinny little girls in ugly clothes used to be somebody else's. Three sisters with no names. Or too many damned names. Different daddies, different folks we stayed with. Couldn't keep the names straight myself so how could anybody else. Who cared anyway.

Sunday in church I missed my mama most. I swear she had skin like black butter. Big brown eyes set wide apart and those sleepy cheekbones.

In church I was always afraid I was going to bump into something or trip over my own two feet. If my mother had been there with us I know it woulda been a whole nother story. Her whispering to us, patting us, guiding us down the red carpeted aisle to a front seat. Ain't you Mama's beautiful little angel girls she'd say and angels we'd be.

Church was where she felt bad about all the bad things in her life she couldn't change, the things she was ashamed of, she said. I could see the little girl she was telling me about, see her shivering like she's naked at the pulpit and no way to hide her shame.

All our secrets we didn't want nobody else to know, she said, all the ugly things people did to us and we couldn't do nothing back . . . people sitting up in church knew, they knew and didn't do nothing but look.

People's mean eyes, the mean words they said under their breath, just loud enough to hear, loud enough to let you know they can see under your clothes. See your underwear got holes, see your ashy skin, your bedbug bites, the scabs in your hair you can't help scratching till they bleed.

Bible don't belong to church. Just a book, she said. Nobody owns it. Not God or Jesus or preachers or church people. Words for anybody. *Old-time singing words she followed across the page with her finger. Words she could taste and smell when she sneaked the reading finger to her lips. Words like funk left over from playing with herself, still there the whole morning in school if she protected her hand, didn't let anything or anybody touch it.*

Rub me here. Yes. Now sniff your fingers, baby. My smell. Me. That's what I saved.

Always liked to read but couldn't read anything after I lost my sons, not even magazines or newspapers. When I wanted company again, started reading again. Found me a nice old Bible in a secondhand store and a picture book called *Atlas of the Bible Lands*. Bought a big fat dictionary too. So many words, weighs almost as much as me.

Started in reading again. Don't expect I'll ever finish the Bible. But I'm not in no hurry. Time's about all I got now.

Here it is. Nice one, isn't it. And here's the part I want to read you.

I groan inside and think, Shit. Please. Spare me this shit. Save it for Sunday. Don't waste it on a sinner like me. Please don't mess up this good thing we got going. We come too far to turn around now. Don't get holy-holy on me now, babe. Worried about belligerent boyfriends or disease or getting jumped by some crackhead, but it's the Bible about to do me in.

Why you making a face. Ain't your best face, neither. Don't you go getting all bent out of shape. Not going to try and save your devilish soul. Ain't about church. Ain't about Jesus. It's about me and mine. Something I want to tell you about me.

Then I see it's a tissue-paper-paged Bible. Soft, kind of reddish cover and a long red silk ribbon sewn into the binding to hold your place. Watching how she spread the pages open, smoothed them and smoothed the ribbon down along the crease, how she barely touched the paper running her finger across the page to the right spot, I knew why, Bible or no Bible, I wanted that day of her hands on me never to end.

Here's one last thing I'll tell youall about the day. You know the old story about the big fish that got away. How the guy telling it keeps cheating, his hands getting wider and wider apart every time he shows how big the fish was. Well, here's a funny thing about the story. Something I never understood before I met her and lost her. The guy's not lying. He feels the empty between his hands grow- ing each time he tells his story, each time the damned fish gets away again. You see, the funny thing is the sorry motherfucker's right. No matter how wide apart he spreads his lying hands, he's right. The story's true.

LAMENTATIONS

WHY CAN'T I leave well enough alone. Wanted some good fucking and got it. Why couldn't I just let it go at that. Older guy hit on me, a nice man, kinda nice-looking kind bound to belong to some nice woman and she's away somewhere for a couple days so he's out tipping around looking for a quickie. Perfect. Cause it's what I wanted too. A no-strings-attached hot one-night stand, rise and fly.

Uh-huh. Ready for some good ole natural one-on-one X-rated adult ting-a-ling. Worse than ready. Long overdue. Hadn't been talking to people for months let alone rubbing up against some nice man's hard body. Still too raw. Still felt like a freak. Afraid a person take one look at me and see in my face all the terrible things happened, see what a terrible mother I'd been, losing my sons. My children gone so no kind of a mother no more. A widow not a wife. Pitiful man I married didn't catch AIDS till he was locked up in prison, but I had myself tested anyway and know I'm not diseased but diseased is how I felt, felt like runny sores all over my face warning people, Get back. Stay away.

Anyway, one night, after I ate my dinner and had my little glass of Paisano chianti and the silliness on TV was making me want to scream instead of putting me to sleep, the prospect of being home alone all evening staring at my own self, feeling sorry for myself, was worse than the thought of other people staring at me. No mystery about what this girl wanted, what chased me into a five-year-old green minidress and peekaboo, irresistible-you heels. Praying, believe it or not, while I bathed and dressed. Praying for a tallish, not too much belly, brown-skinned, slow-smiling man with big hands and clean, neat fingernails, one who wouldn't argue about wearing a johnny. Sort of man who probably didn't really need to wear one because he had good sense, respected women and respected hisself, but he'd be the one to sure enough insist anyway. Praying for a good fuck. Course I know good and well ain't no long-haired, bearded white man sitting up in heaven passing out favors, still I got the habit of thinking *pray* when I want something real bad, when I'm wishing for something most likely a lost cause. My whole life I've been hearing the people around me praying for this or praying for that when they're hurting for exactly what they should know they're not going to get but got their hearts set on it anyway, the same heart telling them they're not going to get it.

Well, shit happens, as they say. And some shit's even good shit every once in a great while. Got what I wanted, what I prayed for. It happened. Found me a nice man and we fucked ourselves dizzy that night. You'd think I'd be grateful, leave well enough alone. Huh-uh. Man didn't rise and fly in the morning, nor in the afternoon, nor the next night neither. Had us a balling good time and started seeing each other regular. Better way to put it, we couldn't stop seeing each other. Girlfriend's nose open and heart stole again.

Why'd I have to find just exactly the man I was looking for. Praying for. And when I did, why didn't I leave well enough alone. Sometimes I think being a spider woman the best way to be. Fuck a man to death. Leave him lying there with a smile on his face, go on about your business.

Scared me to find my story in a book. Thought maybe I was finally cracking up. I'd been around folks who are Bible crazy, church crazy. Didn't like them a little bit. They could be mean. Hurt you worse than the low-lifes doing all the doping and stealing around here. You know what to expect from the low-lifes, you know they're wrong and they know they're wrong, but the Bible crazy ones, they believe they right all the time. Right when they smack you. Right when they don't feed you. Right when they split up little sisters who don't have nothing in the world but each other to lean on. Those holier-than-everybody-else kind of people don't answer to nobody, don't care what nobody thinks. God God God behind whatever evil they do you. God and the Bible. Bible a stick they beat you with if you in the wrong place and ain't nothing but a child can't fight back.

Nothing those kind of people could do for me no more. Bible didn't belong to them, neither, far as I was concerned. Started to read in it and kept on reading because it gave me a lot to think about, helped me deal with the awful stuff tearing me up. Couldn't believe it when I found my story in the Bible.

Never thought about something like being a writer. Hell. Just halfway learning to read but I wondered if I wrote down my story would a woman lost a son in Detroit or Cleveland or Philadelphia or Los Angeles, California know just what I was talking about.

I'm not stupid. With everything I've had to go through I know I'm way past stupid and smart. Wasn't a matter of stupid or smart. After my sons dead and their daddy dead, I decided I wanted to go on living. Had to start all over again. Learn how to brush my teeth, how to breathe, how to walk across a room, how to sleep and wake up. Whatever I was, smart or stupid, before I lost my family, smart or stupid didn't mean a thing afterwards because I was dealing with a whole new world and I had to learn to be different in it or die. The old smart could be stupid in this new world and the old stupid wind up being smart. What I'm trying to say is when I started reading the Bible I wasn't a nut case. No holy roller. It was just a book. Just words. A book shoved in my face by people I mostly didn't like. People who hurt me bad as a child. So it wasn't Hallelujah. Lawdy, Lawd, I done found the light. Huh-uh. More like you out on a dark night in a quiet place like Westinghouse Park used to be before the gangs took over, a dark, quiet place and nobody around but you and you have too much on your mind to sleep, you need to walk and think, so you're walking in the park and notice out the corner of your eye a lightning bug brighting up like a match, then more, here and there. Not many. Enough so you notice, enough to make you stop for a minute and wonder why. Why are they here. Why do they do what they do. How do they do it. Ping. Ping. Little blinking eyes in the night. Something not you. Paying no attention to you. Going about their business. But you see them, they're out in the park with you, so maybe in a certain way what they do is about you too.

Bible ain't no Weegee board guides your finger where it wants you to go. I just kind of shuffled pages till I felt like stopping. Read a little bit of whatever I found. Sometimes the words didn't make sense. Just all these strange names, lists of what could be people's names, could be cities or countries or tribes, damned if I knew. They killing each other or begatting each other and I don't have a clue. Some mornings I found a regular story. Read along a while to find out who's zooming who. Curiosity. You know. Like I used to try and figure out what all those weird white folks carrying on about when I skipped school and watched soaps. Sometimes I'd come across a part like *The Lord is my shepherd I shall not want* I been hearing all my life. Makes a kind of music and that's what I follow as much as I follow the words. Some days I get dreamy and when I put the Bible down, don't have the slightest idea of what I been reading, except it's stirred me up, got hold of me and won't let go.

Remember the old women who wore nurse caps in church, the ones hardly got any hair or voice left but they knew all the verses to every hymn and lined them out to keep a song going and going till it runs out of words and then they start in humming and everybody hums along with them because nobody wants it over, way past words but the song keeps getting better and better and those humming verses when the words run out the best of all.

Didn't read much of the Book of Lamentations first time I found it, but I saved my place. Why I marked my place with the ribbon, why I hurried back first thing next day, I can't say. Maybe just the word. Something about that word *lamentations*. Do you know what it means. I didn't, had to look it up in my dictionary.

Didn't know the meaning and didn't guess right neither. My guess dead wrong. Dictionary said grief and mourning and deep regret. Said it could be a song or poem and that's closer to what I guessed, but lamentations definitely not happy songs. Said it could be a person wailing, letting other people hear the grief inside. The meaning of the word shook me up. How's it not going to shake me up with what I was carrying in my heart. When the Book of Lamentations open in front of me the second time, I read every line. Not a long book. But for me, in the state I was in, reading it like crawling from Homewood to downtown on a bed of nails and hot coals. I shivered. I flinched reading it. And reading it gave me a hurting kind of peace.

Found my story. My song. Got so tangled up in it, scared me for a while. Was I losing my mind. Hiding my face in a book when I knew good and well I needed to get out the house. Open the door and step back out in the world. But I wasn't hiding in the Bible. Just getting ready for what I had to do. Did a whole lot of talking to myself. A lot of trying to make sense of things didn't make no sense no matter how you twisted and turned and worried them. What happened to my sons. Why had they been given and then snatched away. What good was all my love if it couldn't buy them one more minute on earth. Why did evil prosper round here and children die.

Got through the worst finally and started stepping out a little, listening to the part of me wanted to live, wanted to be a live woman again. Got through wanting to die and one the things made it through with me the Book of Lamentations, this story about people beat down so low they got to pray for a reason to pray.

Being here with you like this I'm as close to happy as I've been in a long while. You don't have to listen if you don't feel like it. Close your eyes. Sleep if you're sleepy, baby. You sang for me. Now I want to sing for you. You cried. Now it's my turn to cry some on your shoulder.

> *My eyes flow with rivers of tears*
> *because of the destruction of my people . . .*
> *The children beg for food,*
> *but no one gives them anything.*
> *The old men have left the city gate,*
> *the young men their music.*

A son died playing Russian roulette. Another son killed when a dope deal he wasn't even involved in went bad and they were looking for someone to hurt and shot him because he was the only one home. AIDS killed their daddy in prison. Ask me why I lost three men in my life in the space of ten months and wound up alone with Mr. Mallory in this haunted house and I have no answer for you, all I can say is my life changed and I had no choice but to play the cards dealt me, and I ain't no better nor worse than most people, what happened happened and I'm still here, so don't feel sorry for me, just be careful, be ready, cause rain's gonna fall someday and when it rains it pours sometimes and believe me ain't no handle to shut it off.

Boys are something else, brother. Black boys are born beating they hard heads against a brick wall and the blacker they are the harder they beat that wall it seems, and if they don't knock sense into they own selves, those big hard heads soften up, ain't good for nothing afterwhile but sucking titty and laying half sleep upside titty or beating other boys black and blue. Basically, that's it; except if you're the mother you wind up blacker and bluer than your boys. Be not dismayed what ere betides, the song says.

Can they help it, can they do better? Course they can and most of them try. Cry on your shoulder, cry, cry, cry when they hurt you or hurt somebody else or hurt themselves or just can't do right to save their souls. Crazy country of ours accuses them of everything but being citizens and human beings. Calls black boys mistakes and don't you know I read the other day corrections the fastest-growing business in the nation.

*

Did you ever visit someone in prison. Dungeons what they are, dirty, dangerous dungeons. Die a little bit every time you pass through the metal detector, afraid it's going to start beeping because there's wire in your bra, studs in the stitching of your jeans, wish you could disappear, anything to stop the beep-beep-beeping, the lying machine saying you're guilty and can't even be trusted to enter this dirty hellhole dedicated to destroying low-lifes and no-goods, one of whom happens to be your son or brother or uncle or father or lover, who will be devastated if you don't make it in, him somewhere ringed by guards in a holding pen, bending over, spreading the cheeks of his ass, dying in little bits because he knows the devils are dragging you through shit too, stripping away your spirit, your dignity with traps they set to delay you, deter you, doom any chance anybody who cares will reach the visiting room in one piece. Dogging the visitor like they dog the one dying for a visit, so when a visit finally begins, if it ever does, you spend far too damned much of your precious little time together tense, or numb or fidgeting or fighting, wondering if it's worth it.

Everybody plays the fool, the song says, no exceptions to the rule. Each time I tried my best, fed and washed and dressed my boys and gave each of them my heart. Everything changes the minute they walk out the door. Except you, you expecting each time maybe this time will be different, maybe it's your turn, their turn for something good even though you know better because once they're out your hands, out your sight, the worst things can happen and do, because Evil wraps her arms around them, they're Evil's children, she steals them and raises them and then it's as if the time they were your babies never existed, except the memory of your boys small and helpless and needing you stays in your heart, a mirror in your heart where you see them and see your own face, small and helpless and broken missing your babies, needing them worse now than they ever needed you.

Fast, it all happens so fast. First-born baby boy or girl is the world suddenly beginning all over again. Forget who you thought you were a minute before your child's birth. From the moment you lay eyes on this new little person who just a second ago lived noplace but inside your body and now is free to roam the whole wide world, part of you sings, Thank you, Thank you for the miracle splitting you open, hurting you, changing you, making you holler, making you more and better than you were, and another part of you, sad-eyed, wide-eyed with fear, falls quiet, deathly quiet, listening to the future opening like a crack in the thin ice you're standing on with this beautiful fresh first-born wrapped in your arms.

Guys be hitting on you before you know what the fuck they talking about. Gonna gimme some them goodies, girl. Get out my face, boy. Grab what you can and get out of Dodge is what the guys learn early, early, and you learn game too, the gabbing and growling and goo-goo back and forth that starts out not meaning a thing, just play, just going up and down on a seesaw, then one day your big soft butt nailed flat to the ground and babies in both arms and the seesaw ain't heehaw no more, no sweet man on the other end, and you ain't rising no more, no more game for you cause he's gone, C.C. riding with some other bitch.

How did I manage. How. Hard sometimes when I sit in this bed with a cup of coffee in my hand, hard to think back on both my boys shot dead nine months apart and their lost, sorry daddy rotted down to skin and bones dying in prison, hard to believe I really did get through a year like that. Had to drag my good black dress out the mess hanging in that hopeless closet, brush it, iron the pleats, and it was hard, hard the first time, but if I'd known how soon I'd have to do it again and hear the folks at the funeral home whispering *Here she comes, here comes that pitiful child wearing black again already*, if I'd known ahead of time like I know now what was going to happen, I'm sure I couldn't have made it through, huh-uh, one terrible thing at a time enough, all I could bear because each time I pulled my black dress off the hanger it took every ounce of strength to shake it, brush it, look for wrinkles, and drape it over the ironing board, start checking the pleats, going real slow pleat by pleat, each crease a blessing in a way when I could put my mind to it, work the iron around it, one pleat at a time all I could handle and maybe that's how, maybe it's the only way, I think, anybody ever survives if they do.

Inside of me still raw. I've never tried to explain to anyone before how you can be talking to a person, any old kind of conversation with somebody you know well or not, and in the middle of the conversation you feel this explosion of cold, cold white heat going off behind your eyeballs, deep inside your skull, something like a flashbulb but a million, million times brighter and colder than any damned flashbulb, all light and no sound, the kind of light would explode if you squeezed this whole city into a ball, squeezed it down to lemon size, and then it gets away from you, busts open again, huge in a flash that blows out the back of your skull. In spite of all the fireworks and hurt, you barely blink and the person you're talking to can't see the light. Instead of dropping down poleaxed on the spot you amaze yourself, go on talking with whoever's in front of you because what just happened inside your head is a simple fact coming home to roost, the fact your children are dead and you been left behind has just hit you once more as it has before and will again when you least expect it.

Kicked a gang boy they say, whipped the boy's ass good in a fair fight they say, fair as such things ever are when a bunch from one gang corners some from another gang they say my son whipped him good and then kicked him while he was down on the ground and what else you think he's going to do with his buddies taunting and egging him on because he's big and strong like his daddy used to be, a terror with his big rough hands like his daddy, an easy, good-natured, bother-nobody-don't-bother-him boy like his daddy till he's high on something or somebody pushes him too far then he'd go off, do anything, kick and spit on a boy he beat to the ground and is that why they killed my son in cold blood. Knocked on his apartment door, same ones from the fight the week before, same two gangs still tangled up and shooting each other like cowboys and Indians, same boys been knowing each other since they were little kids, and this time it's about drugs they say but maybe it's about the fight too. KKK cold, fired point-blank with a sawed-off shotgun when my son answered his door. Killed him dead, dead before he hit the floor, but one kicked his big body anyway, kicked and kicked, *Remember me, remember me.*

Jury said my man guilty, guilty as charged. Judge said life without parole. Just me then, a young girl sitting alone in the courtroom with one baby in her arms, another in her belly she got to raise. Jungle where you have to live don't stop being a jungle just cause you try to do right, try to keep yourself and your babies above the worst killing rot and stink of it. Jingle my house keys and my son reaches out for them like any sweet, bright-eyed, curious little boy, like he's going to keep reaching and wanting shiny things the rest of his life till his hand closes round nothing and he sees what's out there glittering like gold is jail keys and he's locked up inside looking out.

Lamentations. Looking at the word, not having the slightest idea what it might mean, my guess was it might be something happy, a happy, dappy, fa-la-la ring to the word, something maybe to do with music, bells and tambourines and drums and long curvy goat-horn horns, you know, kind of stuff they play music with in the Bible days movies. Lester and the Lamentations, I thought that dumb thought too, thought the word sounded like Temptations or Sensations or Sweet Inspirations, the la-la-la names singing groups give themselves. Latin Lester and the Fabulous Lamentations. Little did I know, no clue what I was getting into when I started to read myself the book in the Bible with that name.

PLAYING BALL

NOTHING HE COULD DO would make me love him more. Loved him enough. More than enough to last us both forever and ever and he should have understood but they never do. I don't need him to be any better than he already is, but men don't understand love is love and if it's love it's enough. Men always got to prove something. Or have you prove something to them. So I walked up to the basketball court that day against my better judgment just to be with him because he asked me to. Why do men have to pretend they're better than they are.

Hard for me to sit on a bench beside the court and think some of these boys and men out there may be the ones killed my son. Hard, hard because I see my sons out there with the rest, running, soaking wet, trash-talking, little kids as long as they're scuffling over ball, safe, saved for another day. They jump and fly and chase each other around, play like it's war out there, dog each other and bump and shove, holler like they're making love. Fuss and whine. Smack each other. Hug. All sizes, shapes, colors, one could be my son, one could be the one shot him and kicked him.

She stares so long and hard at one who could be, could be . . . he stares back at her, out the game a second, he's whoever he is when the game doesn't let him forget. He wastes a split second on her curiosity, long enough to let her know he's curious too, and if he wasn't so busy with ball . . . and then he wheels upcourt sprinting after the stampede of big sneakered feet drumming, *plap, plap* past the bench.

He's not, but he could be. She keeps her eyes on him, the bare-skinned wedge of his back, long wet muscles of his arms and legs disappearing into the brawl of bodies, all kinds but many like his, a tangle of flesh piling up under the hoop, smashed together, skying.

One owns the ball. Grunts when he snatches it from the air in one hand, high off the backboard, his other hand swooping in to smack what he owns, smack loud as a gunshot, as if he wants to hurt the ball. Players break out of the pack around the basket. The big man who's come down with the ball grips it in both hands, whips it side to side, elbows flying, a cat with a rat by the throat, then bolts straight up, loads the ball behind his head, and slings it forward the length of the court to a player out in front of the others who puts it up and through the goal before anybody can lay a hand on him.

The one who caught the pass doesn't just lay the ball in the basket, he climbs an invisible ladder, up, up till the arm cradling the ball rises above the rim. In his rainbow headband and giant baggy shorts ballooning past his knees like purple wings, he's a butterfly pinned to the blue sky, a perfect snapshot she'll remember of a man flying like a bird who just might hang in the air forever, and does each time she brings the day into her mind, even though the next thing he does is tomahawk the ball down through the chainlink net, landing where it lands with his legs spread wide, hovering over the ball like it's an egg he laid, before he plucks it up and sets it gently as an egg on the endline, grinning *Too late, too late* like the gingerbread man at the other players never catching up with him.

Once in a daydream she'd soared as high, higher, turned a somersault in midair, in no hurry to come down. Then she's on her feet again because it's time to catch her children who'd been loop-de-looping and floating effortlessly in thin air with her. Her boys are laughing, calling her name as they spin in the perfect blue sky. She remembers juggling them, throwing them higher and higher. Leaping up to join them, their squeals and giggles and shouts. But they are falling fast now. Too fast. Her hands are water. Her whole body water. Water they splash into and drown.

Hey man. How you doin. Where you been man. Gimme some that old-time dap. Yeah. C'mon. Yeah. One more time. Right on. Yeah.

You looking good, man. Must be doing good too, I see, with this fine lady keeping you company. Real, real good. Uh-huh. Young lady my name's Tyrone and if you ever get tired of old men . . . know what I mean . . . some of us young fellas sure like to have your number.

Smile, miss, I'm just playing, miss. Pay me no mind. I'm Tyrone. Ty. This my main man here. We go way back. Ain't hardly old as he is but we go way, way back, don't we, my man. How you doing, main man. Guys always asking bout you. Where's Pops? How come Pops don't come round no more. Real good to see you, brother. Happy to see you back. Not many of us left out here from the day.

Good to see you, Ty. You still looking spry out there. Glad to be back, but we just come to watch. Watch and talk about you when those young boys run your fat behind off the court.

Won't be no running off today. No indeed. Got me a dynamite squad. Just the right mix of old heads and young legs. Could use you, buddy. Always room for my main man. Go on. Loosen up and run a couple hoops for me. Need to catch my breath anyway. G'wan and run. Know you want some of this action. Don't worry. I'll shoo the flies off your honey while you out there.

A roly-poly bowling ball of a man. Big grin. Short stubby legs in cutoffs, thighs about to bust the denim. Fat, dimpled cheeks. Light on his feet even with all that belly and butt he's carrying. The kind of large man fool you on the dance floor, she can tell. Up on his toes, nimble-footed, smooth, slick, all that shimmy and wobble working the beat.

G'wan, git you some, Pops. Know you didn't come out here on a running day like this just to sit and watch.

When the other players surround him, he's all smiles, and trying to look badass serious too, slapping hands, bumping chests, hugging and rocking each other the way they do. Boys. Kids. Always.

A different kind of naked in the daylight when he pulls off his T-shirt. Different from the bed naked. Different from the naked bodies of the younger men. His legs tight and strong as anybody's out there but his thick, naked top is different. Bare skin of the others shiny tar and brass and bronze and gold. Some stripped of skin, just thick plates of muscle seamed with sweat, the hard cords of their insides outside. Black angels, black birds. *Four and twenty blackbirds baked in a pie.* Wasn't that how the nursery rhyme goes. Black angels, sweet black birds baked in a pie, and this court the oven they bake in, sweat draining from their bodies, juice dripping black in the crotches and rear ends of their shorts like they peed on themselves or comed on themselves or bleeding in the heat of the fiery furnace.

Him different because she's heard giggles, coughs, rattles in his deep chest, gasps and grunts, tongued his tiny nipples, nuzzled the graying hairs, pinched and tickled and kissed the folds of his belly, squeezed the love handles at his waist. That's what makes his nakedness different. She knows he could die. The others can survive anything. Didn't they survive killing her sons. Weren't her sons out on the court now in the heat and noise and rush, surviving the meanness of their own deaths to play another day. One dead monkey don't stop the show. Nor two. Her sons slipping in and out of these other bodies. Up and down they fly. Quick and dead. Dead quick. Quick dead. Quick.

Clouds rolling in. Sky greasy dishwater gray now, the no-color sky of most days in the city, no big deal except you notice the gray because just a minute ago sky a pretty blue. The court, the park gray now like the end of a love affair. No surprise, the usual shitty gray of things when they stop being good between two people. Color you expect things always turn out sooner or later unless you're one of the two people just starting out happy together and let yourself forget for a while how close the bluest day is to gray. Don't mind me, she says. I'm telling this story and since I kind of know how it ends, I can't help putting some of the ending up here at the beginning. But what I'm telling is true too. Clouds did start rolling in. Small, white, fluffy and scattered the last time I really paid attention and now the clouds different shades of gray, darker and darker, as large as three or four downtown city blocks of tall buildings up there floating in the air, drifting together, hooking up, larger and larger. On the nature program I like to watch they said giant islands of hot rock slide and bump and crunch deep underground and that's what makes earthquakes. These heavy clouds piling up over Westinghouse Park will make lightning and thunder, an earthquake in the sky.

The rest of the players look more like him now. Grayer. Smaller. The game's slow, sloppy, everybody's keeping one eye on the sky. Then it speeds up again. Like they realize there's not much time left. No smiles now. The air's thicker. Sneakers screech. Ball pounds louder. Everybody's pumped, but holding their breath too. Third game for him and he shouldn't be playing. Or trying to play.

On the court a few minutes at the beginning and a few at the end of his first game. An easy win for Tyrone's team. Next one not much harder, a runaway again and he played a good while during the middle. Hit a shot. Rebounded a couple. Got left behind once, panting, bent over, pulling on his shorts after three quick trips end to end. Stole an in-bounds pass. Threw a long pass away. Holding his own she thought. Good enough she thought. It's going to be all right. He's out there having fun without hurting hisself. Lonely on the bench remembering her sons but she's okay when he plops down breathing hard, sweating, the funk of him, the shake in his muscles, the cute, rubbery faces he makes when he squeezes a sore spot or rubs out a muscle or stretches like a bear after winter. She's okay. She can ride the action on the court. Then he tries to be something he's not. More than he needs to be. Someone he doesn't need to be.

Clouds rolling in. Where'd they come from so fast. Why. How's the wind calm down here while it whips a storm above our heads.

Rain, rain, go away, little Johnny wants to play.

She thought about people praying, always asking for something or another, but they forget to ask for everything to be all right if it turns out they get what they ask for. People forget what they ask for can hurt them. They think they'll know what to do with what they pray for. People wish for things, pray for things, and forget to ask for protection. Whether you have a little or a lot in this world don't do you a damned bit of good, does it, if you're not protected so you can enjoy it. No point in having anything if you can't protect what you have. And if nothing's safe no point in praying. Mize well take what you get.

A chance to play a little ball when he's well past the ball-playing age is not enough. He wants more. And when he gets more, when he holds his own out there, he wants more. He thinks he's getting away with something, getting his wish, and then he finds there's no protection. Got that little chance he begged for and wasn't satisfied. Tried for more, got it, then like me with two beautiful sons, suddenly there is no protection.

Oh, God. Only here. This kind of shit only happens here. Other people don't live like this. Don't die like this. One more time, is it going to happen one more time, one more man snatched from me.

Started off and finished the first game, played lots in the middle of the next until he limped off and sank heavy-bodied on the wet spot beside her Tyrone had left behind.

Think you better stay right here with me, baby. You did fine. I'm proud of my ball-playing man. Saw you grinning after you swished that jumper. Thought you might be losing your breakfast when you leaned on the fence over in the corner. But I was steady cheerleading. Go. Go. Yeah. Yeah, the whole time. My baby can still do it, can't you.

Surprised my own self. Almost a year since I played full court. Shoot around every now and then, a couple of light two-on-twos. No real runs. Hadn't thought about playing till Ty asked me.

Right. Uh-huh. Lucky you just happened to be wearing sneakers and shorts to walk here and watch.

Didn't know what to say when Ty said c'mon and play. Game comes back quick once you step out there. No wind but my legs feel fine. Make it my business to walk almost every day. Fast. Couple miles at least. Jog some with the fellas on the weekend around the reservoir in Highland Park. Do my little stretches and push-ups and sit-ups every morning just about. But shocked myself, how good I feel out there.

You looked good. And now you're where you should be, looking good, feeling good right here next to me on this bench. Don't push it, babe. Game's going to get rained out in a minute anyway. Don't know where all those clouds came from so fast. What's wrong with your leg. Why you keep messing with your leg.

Just a ding. Somebody kicked my calf. A little bruise. Sore and tight is all. Damn. Playing again sure feels good. Body's going to ache whether I'm in shape or not. You know. Price of the ticket. Nothing wrong with my leg ice and rest won't fix. Trade a little hurt for playing time any day.

Nice to see you so happy.

Know what it is. It's the warrior spirit. Don't frown at me now. I know what I'm saying sounds like some dumb knucklehead macho shit, but playing ball's about being a warrior. And how many times does a man get to feel like a warrior round here.

Once you know how to play you don't forget. Blind man could play the game if he got the spirit. All you need's that warrior spirit to keep the old arms and legs moving.

Okay, Mr. Warrior. But don't make me nail your warrior ass to this bench.

Up by four buckets in the second game when he gimps over. Stayed ahead and won by five. Next one much closer. Tyrone's team up, then caught, behind two hoops, then up again, then tied when Tyrone slams into one of the poles holding up the backboard. Nine-nine and first to eleven wins. Too many teams waiting so no deuce game, it's straight eleven, *Next, who gots next.* She halfway remembers the rules he explains from hearing her sons talk, from strolling years ago in this same park, pretending not to be paying attention to what the boys were doing or saying when she sashayed in her pack of girls back and forth past the court.

Time out after Tyrone brams into the pole. He rolls around on the asphalt, moaning, cursing, doubled up, flat on his back like a turtle, squeezing one thick leg to his chest. Waves off the ones who look like they're trying to help him up. Staggers to his feet, hobbles some of the teeniest baby steps she'd ever seen a grown man hobble, him teetering, thinking real hard about each one before he tries the next. Moving a little bit better by the time he reaches the bench. With his back to the court he leans over and whispers.

Take my spot, Pops. Need you, Pops. I know you got the last two hoops in you. You gotta run for me, man. Reach back. Other motherfuckers round here scared to whip these handkerchief-head punks.

Some players on the court against Tyrone's team wearing dark blue bandannas do-rag style. They'd driven up in two spit-shined, midnight blue rides. Fly rides. Big money rides. Strolled in together. Called *Next* and took next, fuck the other teams in line before them. Two weren't playing. They sat on the bench catty-corner across the court. A whole bench for just the two of them. A bench packed full as the others till it cleared like magic when the car doors slammed and the blue bandannas, laughing, profiling, sauntered towards it.

Why do men need to pretend they're something they're not. She'd wanted to ask him the question earlier that day when he said, Let's go down to the park. She knew what was coming. Funny in a way as she watched him lace his sneakers up tight, pull on shorts and a ratty, sleeveless T-shirt. In a way it pleased her. Him wanting to shed some of the years he thought stood between them.

People need lies, don't they, big fat lies sometimes was her answer to the question she didn't ask him then. Lies to keep themselves going. Hard out here in the world and everybody got the right to dream up shit helps them get by. She could under-stand that, did it herself. You couldn't always afford to look too close at the truth of a thing, let alone all the times you didn't know the truth. Nobody's business if you have to fool yourself, leave a thing alone, pretend it's not there till you're ready to deal with it. But the lies men tell to get over on people, the selfish little niggling lies and bullshit they put out to steal from people, hurt people, fool people, those lies fucked things up for everybody.

Poor thing tried to find one more game in hisself, but barely a piece of game left. Didn't have shit left, really. Did he go back on the court because I was sitting there. Him trying to prove some-thing to me I didn't need proved. Was it that warrior crap. Did he really believe it.

Shot an air ball. *Air ball, air ball*, people hollered. Bumped into somebody. Stumbled and fell down when the one he's guarding scored. Bounced his dribble off his own foot and yelled, Foul. You hit my arm. Skin ball.

Foul, shit. You bowed me, nigger. Pumping your arm like a damn billy club. Didn't call no foul till you lost the pill.

You were fouling me the whole time.

Why didn't you call it then. Why'd you wait till you kicked it out. Too busy bowing me is why.

You fouled me. My call. Skin ball.

No motherfucking foul. You just can't handle. Give it up, old man. Your day been here and gone.

Skin ball.

Then the raghead from the bench is on the court, in my man's face. He tugs up his shirttail, reaches down into his baggy jeans.

Blue ball, old gray-ass nigger. My homey say Blue, it's Blue.

Who the fuck asked you. Who the fuck you think you are anyway butting in the game. Who you think gives a fuck what you say. Stay out the game.

Yo. Time out. Time the fuck out. Nigger want to know who I am. See this. See this Magnum, old nigger. This make me referee and all-star and commissioner. Make me Jesus and your daddy too. That's who the fuck I am, motherfucker. I own this raggedy park. Own everything far as you can see. Own you, own your mama and grandma. Own that skinny-leg ho over there you better go on and sit your old self back down beside.

See this 357, old nigger. Ought to put it in your big mouth and shut you up good. But you ain't worth no bullet. You a fly. Some no-ball-playing over-the-hill motherfucker better just go on and get out my sight before I change my mind.

When I say Blue it's Blue. That's who the fuck I am.

He fires twice. Loud, so loud. Hits the ball with the second shot and I'm screaming. Other screams around me. People ducking and running and yelling.

Go home, niggers. Game's over. Blue won. Blue number one. Blue the baddest. Go home, chumps. Rain's coming. I ain't gon kill this ignorant old motherfucker cause he don't know no better. Not killing him today, anyway. Next time you fuck wit Blue you a dead motherfucker. Cause I'm all-world. The commiss. I own this goddamn park. Hear me, old nigger. Own this trifling park and all the niggers in it. Go home niggers before I change my mind and start raining on your sorry asses.

You could run, or back away slow, or sit still like I did too scared to breathe and keep your eye on him, listening to his crazy talk, watch him fire into the sky and wave that long-barreled silver pistol and think to yourself when your heart stops pounding long enough so you can think, That's one hopped-up ain't-going-to-live-long fool, or you could sit still as stone and stare up at the dark clouds and think maybe whatever sends storms down on us sends him. Him sent to do just what he's doing so maybe what he's saying is true. Maybe the power's in his hands. Maybe he's telling it the way it is. Something large, large speaking with his voice, just like it speaks in the thunder. King of the court, life and death sure enough in his hands. Grinning at his crew strutting past, slow and casual to the blue-black cars. Gun arm limp at his side now. Muttering to nobody but hisself. Then he points his empty hand at the bench, sights down the barrel of his finger. *Pow, pow*, like a kid he makes gun noises with his lips. Plugging people right and left as he squeezes off rounds.

Is the sky waiting for him to finish killing everybody, waiting for him to say yes, it's okay now. I'm done, go on and rain. Wash away the blood now.

Big as eggs, the first drops, when they come, don't seem to fall from the sky, they jump out the asphalt, spattering black around his white-lipped sneakers. She hears each drop strike. *Prap. Prap.* Dark holes in the asphalt, splatting the court and she thinks of the grandfather he told her about, an old, dead man spitting tobacco juice in Cassina Way, sitting on the same steps she walks down every day. Rain pouring down around the shooter but not a drop dares touch him as he walks that foot-dragging, shoulder-shrugging, all-the-time-in-the-world, my-world-my-time walk to his car.

The rain hits me. One big drop at a time. It stings, hot or cold, cold and hot. Like somebody way up in the sky, bent over, crying cold, burning tears. Then I remember where I am. I'm shivering, getting soaked on a bench in Westinghouse Park. Hear a gunshot again. Hiss of the basketball dying. Noises too loud for my skull, cracking the bones in my ears. I don't see any people, the blue-black cars long gone, gliding away from the curb like sharks. No, no, I'm thinking. It can't happen again, I'm plumb out of men. No sense in sitting here like a fool, getting soaking wet, letting all those tears belong to another person fall on me. Then I see him standing at the end of the bench, behind it, wet as I am, gripping the rail, staring at the empty court that's full of puddles already, puddles shivering when raindrops hit.

I think he's shaking too, but it might just be me shivering and everything I see all shaky.

Why didn't I run to him when he was out there on the court, throw my arms around him, protect him from the crazy boy with the gun. Me this time the one who dies. Take me. Please, take me. Not one of my men this time. Why did I sit here and let it happen.

Sit like watching a movie on TV. Movie I'd seen before because I knew what was going to happen before it happened. Cold and hot with knowing. Helpless with knowing. Is that why I didn't run to him, try to protect him, beg the fool not to shoot, beg the bullets to hit me. Had I seen it too many times to believe I could change one thing.

Soaked in blood already. His blood I don't need to leave my seat to drown in.

Why doesn't he speak. Does he see what I see, see himself laying out there alongside the caved-in ball in the corner where the bullet kicked it. Does he see the dead body I see. Does he know whose it is. One more black body on the wet asphalt joining all the others. Black bodies twisted on the ground, under it. He doesn't speak to me and I can't speak to him. What kind of noises would come out my shaky body if I tried to use my voice, if I tried to find words. Wailing. He'd hear my body wailing if I try to speak.

When he comes over and drops beside me, his body hits the bench as if he's fallen from a place as high up in the sky as the crying eyes. I wonder what a sane person would think about us. Two wet fools on a park bench hugging each other in the pouring rain. I hear thunder for the first time, close, on its way here, but it's nothing to worry about, nothing that's going to hurt, a little pimple of rumble after gunshots in my ear. All right. All right, he's saying, saying it over and over to somebody, anybody, maybe himself, maybe me. All right, all right, saying it and sucking big gulps of air between the words, saying all right as if he's afraid he won't be all right if he stops saying it. But he does stop. It's just deep breaths now. And then they slow down. And he asks me if I'm all right, as if *all right*'s the only word there is, the only word he can say to keep us both safe till he can say others.

Shit, man. Shit, shit, shit. I can't stop shaking. You were almost dead out there. I believed he was going to shoot you dead.

C'mon, baby. Let's get out of here. Out this goddamn rain. Look at you. You're all wet.

He was going to kill you and I didn't do anything but sit here and watch. That's all anybody did. Watch or run. Watch him kill you.

Nobody's dead. He didn't kill me. It's over. We need to get out of here. C'mon now, girl. Get yourself together.

I saw you on the ground. Over there. Saw you bleeding in those puddles. Your blood in those cold, dirty puddles.

I'm going to pull you up now. No — no — no — no. Please. Don't fight me. Don't push me away. Easy now. Let me help you up.

Why did you have to go out there. Why did he have to shoot.

It's over. Listen to me, baby. It's over. We got to go now. Get out this goddamn rain.

Shit. Shit. Shit.

She lets him help her up. Once she's steady on her feet she wants to run. Far away from this place. Away from him. If she runs fast enough raindrops won't catch her. Won't blister her skin. Won't peel her skin and let the freezing and burning inside. If she runs fast enough, far enough, another city, another life, she won't have to watch the breath leaving his body. Won't have to return here tomorrow, looking for him, mourning him, when even the puddles of his blood have dried up in the blazing sun.

I'm okay now. Now she feels like a fool, shivering in the pouring rain, talking to this man in a calm voice, as if the rain's not there, running down her face, squishy in her shoes. Welts of it, streaks of it. Big drops making her blink when she raises her face to say goodbye to him. Until the moment she decides it's what she must do, she didn't know she was going to say goodbye. Didn't know water drops clung on her eyelashes. Didn't know she would say the other words she had to say and mean them too, abide by them through sickness and health till the day she died.

I love you, baby. Love, love, love you. But I can't love another dead man. I've loved my last dead man. Can't take it anymore. Once more would kill me. Love you but I got to cut you loose, baby.

She can tell he doesn't believe her, doesn't understand the words she says, the words she doesn't. She listens to enough of what he's saying back to her to know he can't understand.

Shushes him with a finger to her lips. Smiles. Then plants a kiss on her fingertip. Passes it on to him. Her fingertip touching his lips while she silently mouths again, *I love you*, then *Goodbye* before she turns her back and walks away.

How long ago. Which finger was it. Of course she knows. She's saved it. Protected it. The print of his wet lips, the rain, her own spit she raises to her face again. Sniffs. Tastes. The sound of that one finger, lifted from his mouth, moving through the air, returning to the place where she would keep it safe is the sound she'll say to someone, someday, that sound of loving him and letting go, if you could hear the way it sounded inside me, you'd know the sound of lamentation.

You mean to say she just walked off and left you standing there. Youall spozed to be deep in love and shit and she all the sudden left you standing there high and dry.

Didn't you hear the man. Said it was raining cats and dogs so he ain't hardly high and dry.

Shut up, Baxter. The brother knows what I mean.

How's anybody spozed to understand what you mean, mush-mouthed negro, if you got the words all crooked as usual.

You the one never listens, Mr. Know-it-all.

Not hardly wasting my time listening to some gumball-mouthed turkey . . .

Whoa. Man's telling a serious story here and youall acting like clowns. Hush. Let the man talk.

Goes to show you what happens to bitches read the goddamn Bible. They get hard-headed. Can't nobody tell them nothing. Bitch tell you in a minute it's her way or the highway. Hard-headed and stubborn. Like what's-her-name, you know, the chick they told, Don't look back, don't you dare look back but she's gonna do it her way and looks and turns to a pillar of something — stone, fire, pancakes — some damned something, serves her right.

Salt, fool. A pillar of salt. Damn. My man telling the story of losing his true love and you butt in with some off-the-wall shit.

Hey, I'm just trying to be helpful. You know. No disrespect, brother man, but these boo-hoo loved-and-lost stories a dime a dozen. You want somebody to listen you got to jazz them up. Salt or pepper or something. Lost count of how many these sad stories I been through my own self. When it's me, though, it's always the bitch end up crying her eyes out at the end and me long gone. Left a trail of broken hearts from one end of this trifling burg to the other in my day. Black hearts, white hearts, all color hearts. Always been a equal opportunity heartbreaker.

Fartbreaker, you mean. All the bullshit coming out your mouth.

Hey, y'all. Let the man finish his story.

Finished, wasn't it. Didn't he say she left him high and dry.

He didn't say high and dry. Old no-talking country negro over there the one said that.

Huh-uh. Said no such a thing. Why you always trying to start something, Monroe.

Whoever said it, don't matter. She left him. Ain't that the point. And the end of the story, right.

Not really. I believed it was over. Didn't want it over but seemed like she'd taken the choice out my hands. Said goodbye. Blew me off with a kiss.

Did my best to change her mind. Knocked on her door. Called her on the phone a thousand times. Wrote a letter. Stuck notes under her door. Waited for her to leave the house and ambushed her in the street, but she ignored me. Never said a mumbling word. Looked through me like I wasn't there. After a while I got ashamed of myself. A love jones no reason to stalk her. I wasn't getting any satisfaction and she wasn't going back on the goodbye. Just hassling her and making a fool of myself so I stopped bothering her. Aggravating myself. Figured maybe if I left her alone a while she might start seeing things differently. Might miss me, might want to see me again. Had to believe she might. What we had between us too good for her not to miss, wasn't it. I couldn't be wrong about it. Missing her just about killing me. Had to believe it was hard on her too.

Tried pushing myself on her, then tried waiting. Tried pride, tried mad, tried saying to myself, Fuck it, the bitch don't want me, I don't need her. Nothing worked. Got to be two, three months and I thought I might have dreamed up the whole thing. How could we be so tight one minute. Then blam. Nothing. Told me she couldn't deal with the thought of losing me. Said losing me would kill her. Then she starts treating me like I'm a ghost already.

Not a word for months. Then she calls. *Mr. Mallory's gone. Could you please come over and help me. Please. Please hurry.*

MR. MALLORY

Dear Mr. Giacometti:

You don't know me. No reason you should or ever will. My name is Martin Mallory. I live in the United States of America and speak only the English language. You may not be able to read these words and I apologize for taking up your valuable time with this letter whether you read it or not.

I am a great admirer of your art. After I came across photographs of your sculptures, I went to the library that very day to find out more about you. The more I discovered, the more I wanted to know. Since that day, your example has guided the work I do.

My work is taking pictures. I'm not an artist but I'm learning from your art to use my camera in new ways. Difficult ways that will probably wear me out before they produce decent pictures, but I want to thank you, Mr. G.

Thank you for what you said about a head, your brother Diego's head, I think, but you were talking about any head, mine, yours, weren't you, when you said the longer you look, the stranger it becomes. You also said a head changes in the split second you look away from it and then look back. Never the same head twice.

I began to understand why I'd been discouraged, ready to give up picture-taking. When my photos were developed, I found little or no trace of what I thought I'd seen before I snapped the shutter. I learned from you to expect disappointment. You admitted failure, even welcomed it. Said it's impossible to copy a world that never stops changing. Seeing is Freedom, you said. Art fakes and freezes seeing. Artists can't copy what they see, you said. They copy their memories or imitate another artist's copy of a memory.

Even with a live model sitting in your studio, you said, you can't copy what you see. Your eyes must choose. Study either model or copy. Lose sight of one or the other. When you turn from the model to shape a portrait or clay figure, it's memory and habit, not sight, that guide your hand. Each pinch or gouge or edge or shadow formed as you remember it. The model always something else, somewhere else.

Should I stop asking my pictures to be mirrors. Will they always be memories, wishes, dreams. Real and unreal. Mine but also strangely not mine. Many years ago, for numerous reasons I'll spare you, if in fact you've been patient enough to read this far, Mr. G, I decided to live alone. Suffered the loneliness and pain of cutting myself off from other people only to discover when I started taking pictures, others still lived inside me. Sometimes when I spread a new set of prints on a table I wonder who on earth saw things this way. Who's caged in my body. Whose eye peeks out the keyhole of the locked door. When the shutter lets in light, are my eyes open or closed.

I've learned from you the world vanishes when anyone looks hard enough, hard the way an artist must. How do you make your peace with this vanished world, with what's unseen, there and not there. How do you keep the sting of its absence present in your work. When I look hard at my photos, a terrible emptiness begins to chew at their edges, pokes its finger through their watery centers, through me. I feel like a blind man who points his camera at a world he'll never see, never be sure of, even when he holds pictures of it he's taken in his hands.

Again, thank you for your example. Thank you for staring hard at the world, for losing it and not looking away, for piecing something together out of nothing, for remembering what's lost.

Through his snores he hears her listening outside his door. The wheeze and snort and whistle and choke of asthma is what she's hearing, not snores, but for her purposes from the far side of the door the difference hardly matters. He's sure he's not snoozing nor snoring because he's been wide awake for hours wishing he was asleep, making up blues verses to keep himself company. *Met myself this morning, flying through my own front door/Met myself this morning, flying through my own front door/Ohh-whee, ohh-whee, mama/Ain't leaving my happy home no more . . .*

In his rambling dreams the city was many streets, then one, then a back porch seen from an alley when he stops many cities, many years away and peers over the tall wooden fence at the back porch steps where she sits, elbows on knees, frozen in bright morning light. Minnie Mouse ankles you could snap like a matchstick, bare and ashy beneath the hem of her long housedress. What shoes would she be wearing. Shoes, shoes, everybody got to have shoes. What face. Her head is bowed. Eyes lost in shadow. Her skinny weight forward where her elbows press into her thighs. Spraddle-legged like she squats on the toilet. If you were a nasty little shaved-head boy on the bottom step, you could peek up her dress.

He looks away before he thinks too much about what her hidden eyes might be seeing. Losing her. She's already gone this bright morning. This woman, this wife in the sunny back yard of a tilted, needs paint, two-story frame house in Washington, D.C., before the war. She wouldn't come outdoors barefoot, but he sees her red toenails, thick net of veins across her high arches. She is too young, too narrow-hipped for all the children she will bear, his children, other men's, the children who live, the dead ones who can't, sleeping in the lap of the five-and-dime housedress from which ankle bones poke, easy to snap as matchsticks.

Nothing could be quieter than that morning. Nothing farther away. Nothing closer. These are messages the floating dream brings with it.

He can't remember talk, what it was they might have been arguing about earlier, inside the house, on the bottom floor they rented, in a kitchen filled with coffee smell, then the sneer of Dutch Cleanser as she dusted the sinkboard to chase roaches. Whatever was said chased her too, outside to the porch, and choked off more talk, neither speaking to the other as he shunned down the crooked wooden steps past her on his way to work. At the gate he didn't turn and wave. Whether she was sitting on the steps or inside the house, visible or invisible through the kitchen window, he'd wave every morning as he left. On the morning recalled by the dream he had wanted her to know how he'd felt lately, what he could not bring himself to say out loud. Why would anyone want to talk about something like that. Why would she want to hear about emptiness and distance. How after he waved and left her in the morning, she disappeared. How once he turned his back and walked away from the porch, the house, their lives together, what she did all day, how she did it or with whom probably wouldn't cross his mind till he saw her again. He kept the feeling to himself. Who'd want to hear it. Why'd he need her to hear it so bad the particular morning he's remembering.

People as good as dead when you weren't around them. He couldn't help it if that's the truth inside him. Till he was certain they weren't dead, he'd just as soon keep his distance, not expect anything from them, not set himself up for disappointment.

If he continued to spy on her over the fence, sooner or later she'd raise her head. And what if she caught him looking. Wouldn't she see in his eyes how sad it was for someone you love to die. And what might he see in her brown eyes. Himself dead too. Why was he drawn to the secrets behind other people's eyes, other people's windows. Haunted by yellow squares lit up at night in the close-packed houses of the neighborhood. Why did he need to watch strangers going about the business of their lives. See them without being seen. Hovering, floating outside in the empty dark, did he spy on people's private lives because he couldn't imagine such a life for himself, a body and feelings anchored, touching, being touched.

Like a sheet clothespinned to a line the cotton dress stretched between her knees. A tight curtain and if he had peeped up under it, would he have seen all the days lying in wait for them, for their scattered children. Days longer than years one kind of dying, years shorter than minutes another kind.

How could he forget her so easily. Out of sight, out of mind. Was it a trick he taught himself. Or was everybody born that way and some people learned the trick of remembering and caring. Why did he forget. Forget what was real in his life. Forget to care. And why was he remembering this morning.

Sometimes when you folded down a corner of a page to save your place in a book, you remembered exactly where you were, what was happening when you picked up the book again and started in reading again, but sometimes everything felt so unfamiliar you'd think you grabbed the wrong book, a book someone else with the same habit of turning down pages had been reading or a book you'd started once and laid aside and lost track of many years before and everything strange now except the hurt page.

A big night for dreaming. The sad back-yard dream one of many in a crowd. Though he could barely recall details of most, two had blended in a peculiar fashion and stayed with him. In the first one he had awakened from another dream of being chased by a bear. Found himself telling the bear dream to a person he didn't recognize. It was important to convince this stranger the dream of being pursued by a bear was not an ordinary dream but a premonition, warning. He wasn't having much luck getting the guy to believe the fear, threat, and urgency the bear dream triggered. Then it came true. He was walking alone along a country road when two big, snarling farm dogs — a German shepherd and an even larger, speckled mongrel — snapped their chains and started after him. Attempting to outrun them foolish; in seconds their powerful paws would rake his back, teeth rip into his calves. He screeched for help — the dogs' owners, anybody with a stick, a gun. Scanned his surroundings desperately for a house to duck into, a tree to climb. That's when he saw what at first seemed another swift, low-running dog charging across a grassy field, headed straight for him. The animal transformed as he stared, suddenly streamlining and enlarging, becoming the huge, bullet-snouted grizzly from the previous dream.

Terrified as he was, he also experienced a tingle of satisfaction — he'd been right to worry, the first dream had prophesied this awful moment. A window in his dream to squeeze in the pleasure of saying *I told you so, I told you so* before he's torn apart and eaten alive. Also a moment to hope maybe dogs and bear will get tangled up and distracted, give him time to reach the cottage that has sprung up just a few yards ahead. He knocks frantically at the front door, races around the house searching for another way in. Oh shit, Oh shit, he's thinking as he runs. This close to escaping and nobody's home, the sucker's locked up tight. Then he's inside looking out, drinking tea with an old cracker farmer and the farmer's young, black-haired wife while howling dogs, a growling bear, people with guns, radios, loudspeakers, flashlights scramble around outdoors.

How long had she been listening at his door. Had she been there while he dreamed. Could she follow the stories unfolding dream to dream. Would voices and animal noises, the thunderous thumps of his heart force their way through the din of asthma. Most likely she'd been standing with her ear to his door only a minute. Was her boarder dead or alive all she wanted to determine. He'd fool her one morning. Hold his rattling breath, pinch his nose holes shut. Force her to wait and wait and wait for a sound till she had no choice but to knock, knock again and again. Louder. Calling his name, Mr. Mallory. Mr. Mallory. Shouting, finally pushing through his door.

Morning, miss. He'd greet her stark naked, wearing only a Morning miss smile.

No. No, he wouldn't. He liked her. Liked living here in her house. Liked her habit of checking on him. His guardian angel. If he heard her in the hall listening he knew he was not dead yet. Nothing gained by playing a nasty trick on her. He liked the girl.

Worried about her. Couldn't imagine where she found strength to survive the bad things happening to her. Someday they needed to have a long talk. Many talks.

Much better here than in the senior citizens' high-rise where every week it seemed some coughing, watery-eyed one or bedsore-ridden one or inch-along, dead-smelling one finally kicked the bucket. His room had been next to the elevator. Through cardboard walls he'd overheard the news. Who was sick, missing, had passed. Who received a visitor and who didn't. What had been served that day in the cafeteria downstairs it was a crying shame to put on people's plates and call food.

Bells pinged when the elevator doors clattered open. Chimes to awaken poor souls who fall asleep the instant their heavy-lidded eyes droop shut. *Ping-ping-ping* for the ones too blind to see oversize numerals lighting at each floor. Chimes for the ones who forget to punch a floor. For the ones who play all the buttons. Last call for the ones hearing nothing as they drop nonstop to the basement and out the back door to a meat wagon. Or the one who can't make up his mind to get on because he doesn't want to be smashed in the face and robbed again when he steps off. *Ping-ping* for the lady who understands nothing about counting chimes or lights signaling floors, who's puzzled by exile, the hospital-sized, piss-reeking boxes rising and descending, doors wheezing open for what. Chimes for the one who won't get off the first or third or fifth time the elevator stops at her floor, maybe never unless some kind, less fuddled soul says, Miz Smith, I think this one's yours, dear, and leads her by the hand.

The one he named Mrs. Mumbles. Until she slipped on the ice and broke her hip trudging up one of the steep streets surrounding the high-rise like a moat, she had dressed every day in church clothes, complete with hat, gloves, hose, heels, powdered her face, and made it her business rain or shine to go somewhere, a visit or an errand, a bus ride nowhere in particular with her senior citizen's pass, just out the damn building. Busy, earnest, bandy-legged Odetta Eleanor Washington, a tiny lady he called Mrs. Mumbles because she never stopped muttering, her big pop eyes roaming, little hands twirling, busy trying to enter a conversation she doesn't let anybody distract her from too long. He could almost see comic-book balloons full of words no one hears but Mrs. Mumbles sailing in the air above her head. They're rising and gliding away but she's determined to keep up, catch the attention of familiar voices talking up a storm, people from her real life before she landed in the high-rise, family and friends who for some cruel reason won't answer her now.

Where were they today. All his lost ladies. Poor Mrs. Mumbles with her shattered hipbone, blind Miss Gillingham, the girl on the back porch steps who was his wife. Once upon a time he believed his life didn't float like a bubble, it trailed him like an oil slick. He leaked it like an incontinent old man. It stank. The sour, stale funk of this last bed, this last room. He slipped through people's lives like flu. Drained and dirtied them, marked them with his spoor. He knew better now. Now he doubted anything he'd ever said or done had made the slightest difference for anyone.

Boxes of overexposed snapshots, undeveloped negatives, unsent letters. Here he was, his skin wrinkled, soiled laundry, the gears of his body just about to seize and send him on his merry way and he's curled in bed, covers over his head, listening for a girl to tell him whether he's alive or dead. Oh Lawdy, Lawd, alive or dead and still he's not quite prepared to get up and start the work he couldn't finish if he owned more lives than a cat.

He's heard of whole towns drowned like kittens. Citizens ordered to evacuate, rousted from their homes, their farms by sirens, bells chiming, *ping-ping*ing. New England valley towns turned to reservoirs for thirsty cities. Towns someone declared nobody needed anymore so a dam opened, low-lying plains flooded. Citizens warned for weeks by clamoring sirens and chimes. Years afterward at night the lights of the drowned towns they say still pop on, stars beneath black water.

Dear Mr. Giacometti:

Me again. Mr. Mallory here again. I'm both disappointed and relieved not to have received a reply to my first letter. I set it aside after I'd written it. Intended to reread it in a cooler frame of mind, then draft a clean, revised copy I hoped would be an improvement on the original. As if I didn't know better, as if you hadn't pointed out the foolishness of wasting time and energy tinkering and tinkering to achieve an appearance of something finished once and for all, as if anything could be completed while we're still alive and breathing, still continuing to see. Vanity, the urge to impress you, to make the letter perfect, kept me from mailing it. Then I realized I didn't know where to send it. Wasn't sure whether you are alive or dead.

From various brief accounts of your life I recalled many years in Paris, international fame, a serious illness, cancer perhaps, and a trip, your only one, to this country during the 1960s, New York for a show at the Museum of Modern Art, then nothing closer in time. No memory of a birth or death date. Rather than discouraging me, all the above, especially the thought of you somewhere beyond the reach of words, frees me, puts my project of writing to you in the proper perspective, outside ordinary day-to-day time, into a space where your figures live, fixed and dancing, metal and flesh, entering and leaving time through the needle's eye of each beholder.

How can I make photos that invite a viewer to stroll around them, as they might stroll around one of your tall, tiny women on her pedestal. I want people to see my pictures from various angles, see the image I offer as many images, one among countless ways of seeing, so the more they look, the more there is to see. A density of appearances my goal, Mr. Giacometti. So I snap, snap, snap. Pile on layer after layer. A hundred doses of light without moving the film. No single, special, secret view sought or revealed. One in many. Many in one. If I ever get good, my pictures will remind people to keep a world alive around them, to keep themselves alive at the center of a storm of swirling emptiness.

Invisible views. They are what attract me to your art. You force me to see something not there. See missing ingredients I must supply, if I dare.

I don't wish to sound mysterious or silly. I'm touched by what you do, touched so strongly I need to understand why. Tell you. What I mean when I say invisible views is this: our eyes take snapshots. Like a camera. A million, million frames day in and day out. Too quick to keep track of. Each one disappears instantly, leaving no trace behind. Except from these snapshots we build a world of things with weight, shape, things that move and last. We believe in them. Depend on them. See a world out there, separate from us. Force of habit turns to certainty. We forget how spirit and mind piece the world together glimpse by glimpse. We forget our power. Forget that one naked, sideways stare, one glance away changes everything.

Your art, Mr. G, warns me not to forget. I thought of you

the other day when I saw a picture of a magnified letter *I* in a magazine ad. Without the caption beneath it, no one could have guessed what they were looking at. Just a field of dots and dots and more dots speckled inside dots. Dot, dot, dot, one after the other, inside the other like the snapshots our eyes take.

A baby knows the world disappears when it shuts its eyes. It wails, trembles. You have to hug it tight and rock and rock till everything's all right again. It knows the world's gone and lets out a howl lets you know it knows. Takes a while to figure out what most of us figure out, if we're lucky. No point in making a fuss, just keep yourself remembering while it's not there and usually the world starts up again. Babies learn words, stories, and soon enough get to be just like everybody else. Learn that what happened before is connected to what's happening now and what happens next. Learn these lies and then here you come, Alberto Giacometti. Stop, you say. Break it down. Remember, you say. A man? A picture? Look closer, you say. It's just dots with dots inside those dots and inside those more dots down to the dizziness where even dots disappear. You undo our trickery with your tricks. Strand us in a blizzard of black dots. No story. No picture. No solid little stand-up people on stands. Whimper and wail time again.

Did you know you were sculpting Africans, Mr. Giacometti. High-butt, skinny Watusi warriors rippling down a city street, crossing an intersection in the corner of someone's gaze, your flying people with their steel cable legs and chunks of lead for feet, yet lighter than air, invisible when a passerby halts midstride and turns to check out what she thinks she just might have glimpsed over her shoulder.

*

When I heard her say Mr. Mallory's gone what I thought of first was the basketball that punk killed in the park. Not the bang- bang shooting part but the way the ball jumped like somebody invisible had booted it real hard even though the ball just sitting there on the court minding its own business. It kind of jerked up and tried to scoot out the way like a kicked dog but it couldn't move fast enough. Wobbled to the fence, gave out one last pitiful wheeze I thought I heard but probably didn't because the ball too far away, off the court, up against the twisted wire fence where it'd slunk off and settled down to die. Had such a clear picture of the ball in my mind, it brought back the whole afternoon, the park, the walk with her, the night we'd spent together before the walk, everything in the picture of the ball jumping and scudding along the asphalt, the air wheezing out. Heard all the air going out the house on Cassina Way when she said Mr. Mallory's gone. The last straw, the straw breaking the camel's back, something ending, something she couldn't handle, the walls of the house on Cassina sucked in, collapsing, not a noisy crashing, just slow-motion video with the sound turned off and she's sitting on the edge of her bed with the phone in her hand and can't get out the damned way.

I thought maybe I should dial her back and find out more about what had happened and what I could do to help. Had sense enough to let that thought alone. If she wanted talk, she could have stayed on the phone talking. The idea she might need more from me than talk hit me too good to be true and it's probably why I hesitated, staring down at the phone a dumb minute as if she might crawl out the damned thing or I could crawl in. Couldn't count how many times I'd told myself I'd finally got my head around the idea of not seeing her anymore. Enough times to convince myself the story was true I guess because hearing her voice, wishing I had wings to fly to Cassina Way, I'm wondering why I'd bothered bullshitting myself, what crazy kind of twisting-myself-inside-out gyrations I'd been performing to believe such a bald-faced lie.

In all the time since I'd started going to Cassina Way, I'd only seen Mr. Mallory once and it wasn't in the Cassina Way house and I didn't know it was him till he said his name twice. Heard him in her house on plenty of occasions. Coming and going through her front door I'd hear those rusted-out windpipes of his groaning and sputtering when I passed his room. Mr. Mallory could call some hogs, boy. Except for me hearing the coughing and wheezing, he could have been a made-up person she kept in the house for company. Wouldn't blame her if he was, after all she'd been through. Couldn't really blame her if that's who I was too.

Anyway, one person's bad news, good news for somebody else. Felt sorry for Mr. Mallory, but grateful his bad news had moved her to call me. Grateful and scared. And even though I didn't know him, even though he was old and sick and probably ready to go, I was sorry too.

Tried to remember on the way over to her house what the old man looked like. A freezing winter day the day I'd seen him so he'd been bundled up like everybody else in line at the post office. Big plate-glass windows of the post office steamed up with people's breathing. Couldn't see in or out. From the street the inside must have looked like those giant, cloudy fishtanks in the Highland Park zoo. Close to the holidays so it's packed. Lines of people looped from door to counter and back, joint jumping like it did Saturday nights when the state liquor store used to be in there before they moved it down the block to a larger storefront.

Fella behind me in line, guy I played ball with in the old days, is telling me his son's graduating community college and his twin daughters on the honor roll in high school but the youngest boy, the last one, runt of the litter in junior high, just won't do right. A hard-head. Won't listen to nobody. Got to do it his way. Skips school. Driving his poor mother crazy. Sometimes I just want to kick the little jitterbug's ass. You know. Knock some sense in his knucklehead. Old people would smack you in a minute, you got out of line. Good old-fashioned ass whuppings didn't do nobody no harm, did they. Do the trick sometimes. Didn't hurt half as bad as the stuff you could get into if somebody don't take you aside and slow you down. Soften up that hard head. His mother says, No. You can't hit my baby. She's right in a way, and it probably wouldn't do no good anyhow. Kamal getting too old to put my hands on. Hard-headed as he is he just might try to fight me. Then what. I'd have to hurt him or let him hurt me and then he's out the door either way, ain't he. Maybe I should cripple his contrary ass. Let him chill out in a body cast a couple of months. Kids today drive you crazy, man. You lucky you don't have none worrying you.

Like they were sent to prove a point, two boys bop in. You don't have to turn around to know when somebody opens the post office door, blast of freezing air comes whistling through your clothes, but I'm sideways listening to Snobs, Snobs what we called him at the court anyway, so I see two kids wearing enough hooded jacket for eight kids and those baggy pants and Godzilla sneakers saunter in, look around, head straight for the counter like not a soul in the post office but them.

Where them little motherfuckers think they going. Snobs still talking to me but loud enough other people hear him because everybody has noticed the two young men in their matching blue-on-blue football parkas, gang colors, and the whole place gone quiet.

Quieter when they get to the front of the line, ignore other customers up there, lean on the counter, and state their business. Somebody is shushing Snobs. Several people trying to catch his eye are nodding, *no, no, huh-uh* on their lips because Snobs on a rip, not exactly loud talking yet but in the stillness you probably could make out what he's saying from any spot in the room. The two bangers don't seem to be paying any attention. Occupied with whatever brought them in. Medium-sized boys in XXX-large parkas. Heads inside hoods, with watch caps pulled down over their ears, what those kids gonna hear even if they didn't have Walkmen plugged to their skulls.

I been in a war, man. Shot people and people shooting at me daily. Now I'm spozed to let these punks stroll in here and bogart my turn. What's wrong with everybody. Why don't somebody snatch those little niggers. They need a good ass-whupping.

Cool it, brother. Women and children and old people in here. Don't want nobody hurt in here. Not worth it, brother.

What you talking about. Who's gonna get hurt. You think I'm worried about getting hurt by them punks.

Other people, my brother. People's scared. Look round you, friend. Know just how you feel. I'm gritting my teeth too. A goddamn shame. I'm pissed off as you, believe me.

Put my arm on Snobs's shoulder, amen what the other guy's saying. If there was time, I'd tell Snobs about the silver Magnum, the basketball blown to kingdom come. My rage. My guts churning. How I almost bum-rushed the fool with the gun. Almost, but didn't. And cursed myself afterwards for being a coward, for not taking a goddamn bullet if that's what I had to take. Shaking with shame and humiliation cause I didn't go for it. Same shame and helplessness rising in my throat now. But now not the time nor place neither. Not for my story. Not for dying or getting other folks killed.

Easy, man. Don't know what they got up under those big coats. If they're not packing, their buddies are, and a bunch of them just up the street round the corner where they always hang. Guns. Plenty, plenty guns. They got guns and like to use them and don't give a fuck who they hurt. Bust in here turn the post office into a shooting gallery. It ain't about you, Snobs. Ain't about you or them. It's about guns. Guns killing people.

Snobs staring holes in the backs of those blue parkas the whole time people trying to cool him out. Mouth tight. Eyes slits. Grim killing mask of a face. Veins popped in his neck, chest pumping. When he turns and looks me full in the face, tears in the corners of his eyes.

Forget those ignorant punks, Snobs. Just kids. Don't know no better. Fuck it. Let it go, man.

An old woman in line across the way who must have been following his every move slides over and stands close to Snobs, holds on to the sleeve of his overcoat. She squeezes his gloved hand, then pats his back, rests her hand on his shoulder, where mine had been.

You're a good young man, young man. I know you are. We all know. A smallish, tan woman, plaid knit cap with a fuzzy pompom hides her hair. She's layered against the bitter cold, a puffy penguin above her white plastic boots.

When she scuffs back to her place Snobs not okay but he's started pulling back inside himself. Doesn't look up when the boys, finished with their errand, pass by, waddling almost in the monster coats, their droopy-bottomed pants mopping the filthy floor.

Excuse me, young fellas. My name's Mallory, Martin Mallory, and I wonder if you gentlemen would allow me to take your picture, please.

An old man with a shopping bag, three or four bags inside each other from all the handles twisted in his hand, has stepped into the path of the blue parkas. So much going on I don't really hear the ragamuffin-looking old guy's name till he says it again, *Martin Mallory*, and my legs turn to water right there in the post office, hearing his name, feeling the loss of her jump up and catch in my throat, raw and fresh like I'm just finding out she's gone when he sticks out a hand for the young men to shake.

After a long, long pause in which the boys exchange nods and looks I can't read with their hoods in the way, one of them slowly extends a fist, nudges the old man's mitten.

I'm a photographer, young gentlemen. Or aspire to be. With your permission I'd like to snap a few pictures of you.

More looks back and forth, more shrugs and finger signing and head jerks I can't read. Like I said the post office real quiet before but nowhere near this new quiet. Everybody probably thinking what I was thinking. Oh shit. Thought the worst of it over, and thank goodness nobody jumped bad, nobody hurt this time round, the short-fuse, fly-off-the-handle bangers on their way out but now goddammit some nutty old man pops out of nowhere and won't let well enough alone.

Only require a minute of your time, young gentlemen. Let me get my camera out. Give me a second to focus and you can continue on your way. Don't need you to pose. I'll be snapping as you go. Once I point the camera just pretend I'm not here.

Thank you. You did mean, yes, didn't you. Very kind to let me impose. No more than a minute of your time.

A general sigh of relief. Some folks look away from the entrance, the old man bargaining with the boys. It's going to be all right after all. In spite of. They didn't knock him out their way. He didn't try to lecture them about jumping lines. Some people might be hoping he'll pull a Mach-10 out his shopping bag and waste the bandits but most are ready to go back to standing in long lines, finishing their post office chores.

Me. Of course I can't take my eyes off Mr. Martin Mallory, her Mr. Mallory who up till that moment, until I heard him pronounce his name a second time, had only been a name to me. Tall. Taller in his nappy ancient lamb's-wool Russian hat. Slim. You can tell he's skinny inside the bulk of the army surplus overcoat. Small eyes under a high, wrinkled brow. A very large nose. Way past funny-looking big to peculiar, dignified big. Like the nose arrived first and spread out over everywhere and the rest of his features had to scramble on board for the ride. He pulls off his holey mittens, tucks them in the big coat's deep pockets. Hands oversized as the blue parkas, his king-size triangle of nose.

Excuse me, young men. May I ask you a question while I'm working. You are our soldiers, our blue warriors, aren't you. Where were you when we needed you. When the police army attacked John Africa and his people, when they slaughtered women and children and burned down our neighborhood. We needed you then. Where were you.

Say what, old man.

Huh.

Tell me. Please. I want your answers in my pictures.

You tripping, nigger. Chill. Diss Blue, you be wearing that bag on your head. Wit a cap in it.

Needed you then. Need you now. Talk to me, please.

Old dude whacked out.

What you smoking, old man. Turn me on some your shit, grandpop.

Mafucker's crazy, man. Fucked up.

They wag their heads and sign with their hands, lots of threatening, herky-jerk movements, I can't tell if they're getting ready to jump him or profiling for his camera, then another blast of cold air and they're gone. Mr. Mallory shrinking as he puts his fold-up camera away and slips back into the end of the line, one more bundled-up person in a bundled-up crowd doing their best to do what they got to do and stay warm on a bitter cold December afternoon.

Guns and pictures, Mr. G. Those with the guns own the Big Picture. They say the Big Picture is the truth. Love it or leave it, my fellow countrymen say. Their Big Picture only a snapshot, but the ones with the guns say, Here's the way the world is, has been, and always will be. Forget whatever else you think you see or hear or smell or touch. Big Picture's all you'll ever need to get along.

My camera shoots but it's not a gun. And even if it was a gun, it's just one gun. Bang, bang. I'm dead.

Bang. Bang. Dead whether I snap pictures or not. Big Picture answers with a volley of atom bombs, blows me and my little pop-gun camera to smithereens.

*

When Mr. Mallory lays down his head on her pillow to die, he whispers to the empty room, I'm sorry. So sorry. Whispers to the yielding softness, the smells of her more pungent as he burrows deeper, ashamed of himself for rooting in intimate places where he has no business being, alive or dead, her dresser drawers, the jumble of closet, a jewelry box, her clothes, shoes, finally her bed, where her spit and stains and heat have marked the sheets and pillowcase with a map of her body, a secret copy too close a version of what it maps for him to touch without her permission, too close to touching her without permission, this panting and rooting and twisting in her bed the way a dog wallows when it finds a fresh carcass in the woods and riots in the wet, dead skin, wearing it, becoming what it hungers for. He's ashamed of dying where he knows she'll be the one to discover him, knows she'll be shocked, disappointed, scarred, but he's surprised to find he doesn't care about shame or scars or discovery, none of it matters, it has no power to stop him, not now, not a lifetime ago crouched in the dark on his knees spying through windows, he cares only about the circle closing, how easy it is after all to go back more years than he can count to the first woman whose bed he shared, the woman he married and deserted, who bore his children in the tilting row house behind a tall fence before the war. She's here, lying next to him. Asleep in this pillow he hugs drowning him in sleep. Her sleep. Sleep smell of the woman who lives in this house, this blue room he's never entered before, bed he's never laid his sore, tired body across or squirmed into, dug into as if, as if he must bury himself before the thunder of enemy artillery starts walking down on him.

He stops to ask himself which woman. Which face, which ears and eyes. I'm sorry. So sorry.

Both women lost their men. In one story it's him, in another it's not him, but he's sorry, so sorry, as if it's always him, the one forever missing. In one story he doesn't own a camera. In another he's stopped taking pictures and the dusty camera buried in shopping bags accuses him every day and all he can do is whisper, I'm sorry. Sorry.

Why must it always be about sorry. Living sorry. Dying sorry. Who invented, who owns this word he's crooning to himself here at the end in a stranger's bed, a stranger's house where he stays alive eavesdropping on someone else's life, a scavenger, roaming the crowded blocks of the city, surviving on what he steals through the yellow squares. He hopes they forgive him, the ones he spied on, the ones he can't touch but hurts. He asks forgiveness each time. Promises he'll give something in return for whatever it is he can't help stealing. Pay back with the pictures he takes after he wins a camera in a poker game. The squares of light he stares at through the eyepiece are what he'd give in return if he knew how, if he could hold the bright water of them in his hands, in the cups shot full of holes that are his photos.

He's pulled down the bedspread and sheet, rolled his naked body into the hollow where she sleeps, rubs his skin into the scents hoarded there, perfume of her on his fingers he brings to his cheeks, massaging it into his pores so he smells her, inside and out with each breath, each bitter-as-iron, burning clot he drags from his rotten lungs.

Which woman, which girl is he asking to forgive an old man's cracked, parched, never-quite-clean-again skin that will leave flakes though he washed and tidied himself as best he's able so she won't have to deal with the mangy stink of him spoiling her bed. Is he sorry because he's been sneaking through her things, sneaked into her bed, or is he sorry because he can't remember who lives here. Who he's deserted and forgotten. Soft eyes, soft voices, hair, flesh all one, no one, anyone, either one. Who will see this last snapshot of an old dead man in a rumpled bed, an empty room, he takes just for himself and nobody else. Click.

You okay in there, Mr. Mallory. Who's calling through his door. He'll pretend he knows. Pretend he can answer, pretend his words will shape this dream.

I'm fine, miss. Stupid old body won't stop coughing, that's all. Bark, bark, bark. Coughing goes away sooner or later. In its own good time. Hope my barking's not keeping you awake, miss. Can't bite but I sure do bark.

You didn't wake me, Mr. Mallory. I can sleep through anything. Up puttering around when I heard you. Just wanted to make sure you all right.

Thank you. I know it sounds terrible. But I'm fine. Just a spell. Just a matter of time.

Words not out of his mouth good before he's doubled over, a long, gagging, barking spasm that ends by jerking him upright in the bed, yanking him around like a puppet on evil strings.

She pushes through his door. First time since she rented him the room is what he thinks, seeing her face flicker in the shadows at the foot of the bed.

You okay, Mr. Mallory.

When he can talk, after he spits in the Crisco can he keeps beside his bed and swipes at his eyes and nose with the sleeve of his nightshirt because he doesn't want her to see his bloody snot rag, he thanks her again for her concern, hitches himself up straighter in bed, nods and smiles as generously as he's able, pitiful, weak piece of nastiness as he must seem in this young woman's eyes who's crashed suddenly across what he believed was the sturdy threshold of his room.

Anything I can get you, Mr. Mallory. Any medicine you take when it gets bad.

No, miss. But thank you. Surely as a spell comes, it goes. In its own good time.

You certain there's nothing I can do.

You've done it already. Being kind. Stepping into a sick old man's dark room. You've already helped immensely. Thank you.

Better go, then. But you call me if you need anything. Hear. No way I'm not going to be up a while.

Maybe, miss . . . maybe since you're here already you could sit a minute. Company a minute would be nice, since you say you'll be up anyway.

Sure, Mr. Mallory. Sure. Happy to sit a minute, if you're willing to put up with me.

More than willing, but I don't wish to impose. Just a minute or two.

You're not imposing, I promise. This one of my up nights. Could feel it coming. Told you I can sleep through just about anything and I can. When it's a sleep night. And thank goodness most nights are sleep nights, but ever so often, just like you say a coughing spell comes on you, one these up nights comes down on me. Nothing I can do about it, neither. I'm up. Gonna be up no matter how tired I am, how hard I try to fall asleep, sleep ain't coming. That's why I heard you. Tonight's one those up nights.

I'm sorry. He hears himself say the words and they have a familiar sound, *sorry, sorry,* spoken to a woman not the young woman who sits in the ladder-back rocker he found in the Salvation Army loft full of crippled furniture. Castoffs and castaways, every piece coated with dust, cobwebbed and spiderwebbed in the smoky shaft from an unexpected skylight.

Daughter, you remind me of someone I knew once, long ago before you were born. Before your mother born, probably.

He's seized again. Racked by a fit of coughing. Room swirls, turns the rusty color of blood, then explodes. Fiery specks and dashes flashing, darting in the pinkish space behind his closed eyes.

She's said something he missed. The word *nice* in it, the rest scattered by his coughing. He thinks he's scared her away. His illness and age spraying the room, raining on her. No wonder she escaped as soon as his head jerked away, his eyes squeezed shut. No. She's handing him a tall glass of water she must have fetched from her icebox because it's cool in his hand, cold on his lips. He shudders as cold water shudders step by step into his gut, shivers with the iciness of it, the unexpected gift.

Not too cold, is it.

No, no. Feels good on this raw throat. He gulps it down. Effort of swallowing, the battering waves of chill passing through his shoulders, chest, belly exhaust him. He must be feverish. Light-headed, a desert.

Some more, Mr. Mallory.

No, thank you. I'm fine for now. Don't mean to stare but I can't get over how much you remind me of her. A woman I was married to once. Something about you brings her back. Still married in a way, I suppose. Haven't laid eyes on her for ages, but we never got unmarried to my knowledge so she's still my wife by law, isn't she. You don't look like her exactly. Don't think I remember exactly what she looks like, to tell the truth. But that's not quite the truth either. I remember her doing certain things and she's there, in the middle of what I remember, but not so I can see her exactly. Not that I do a lot of thinking about her anymore. What would be the point. She'd be different now, wouldn't she. Old now like me. If she's still alive. You're like a snapshot of her young, a picture I never saw before, and it might not even be her, but it takes me back, right back, and I remember how her face made me feel.

One, two quick, tight coughs remind him it's not over. He clears his throat and says, Water helped. Still barking but I'm better. Better if chattering at you's better than barking at you.

What was her name.

Would you think I'm a terrible man if I said I don't remember. Well, until a second ago I didn't. Hadn't said her name in years. Didn't believe I still had it in my head till you asked and it popped right out. That's how long it's been. How much I've forgotten. Flowers. Edith May Flowers before she was Mrs. Mallory. Pretty name, isn't it. Glad I remembered it. Didn't know I did till you asked and I said it. Surprised myself. You know, like you surprise yourself coming across something down in the bottom of a drawer you didn't even remember you'd lost.

Did youall have children.

Yes. They'd be old now too. Much older than you. Wouldn't know them if I passed them on Homewood Avenue. Babies to me. Always will be cute, chubby little babies. Lap babies sleeping in her arms. In mine. Perfect little toes and fingers. Curled-up legs, don't know why they made me think of turtles. Wouldn't recognize them with long, straight legs striding down the street. Little babies. Hope she stayed alive. Hope our babies not orphans.

I'm sorry, Mr. Mallory.

Nothing for you to be sorry about, child. I'm the sorry one.

Walked out on them, on her. A pitiful excuse for a man ever since. An old story I haven't told in years. It's not the part of my life with her I was thinking about when I said how much you're like her. Edith May Flowers. Saying her name is what's bringing back the sorry part. And me the sorriest part in it. I'd forgotten her name.

Hard for me to understand you forgetting something like that. I mean your wife's name, names of people you love. But like you say, it was a long time ago. Makes me wonder if I live another fifty years, what I'll remember. Whose names I'll be able to call. I think I know. I could say right now I'm sure I know, but I don't really know, do I.

Like her in many ways. She would have brought water. If she heard an old man coughing she'd worry about him, even if he's a stranger. A softhearted person, a good person, and shy, private like you. Could tell by the way she walked she didn't trust the ground under her feet. Both of you know it can crack open, suck you down or leave you stranded, nothing but a big black hole everywhere you look. She would have knocked, though. Knocked and waited for me to say come in. She'd be worried about what was happening on the other side of the door, but she would have stood and waited.

You left her.

No choice. Believed I had to leave if I wanted a life. Stole myself. Like a runaway slave. Stole myself and the price was leaving my family behind, my people behind.

More shakes, shivers, the spewing, spraying helplessness. A long silence afterwards as if both people in the room are stunned speechless by the coughing fit's power. Through his shut eyes he watches her watching him, listens to the rocker creak, the silence after it stops, silence growing, drifting, forgetting what's supposed to come next, what came before, the room's slow, deep breathing, silent intake and exhale and drift.

Daughter. Did he think the word or say it. She doesn't stir. Half listening or past listening. If he had her attention once, he's lost it now. He's lost interest too in the sick, dying old man she's been kind enough to try and help. Why should he punish her kindness. Why rattle the chains and bells and spikes of his story. He couldn't remember how to tell it anymore. He'd failed to stay in touch with his story, the way he'd failed her name, the way his photos failed to stay in touch with his eyes. Who was this child rocking up and back slowly, slowly in a ladder-back chair. He puts a baby in her belly, in her skinny arms. Up and back. Her smooth skin and perfect, bony limbs. Her face another's face, missing, blending, born again. He'd called her daughter. A slip of the tongue. Or what he'd been calling her for a while in his mind but had feared saying aloud. Scared he'd chase her away. Who'd want a dying old man, a man with no story he remembers how to tell, for a father, a grandfather. What scum-bottomed rock had such a man crawled out from. He'd deserted her. How could he ever be trusted. Why would she want to be his orphan daughter. Why would she step again into thin air over the black pit he's opening at her feet.

Daughter.

You all right, Mr. Mallory. My eyes getting kinda heavy. Maybe I'm ready to sleep now. You okay. I think I might have nodded off a little bit already.

I'm fine. You go sleep, please. You've done more than enough.

Call me if you need me. Promise. And don't forget to call loud.

He covers his mouth with the filthy rag he was too embarrassed to pull out till this moment when she's turning to go. She pats his foot poked up under the bedclothes. Needs the rag to quiet the hacking coughs caused by the drip, drip of mucus down the back of his throat, a reflex he can't stop but sometimes tames by tightening his neck muscles, grunting, exhaling, a dry wheezing heave he hides behind the rag so he doesn't draw her any deeper into his sorry story.

You can imagine how shook up I was to find Mr. Mallory laid out in her bed. Bed I had claimed just a few months before. Like finding your daddy in your wife's bed. Or your mama in your love bed. Great googa-mooga. What the fuck's going on here. There he was big as day. Old, crazy, hog-calling, crusty-butt, sprung-dick, goat-smelling man naked as a jaybird curled up in her bed, both arms wrapped around her pillow, big dark stains where he'd sucked it like a titty, black stains like he'd bit down and drawn blood.

I was mad. Then felt bad for him. Who'd want to die this way. All your dirty old man's secrets swinging in the breeze for anybody to see.

She had pulled up the sheet from the bottom of the bed and covered him head to toe she said. He was naked again because I needed to see all of him, check for signs of what might have killed him, what dying did to him, did to her bed. When I flipped back the sheet like opening the shade on somebody else's window and peeking in. No, not peeking. Snatching the damned shade off so the whole wide world can get in Mr. Mallory's business. Poor old man, I'm thinking. Realize I'm feeling sorry for myself as much as for him. Didn't I lay where he's lying and come close to dying. Didn't I ride as near to the edge as I could, grinning ear to ear cause I thought I was getting away with something. Smiling because the kind of ride it was don't believe in death. A damned fool cause in a minute, any minute I could have ended up just like this pitiful old guy. Closer to death than I thought I'd ever care to ride, but couldn't care less, long as I was riding. She took me so high no place to go next but down. Way, way down from the mountaintop this woman had me believing was my natural home.

She doesn't watch me examining him. Sits, elbows on knees, squatted on the dresser stool, weight of the world on her thin shoulders. She looks bad. Wild. Not riding wild but coming apart wild. How else she supposed to look. She had every reason to be looking worse than she did. One more dead man in her house. And her so beat down, no choice but to phone another dead man for help.

Didn't really want to study him, and maybe I didn't have to and I sure didn't know what I expected to find, but study I did for a quick minute. No trace of anything particular that might have killed him, no marks except signs of age. A lean, stringy body, big-boned, knotted, wrinkled, scarred, knocked around. Not dead long enough to have the peace and quiet of being beyond any more hurt. A body swollen in places, flabby in places, shriveled in places, parts that had failed him, stopped working the way they should, stopped looking how they should. I covered him again, learning that quick the things about his dead body I'd never forget. Sagging pouch of balls, harmless stump of gristle in the gray hairs above it. His long, sucked-in cheeks, wrinkled like the ball sac, gray whiskers poking through dry skin like little porcupine quills and won't stop growing for weeks they say.

Just a minute with him and an itchy feeling like I needed a shower even though I hardly laid a finger on the body, and then I covered him up again and went over and stood behind her, both of us staring at the lumpy sheet but seeing different things under it, I'm sure.

He's gone all right, I said, feeling like a goddamn idiot soon's the words out my mouth. She didn't say a thing. What was there to say. Of course he's dead. She wasn't asking me if he's dead. She knew damn well he was gone, knew better than I ever would. All I did was hold the palm of my hand above his mouth. Rest a fingertip on his neck where a pulse should be. Listen for his chest. She'd told me already how she tried to fight life back in him. Pried his lips open and blew in her breath. Pumped his chest. Slammed his heart with her fists. Done all that before she phoned me. She didn't need a death expert.

He was so cold. So cold when I found him, she said. Ran my hands all over him looking for a spot wasn't icy to my touch. Cold, cold, cold. Everywhere.

Must have come in here looking for me. Must have known he was dying.

Could have been delirious, you know. Wandering around till he couldn't wander anymore and dropped down in your bed.

No. I think he knew. Think he was looking for me. He didn't want to be alone at the end. Wanted me to be here for him. And I wasn't. See, things got different between us. We started talking. Found out he wasn't a nobody. He talked to me about his life. Asked me to help him with his pictures. Those boxes in his room. Pictures. Full of pictures he took. If I die before I finish my work, he said, Burn them. Burn everything. How am I going to do that. How can I burn up the poor man's pictures.

He made me promise. And promise not to look. Nothing to see, he said. Negatives, he said. Just burn them.

I try to get her up off the stool but she won't budge. She weighs nothing, just skin and bones but I couldn't lift her with a crane. I remembered rain. Soaking weight of it on her shoulders in the park.

I lean over and wrap my arms around her. Hug her. Make myself a hood, a roof, but the heaviness of rain passes through me, each drop striking her and nothing I can do but hold on, not give in to the drenching weight, hold on to the slow, slow sway of her shoulders, her back trembling against my chest.

I can't go in his room and take his boxes and burn them. Be like him dying all over again. Why'd he ask me to do something like that. Why'd I say yes.

Pictures nobody's seen yet. Not even him. Pictures of I don't know what. Some of me, maybe. I'm in there. He took pictures of me.

I saw him with a camera in the post office three or four months ago. Around the holidays. Stopped some gangbangers in there and asked them if he could take their picture. Didn't know it was Mr. Mallory till he said his name the second time. Often as I've been in this house I never saw him here, you know. Not once. Heard him snorting and wheezing plenty, but never saw his face.

Big boxy old-fashioned fold-out camera in a shopping bag. Right before Christmas and it got pretty ugly in the post office that day. Thought those kids might hurt him. But they let Mr. Mallory do his thing. Shocked the hell out of me. The whole business. Crazy kids, your Mr. Mallory, then you, right up in my face, wringing my heart.

Got to thinking soon as it was over, Hey, I've seen this old dude and his shopping bag before. Lots of times. Matter of fact couldn't remember a time when he wasn't around. Know what I mean. How you get used to seeing a person in the street, seeing them everywhere you go around here and after a while they're just part of the street. Don't see them anymore, don't pay attention, they mize well not be there. Somebody has to point them out. Or you got to trip over them or hear something bad happened to them or hear they're gone before you see them. Well, almost broke my neck tripping over Martin Mallory that afternoon in the post office.

He used to go out regular. Stay out all day. Then he cut way down. Got to where I shopped for the few little things he needed and as far as I know he hardly ever left here. This last month or so after the cold weather started to break he got real busy again. Sick as he sounded he's gone every day with his shopping bags tucked up inside each other and his camera in them.

When I saw him in the post office that's what he was carrying. Lotta shopping bags, big box camera inside. Looked too heavy for a frail old fella like him to handle.

When the asthma didn't put him on his back, Mr. Mallory could do just about what he wanted to do. Bad leg and all he'd walk these streets every day. Years slid right off him when it came to that camera. Walking with it. Talking about it. Camera his toy. And him just like a kid playing with it. He'd be telling me something about picture-taking and change right in front of my eyes. Be all excited, just like a little boy. That camera could turn him to a different person. Different acting. Different looking. Had the nerve to flirt with me when he took my picture. And silly me couldn't help flirting back. Nothing nasty about it. He'd flirt, kinda shy flirting like your nice old granddaddy would flirt. Not because he's trying to run game. Not because he wants something. He's just playing. Having his fun making me smile. Teasing me about being a woman. Letting me know, whatever else he is, he's a man and the man part thinks I'm good-looking. Said he was going courting again soon and needed some courting practice. Wanted me to feel courted when he took my picture. Kept saying that old-timey word, *courting*. Told me any man, even one dried up as him, couldn't help courting me.

You used to tell me he never spoke. Like living with a ghost you said. Didn't you say you thought he might be a little bit off from something happened to him in the war and didn't speak or act like normal folks.

He changed. Or maybe it was me changed. Maybe I was the one started it the night he was real sick and I went in his room. Things different after that. Kept each other company. Not often, not much. He still stayed mostly to himself, but every once in a while he'd get to talking. Talk, talk, talk about everything. Stuff you'd have no idea he knew. Places he traveled. Different kinds of people he'd met all over. Talk about picture-taking. Could have been lying for all I know. Could have been telling stories he read in books. Didn't matter. He talked and I liked to listen. Enjoyed listening. And he'd listen to me.

Kind of like we had this agreement between us not to talk and it lasted a long time and seemed to be the only way to act around each other, the best way, because we both wanted to be alone and respected the other person's wanting to be alone. Then one day we got tired of the old way and pushed on through to something new surprised us both. It just happened. Sneaked up. We broke the old rules. Couldn't see how the old rules kept us pinned down till one day we acted different and things I didn't believe could change started to change.

You probably think I'm crazy but it's like I hoped Mr. Mallory might help me get back with you. Had this idea of fixing a real nice dinner. Cook the best dinner I know how to cook and I'd invite you over and the three of us would sit down to this fabulous meal like a family. Be all smiles and talking and everything would be all right.

I'd sit around sometimes daydreaming what I'd buy at the grocery store and cook. Wondering what might please you and him and me. Just a matter of waiting for the right moment. A time when we could relax and talk to each other. When he'd be easy with you and you with him and I could sit myself down at the table with both of you and know everything was going to be all right. Seemed as if maybe something like that might be possible if I took my time and listened to what Mr. Mallory had to say. And let him hear some of what I needed to say. Then maybe say to you after I'd given myself a little more time to get my feelings together and words together.

Got it all ass backwards as usual, didn't I. Hoping he could bring you back. Believing he might. Counting on him. Letting myself listen, letting myself start to talking again. Scheming. Making plans. Not letting well enough alone. Now he's gone too.

How'd he turn so cold so quick. He was alive this morning. Heard him in his room snoring. Don't it take people a long time to get cold.

You're shivering, baby.

I'm not going to burn his pictures. Don't care what I promised. You got to forgive me, Mr. Mallory, but I can't. Just can't.

I better call and let somebody know Mr. Mallory's dead. Police and funeral people, I guess. I've never done this before and you've done it too many times but we need to figure it out and get the process started.

No. Before you do anything I need you to step in his room with me. I want to look in the boxes. See if what he said's in them. Come in with me, please. I can't do it alone.

She's on her feet. A wall of rain between us. Rain wetting the sheet covering the old man's body. If it had to rain, why didn't it just go on and pour, wash this gray day away.

Mad. Sad. Then I'm mad again. Not at him. Wasn't Mr. Mallory's fault things the way they were. Sounded as if he tried to help her, not hurt her. I was mad because more bad happening to her. It should have been my head on her pillow, me guarding her, not some dying old man saving a place for me. What kind of goddamn place is that, anyway.

Pictures. Boxes of pictures she'd promised to burn. She could start with this one. Practice on this pitiful picture of me standing here dumb and helpless. Behind my back the room's dark corners begin to lift and curl up at the edges. Blacken, start to smoke, eye-stinging chemical smoke of film burning, grayish smoke twisting, climbing. The photo twists, losing its shape, melts, cools to ash. Rain and ashes cover her bed. Darkening it, turning it to mud. If I lifted the sheet again, whose face would I see.

Dear Mr. G,

Have you seen the paintings of Mr. Romare Bearden. He's my fellow countryman, and I'm proud to say of African descent, as I am. I've read the color line is less a problem in France than here so perhaps you've bumped into Mr. Bearden since you both resided in Paris a good while. Maybe you're friends. They say artists of all colors meet and talk in great cities like Paris. The idea excites me. Those gatherings and conversations might change a city, its history, its future.

I understand now the first letter I addressed to you was an attempt to enter such a conversation, begin a dialogue that somehow might lead to an actual meeting, my far-fetched dream of sitting at your feet as an apprentice.

I'm curious about your familiarity with Mr. Bearden because his art shares much with yours. His paintings are many paintings in one, overlapping, hiding and revealing each other. Many scenes occur at once, a crowd hides in a single body. Time and space are thicker. I'm seeking the truth of his painting when I stack slices of light onto each square of film. Different views, each stamped with its own pattern of light and dark but also transparent, letting through some of the light and dark of layers beneath and above. Like a choir singing. Each voice distinct, but also changing the sound of the whole, changing itself as it joins other voices.

Here I am talking to you about a choir when to tell the truth I'm a total ignoramus when it comes to music. In the schools I attended as a boy they taught us nothing about any of the arts. When we should have been learning to read music, we chanted stupid little ditties about darkies and plantations that made me want to crawl under my chair. Luckily music wasn't spoiled for me. I've always listened carefully and enjoyed all kinds, especially the blues, jazz, and gospel songs I heard growing up. And though I lack words to say how, our homegrown African music, like your sculpture and Mr. B's paintings, helps me with my picture-taking. In the piano solos of Mr. Thelonious Monk I hear familiar tunes drifting in and out, hiding and uncovering each other, old songs playing something new, music no one's ever heard before.

Since I'm fussing about my school days, I'll also share one pleasant memory. An illustrated storybook of Greek myths I loved so much I stole it. I dreamed of having the golden flesh, the huge muscles of the half-naked gods and goddesses who did whatever they wanted to do, ruling the universe according to their whims, fighting and squabbling with each other the way we did every day in the schoolyard.

One tale in particular stayed with me. Not a happy one. About a snake-haired demon, Medusa, whose terrible stare turned men to stone. Do you know the story. The hero must figure a way to fight a monster he must not look at, whose looks kill. He polished his shield till it was bright as a mirror and when Medusa attacked, she saw her reflection in his shield and became harmless as a statue.

I never forgot the drawing of Medusa's face. Her red-rimmed, spidery eyes, the nest of snakes hissing and wiggling atop her head. It was Medusa I thought of years later when I saw a photograph of a black boy's face that turned me to stone. The boy's name was Emmett Till and he was murdered by white men in Mississippi forty years ago. His battered features and the witch's face blended in a nightmare that still haunts me. Medusa's story made me uneasy from the beginning. Nasty as she was, for some reason I felt sorry for her. Turns out the hero didn't go after her because he was trying to rid the world of evil, he just wanted to steal her evil power for himself. Chopped off her head and carried it around to freeze his enemies.

You probably know the story. Why am I recalling it now. A stare that freezes and kills just the opposite of what you do, and Mr. Bearden and Mr. Monk. You turn things loose.

And I keep pulling the trigger, snapshot after snapshot blasting holes in the world, pretending nothing changes, the ducks still sit on the water untouched, calm, waiting until I'm ready to shoot again. My pictures are pretty postcards with the world arranged nice and neat. But I don't want to hide the damage. I want to enter the wound, cut through layer by layer like a surgeon, expose what lies beneath the skin. Go where there is no skin, no outside or inside, no body. Only traffic always moving in many directions at once. Snapshots one inside the other, notes played so they can dance away, make room for others. Free others to free themselves.

Excuse me for putting it this way, but is your art a lost cause. You, Mr. G, and Mr. B and Mr. Monk all lost causes. No solutions to the problems you set yourselves. And in that hopelessness, are you kin to the rest of us who walk the earth, all of us who must risk losing what we see if we truly want to see it.

Are there gypsies in Paris. If they're there, I bet your Mediterranean blood has led you to their caves. Have you heard their flamenco music, their deep singing. It reminds me of our gospel shouts and chants. Music full of violent unwelcomes in strange lands, the pain of exile, war, hunger, yearning for a home never seen, never touched except as absence. I hear layers of ancient suffering in gypsy music, hear what I wish my pictures would say, if they could sing.

She watches him scuff his pigeon-toed shuffle up the narrow corridor of Cassina Way. He looks old today. Poor dead Mr. Mallory old and weighed down. The slump of his shoulders, the stiff-kneed walk. She remembers the story he told about his grandfather coming home from gambling all night. People swore they could tell when his grandfather had a lucky night because he always seemed much older dragging home in the half-light of morning if he'd won, bogged down by everybody's bills and change stuffed in his pockets. His grandmother would plant herself on a chair at the front window of the Cassina Way house long before dawn to wait for her husband. In the story his grandmother breathes easy for the first time in hours when she catches sight of her man, then her breath stops because there's a fellow in the shadows creeping along behind him with a gun. If the story were happening now, happening just before the man with a gun is visible, the grandson would meet his grandfather, one coming, one going, the two of them face to face in the cobblestone alley, close to the same age, same size, brothers maybe or a pair of slump-shouldered, tired-eyed, weary twins. If she could, she'd enter the story and have them smile, slap each other five. Lighten up, Grandson. Don't be so blue, Granddaddy, because she knows the shadowy, slinking man with a pistol he's trying to hide pressed against his thigh will miss his target, miss and run away because as he squeezes the trigger, glass shattering, a woman's scream will make his hand jerk. And she knows the woman's hand, cut and bleeding from smashing the window to warn her man, will heal, and the scar become a story grandmother will tell grandson and then one day long afterwards the grandson will tell it to her. Knows she'll love him as she hears the story and love the slump of his shoulders, his pigeon-toed walk, even when he looks old enough to be his own grandfather walking up Cassina, leaving her alone feeling old as somebody's grandmother, watching from the front window.

And she knows he loves her. If she ever doubted it, the events of this long day removed any doubt. He'd filled out papers when the hearse arrived to take Mr. Mallory away. Carefully read then explained the forms he handed her to sign. Dealt with the paramedics, the ambulance people, the cops. Phoned Wardens to arrange a funeral and burial. He'd taken care of most everything. Treated her like he'd never been chased away. Took charge when it was clear she couldn't. Made it all as easy as possible.

She'd called out his name when he'd knocked. Let him fold her in his arms as they met in the doorway. A deep folding like a velvety cape or sheltering wings that had made her feel so damned good the first night dancing in Edgar's. She knew he did what he did because he loved her, not because he wanted her to feel beholden, not because he thought his helping her might buy back her affections. He could have acted that way. Could have had her feeling like a whore. Could have broken her heart double. Or played cool and proper, doing what he did because he was a gentleman and would have done the same thing for a puppy dog in her circumstances. Huh-uh. His doing was soft-eyed, open-mouthed love. In each little vexing duty and painful chore she'd heard the kindness in him saying loud and clear, This hurts me too, these things hurting you, and I'd do what I'm doing just this way, with my heart and soul aching, even if you weren't around, even if I might never see you again.

His hands on her first thing at the door cured any doubts. Doubts she didn't really feel but knew she deserved because he was a feeling, hurtable person just like her and she'd hurt him, yes she had, deeply as only one lover can hurt another. She'd walked away from him after the terrible day on the basketball court. Demanded her space. Demanded distance. Kept him distant. Withholding any expression of her love. Refusing all signs, the grasping after her of his love. Knocks on her door. Notes shoved under it, letters in the mailbox. Call after call. All those accidental times he just happened to wind up in the Shop and Save or post office or walking down Homewood Avenue when she did.

And after all that, even now with Mr. Mallory dying to bring them together, when she decides it still isn't time, decides she must ask him to leave again, she kisses him on his cheek, a quick peck, then feels so much the hypocrite, she slides her lips around and brushes his, then mashes his mouth with hers till it hurts, saying when she can talk again, One more day, please. Tonight I need to be alone and then tomorrow we can talk. Please call tomorrow, early. Or I'll call you. Either way. Another quick kiss to seal the bargain, a kiss to shut his lips because she can't bear hearing what he might have to say, his objections, his confusion, his hurt again, or him with another plan, telling her why being alone tonight was a big mistake or just saying I love you or I missed you, whatever might come out his mouth she needs to press it back, silence it with hers, with the hot breath she breathes down his throat, as desperately, as sure she has no choice, as when she tried to start up life again in Mr. Mallory.

Why had she wanted this night alone, why had she demanded it of him, of herself, why'd she risk hurting him once more, hurting herself again for God knows what reason she asks when the door closes and in fact, at last, she is alone again in the house on Cassina Way.

She stops herself from stopping at Mr. Mallory's door. Stops anyway. And as she expected, it takes a while, it's a struggle not to hear what's not there. Then she briskly steps away, hears the tapping of her high heels, kicks them off and they clatter in the emptiness.

Can she do this alone thing one more night, as she did it for months. She doesn't have to be alone if she really can't stand it, does she. She can pick up the phone. Walk out the door. Jump in a taxi and alone's over that quick. A coward's way out if she turned out to be a coward. So she'll chance it. Stay by herself. Be by herself because she can end it when she needs to, can't she. When she needs him.

Not fair to him. But she loves him. So fair has nothing to do with it. She loved her husband, her sons. Loved Mr. Mallory. Each man for different reasons because they were different men and she was a different woman with each one but also the same woman who didn't know any better, any other way. A woman full of love. Didn't know how not to love if she loved. And no goddamn way that's fair, either.

It's not dark yet outside but inside the house never more than a shade drawn, a light turned out from dark. In this dark alley of a house. This tunnel, every passage closed down now but one and she hits the lights as she hurries (hurries?) upstairs and then stock-inged feet slip-sliding on the vinyl runner to her bedroom.

Jesus Mary and Joseph. She'd heard somebody, somewhere, a white woman, the first one she's sure, shout those holy names, run them together like all three saints had surprised her, butted in suddenly, someplace they know good and well they shouldn't. Saints to blame, saints who just pitched one last straw on the load about to break your back at the end of a wearisome day. Saints disrespected, bad-mouthed, and better answer if they know what's good for them, they better explain why, after everything else she's had to deal with today *Jesus Mary and Joseph*, why in hell did she have to sink and sink and feel sick and doomed a split second like she was over an edge and never going to stop sinking as her behind dropped to the bed and bed wasn't there, not where it was supposed to be anyway *Jesus Mary and Joseph*. Brams her ass *thunk* on the hard box spring. Why'd she have to suffer a fall from grace, a fall to the everlasting pit in that split second it took to cover about six inches where the mattress should have started and didn't. Once she'd let herself go, she couldn't stop from sinking down past the usual comfortable landing place. Bounced up again from the unexpected hardness scorching her buns. Bouncing up like she had something urgent *Jesus Mary and Joseph* she just remembered and had to tend to. But no. She was alone in the empty house. Mattress missing from her bed is all it is. Nobody she loved needing her, calling her name. No names she could call. Nothing to do now that she's on her feet again but skin her dress over her head. Fetch a nightgown from the dresser. Sit back down again, carefully this time, remembering what's missing this time. Roll off her stockings. Slide down her panties. Undo the bra and let it slip down her arms. Pull the long cotton gown over her head. Ease back on the naked box spring. Scrunch up to the head of the bed where two black overstuffed backrests she'd bought at Sears sit against the wall looking like twin headstones.

She thought the cemetery word and the backrests hovered sad, spooky, draped in black crepe, but she refused to think it again. Refused to give in to the treacherous way things could change themselves right in front of your eyes, change and hurt you with a power you always forgot they possess until you looked at them a certain way, changed their names or twisted their names or forgot their names so they own all the sudden new force of what they aren't. Of everything they could be, might be. Two ebony love pillows she'd bought as a surprise for him and a treat for herself. For him to rest his stiff back on. For her to lean against and read. Bed like a sofa or a booth in the nice Chinese restaurant where they'd sit and have their tea, chat the evening away with a warm bellyful of noodles and shrimp. One of those cushy black lumps propped under her hips so he could tear her pussy up. Wouldn't let them be blank, staring eyes, neither. Wouldn't let them be the graveyard word she'd almost said aloud when she looked at them with different eyes, eyes that had found a dead man in her bed.

He'd dragged her mattress out into Cassina Way. Hadn't asked. Just did it. Bumped it down the steps, yanked it into the alley, left it in the vacant lot next door where it wouldn't bother anybody he said till he could borrow a pickup and haul it to the dump. Or maybe the damned city would cart it away if they ever got around to cleaning up around here like they're supposed to. Fuck it. Either way. He just got it downstairs and out the house so she wouldn't have to look at it, after he understood she meant what she said and needed to stay the night.

Where will you sleep, he'd asked.

And it had sounded strange coming from him because it sounded more like a question about those months of separation he didn't dare ask till now, and funny too because the answer to *where* didn't matter now or before because his concern not really *where* but *who* will you sleep with if it wasn't going to be him. Strange because he didn't understand and he should have understood that if it wasn't him she was sleeping with, if it was anybody else, it wouldn't mean a thing, not to her, not to him.

She hadn't thought of where she'd sleep this night till he asked. Not in a bed where Mr. Mallory just finished dying is one answer his question had in it, answering itself. But she wasn't afraid. Why would she be scared of ghosts after living with ghosts for so long.

In my bed, I guess. Where I always sleep. He'd dropped his eyes when she answered, and went on about finishing the business needing finishing.

Mr. Mallory owns all the beds in the house now anyway. Just two left. His in his room, the bed in her room he'd died in. Her sons' beds gone. Shipped out. Given away or sold, she didn't remember. Wished the beds had turned themselves to fireballs. Bursting into flame a second, then swoosh, gone, no trace. Didn't happen that way and she doesn't remember how it did, except after her first son gone she'd hollered at some kind soul who was only trying to help, *Just get it out of here. Can't stand the thought of him never sleeping in it again. Kill me to live in the same house with his empty bed.* And worse the second time because she'd worked so hard to teach herself not to expect her second son to sleep in his bed. She'd gotten used to the unwrinkled bedspread, the emptiness, his absence when he stayed out all night, stayed away days at a time and just a boy, her ham-handed, big hard-head boy out in the street doing dirt but she kept a place safe for him, clean sheets, clean house, and made sure he was sure it would always be there, no matter what else went down, he had a mother who loved him and saved a space for him, protected it, keeping it when he was absent because she needed him, they needed each other, didn't they, especially now, the only survivors, the last two left. Sometimes, on the rare nights he made it home, she's so used to his absence, takes her a minute to believe it's him. She must be dreaming. Who's this overgrown boy stealing her baby's bed. A body too big for the bed stretched out in it and she's ready to get the broom, her butcher knife, and chase the stray away. Emptiness more real than the big snoring body. Absence keeping him alive. Something she was used to and could count on. Empty bed less a shock than the sight and stink of him crowding the room. So when he too is shot dead, nothing new about his empty bed. Empty as it should be, as she'd taught herself to expect. Why then was it harder to give it up. Harder the second time to say to whoever was listening, *Take it out of here. Please get rid of the damned thing.*

Without being asked he'd tipped her mattress up off the box spring, trailing bedclothes, pillows tumbling to the floor as he lifted, grunting, muscling it at first then walking it upright on end through the door and down the hall like you'd steer a drunk. Bumpty-bump down the steps into Cassina Way.

She'd thought about tucking clean sheets over the box spring but didn't. Kicked the pillows out into the hall, one bloodstained for sure, the other she didn't care to find out about. Kicked them again and they churned topsy-turvy, one over the other down the steps. Her following them down, nudging them with her foot through Mr. Mallory's door. His pillows now. Like the beds were his.

Up the steps, in her room again *where will you sleep* she'd picked up the black Sears backrests from where Mr. Mallory must have set them on the floor. Placed them side by side, a loving couple at the head of the bed against the wall where they belong. This would do. She could deal with the bed, the room now. Sleep here now. Dying, he'd claimed her pillows, her mattress and bedclothes. She'd keep the rest, something for herself, something she wouldn't let go.

What is your first language, Mr. G. I'm supposing you speak more than one, given your birth near a border where many countries connect. They say it's common for people who live in Europe to speak several languages. But even in Europe with numerous countries close together doesn't everyone own a first language. The language in which you learn to feel. A body language of smells, noises, colors, movements of the first people who care for you when you're helpless, who teach you to crawl, walk, talk, who hold you and smile at you and feed you and clean you, and if you're lucky and loved, sing to you, rock you, tuck you into the warmth of their bodies so you forget you are not them and they are not you. A first language of feelings without names, many feelings inside each word you learn.

I ask because I also speak more than one language. But my first language has no country, no name, or many names, most of them ugly. It's an orphan language. It orphans me when I speak it. Marks me as not belonging anywhere to anyone because I speak this despised, motherless, fatherless tongue.

For a long time I was confused, didn't know better than to believe what others said about my way of speaking. I had to teach myself to remember the love and power of the language spoken by the people who taught me to feel, to live in a body. That language is what I want my pictures to speak.

What is the language of your art. Did you ever feel it was hated, a language that tainted you, cut you off from others, mocked you, mocked your efforts to share mind and heart. Did anyone ever say you must shed your first language and embrace another if you wish to be taken seriously. Was there ever a time when you wondered if your first language counted as language after all. Or could it be babble, babytalk, ignorant, nonsense sounds and gestures that might entertain but could never be considered more than a distraction, a curiosity, a minstrel tongue you must rip from your mouth if you wish to grow up.

I must recover what the oldest voices taught me. I keep working to keep myself alive, the voices alive inside my work. Did you know they can transplant people's organs now. Livers, kidneys, eyes. Sometimes, on the best days, I can hear the camera thrumming in its bag like a heart packed in ice I'm delivering to save someone, and I believe this time, even if never before or never again, this time I'm going to find what I'm looking for, what's been looking for me. I believe I know what I'm after, and the voices guiding me, granting me a moment's certainty, speak my first language. You would understand it if you heard it, Mr. G. And of course you're there, there in the chorus with Mr. B and Mr. M urging me on.

Hellooo.
　　Hello.
　　It's me.
　　I know it.
　　Did you think I'd call.
　　Dead to the world. Not thinking much of anything. Is it morning.
　　A long day, wasn't it.
　　Yes. Yes it was.
　　You'd think I'd be exhausted. You'd think I'd have sense enough to get myself a good night's rest.
　　Are you okay.
　　It's an up night. Okay or not okay beside the point. I'm up is what I am and now I'm waking you up too in the middle of the night.
　　Good to hear your voice, anytime.
　　Do you think I'm crazy.
　　Of course not. No more than you should be. But hey. Easy on questions till I'm awake good.
　　Didn't really expect an answer. I'm all wound up. Sitting here talking to myself for hours so don't mind me. Asking and answering questions all by myself. Wasn't making much progress. Going backward, probably. Realized I was sitting here in the dark pre-

tending you were beside me. Wanted you listening. Needed to hear your voice. But see, I've got to learn to help myself. Love's not enough. Love won't do it. I've got to find out what's inside me I can lean on besides love. I want you to know this.

I know it.

No, you don't. I don't even know what I mean and I'm the one saying it. Huh-uh. You're a man. It's different for you. Love's different. A man can love. I mean some men have it in them to love. A woman just better not expect it. Better not ever take it for granted, because the ones can love come few and far between. Some men have it in them, but it's way down the bottom. Usually youall lost track of it. Or hiding it cause you're scared. Usually youall don't know how to find it even when you try real hard. Till it's too late. But sometimes it's down there. Trouble is it gets stuck. Youall keep it buried deep down, too busy with the silliness of being men. Trouble is, love's what being a woman's all about. Start at the top of her head and go down, way down and it's love, love, love holding a woman together. We can't help it. No more than you can help all that busyass silly business of being a man.

Slow down. Lemme catch up. You're laying a whole lot on somebody just opening his eyes.

Don't matter if you follow me or not because I already changed my mind. Just been telling you what I used to think and don't think now. Why I had to start over again time after time each time I lost a man. When I saw you almost killed in the park, knew I couldn't go down that road again. Starting over, I mean. Giving everything, losing it, then starting over with nothing. Not a goddamn thing. Nothing. Huh-uh. Had to be something of me wouldn't die if I lost you. Wasn't even about you. Loved you then and love you now. It's about me. About having something left I can count on if there's no you.

It can't never be just about you. Won't never be my head on a tray you can just take with you when you decide to go down. Not like my boys did. Not like my man.

Now. Do you have the slightest idea what I'm talking about.

I might. But you got me scared to say yes.

Don't be cute. I'm not playing. It's the middle of the night and sometimes it's my boys playing around here or Mr. Mallory or their daddy, God rest his sorry soul, trying to sweet-talk me into laying down beside him again. I'm dealing with all that. All them and you too. So talk to me. Tell me something I want to hear or need to hear even if I don't want to hear it.

We'll do it your way. Any way. As long as we do it together. That's all I can say. I'm here and you're there but I'm with you. And you can take that to the bank. Keep talking to me. Talk yourself to sleep if you need to. Leave the phone off the hook and I'll keep listening whether you're talking or snoring, if it's only air crackling through the wire.

Better not hear *you* snoring. I'm trying to tell you something important.

I'm wide awake. All ears, babe. Tonight and any night. Every night for you.

Listen. I thought it was time to die when my sons died. Then, right at the edge, I found out I wanted to live. Found myself hungry, greedy for life. Wanted my life so bad I felt guilty. Worse each time. Lost one son, then lost another and their daddy in between, dead in prison. How am I supposed to live through something terrible as that. Almost didn't. People tried to help. My friends. My sons' friends. But after the funerals, after I got the last one buried, I didn't care nothing about anything. Let myself go. People got tired of me. The few I called friends stopped coming around. Just me and my ghosts and Mr. Mallory who mize well be a ghost locked up in this house with me.

I'm pitched across my bed one night not sleepy really but no desire to be awake neither, an awful kind of whipped dog feeling like when I fought with my man and he got tired of me up in his face arguing and knocked me down on the floor and then he's gone wherever he goes when he hits me and stomps out and slams the door behind him. Hurt, hurt, knowing some of it my own fault, got myself to blame for some of what's happening to me and thinking maybe that's why all of it happening, because I deserve it and no man with good sense would put up with terrible me so I'm crying cause he's out the door, crying because I'm bad and here I am all by myself and miserable cause I done it to myself. I sigh and think what a pitiful case I am. Sigh again but funny now there's a little relief in it. He's gone. Don't have him around to deal with till he comes home, if he ever does come home. Only my own self to worry about a while if the baby slept through the hollering and screaming and door slamming. Unhappy as I am, I'm free too. Got a little time to myself. Time to be the person I can't be when I got to tip around him. He's out in the street doing his dirt and I don't want to go there but a kind of street in my mind. Feel kinda guilty it's there, but it is and I go and don't feel much better, but the little better helps me through the worst. I'm remembering the door slamming and how the air goes out of me and I mize well be an old empty sack of nothing but I'm not. Something inside me sighs a little bitty sigh of relief. Hey girl. Here's a little taste of how it might feel if things were different. If you just had yourself to worry about girl so go on and worry about yourself a while. While you can. While you got breath in your body.

I'm pitched across the bed one night remembering how that feeling used to feel, alone at last, a sigh of relief, baby sleeping, quiet night ahead.

Remembered I was somebody besides what other people needed from me. Started taking a little bit of my life back. My time. I'm stuck with my life, one way or the other, whatever mess it is. How can I ask for a life after my sons shot down in the street. But I did. Wanted it bad. Wanted it no matter what. They're gone but I wanted what was left. Don't want you if what I have to give up is the little bit of me I found after I lost them.

You there. You still listening to me ranting and raving.

What do you think. Don't you know by now.

Wouldn't be running off at the mouth this way if I couldn't count on you giving me the benefit of the doubt. Isn't that what you told me your grandfather famous for saying. Give a person the benefit of the doubt.

He said it all right. How he lived too, according to everything I've heard.

Listen. It's three-thirty, four o'clock in the morning and I'm so weary my eyes bout to fall out my head but sleep's not in me yet. Do you understand.

I understand.

No you don't. You're not supposed to. You're giving me the benefit of the doubt and I love you for that and it means more than understanding because goddammit I don't understand my own self tonight. But I need you to listen.

We'll get through this.

Do you think I'm crazy staying here all by myself in this bed where Mr. Mallory just died and wanting you, needing you and keeping you away so long and waking you up in the middle of the night or morning or whatever the hell it is to listen to me rant and rave. Don't answer, baby. Listen, please.

I wanted to be the best mother in the world for my boys. Tried to be something I didn't have any idea how to be really, since I never had a mother I could remember past the time I was a little, little girl. She was everything to me. Perfect. I think that's what I tried to be for them. Everything. And everything's too much for one person to be for another. I couldn't be the angel mother I remembered. My boys didn't need no angel for a mother anyway. Nobody does. And my mama, God bless her soul, wouldna been one for me if she lived. You know what I mean. Some of all that's tied up in me losing them, in me failing them, but it wasn't just about me.

You remember the story I read you about the city God destroyed in the Bible. People of that city no better nor worse than other people. Plenty to be sorry for. Plenty of doing exactly what they know better than to do. Plenty mistakes like everybody makes so why did God's hard hand come down so heavy on them. Why did he smash their city. Kill their children, starve the people, take away everything. They needed to know why. City gone, families gone, and understanding why he took away everything sure wasn't going to bring none of it back, but they got down on their knees weeping and wailing and begged to know. Just like I begged to know.

Hated the part of me begging. Hated the part of me to blame. Hated the suffering part. After my sons gone seemed to be nothing about me I liked. About to choke to death on my own sorry self if I didn't lighten up. Had to give myself the benefit of the doubt. Got off my knees. Stopped asking why. Couldn't be a why. Not a why I'd understand anyway. What good would it do even if I could know why. Wouldn't bring my boys back.

Said to myself, Git up off this bed woman. Fix yourself a bologna sandwich or comb your nappy hair or scrub out the sink or read your Bible or play with your goddamn self. Take what's left. Take it. Be glad it's there to take. Be grateful. And I did want to live after all, even if the whole world coming apart. Found a corner of me wanted life. Close as I'd come to losing it, it wasn't gone. Sure I felt ashamed. Sure I felt guilty. But I wasn't sorry to find that little corner. Huh-uh. Cursed it out sometimes, but I was thankful too. It's the part you know how to touch and raise up in me.

Tomorrow, you can forget all this silly talk. Okay. We'll have lots to deal with tomorrow. If you're still with me. And I believe you are. I love you. But I'll never let you nor anybody else take me down to the edge again. I love you. But I'm not going to hold my breath while you're out running the street. I'm not going to let you take me out there with you and get me killed too.

My house full of men like yours full of women when you were growing up. Loved my men the way you said the women loved you, spoiled you. Gave them all I had. Didn't hold back a thing. And they knew. No way they couldn't know. Feeding them, ironing their clothes, staying up all hours to hear them come in safe at night. Mothered them the way I wished I'd been mothered. Loved them like I dreamed my mother would have loved me if she'd stayed alive. They knew how much I loved them but went on and did their dirt — gangbanging, dope, Russian roulette with a loaded pistol, fucking every woman or man or alley cat or whatever they were big enough to fuck. Knew the foolishness could kill them and might kill me but that didn't stop them. Guess they didn't care. Damn them. I love them so much. Don't matter to youall what kind of mess you leave behind, does it. Who you leave behind to clean it up.

Never putting my life in somebody else's hands like that again. No-no-no-no. I gave it all to them. And they killed themselves. Had to know they were killing me too. Almost did. I'm sorry, youall. So, so sorry.

Never again. Don't you dare think for a mad minute I'm going that far with you. Teaching myself a different kind of love. Love with some room in it for me. Nobody's angel mother no more. And if my kind of love not good enough for you, I can live with that too.

Helloo.

I'm here. I'm listening.

I know. You better be. And by the way, I went in Mr. Mallory's room again.

Thought you said you'd wait for me.

I am. I am. I need to go in with you and sort out his things and decide what to do with them, but I had to go in again by myself too. I think he would have wanted me to come in alone and say goodbye. He was looking for me at the end. I know he was. So I had to go in alone and say goodbye. Say everything's all right, Mr. Mallory. You know what I mean. He probably thought I'd wake him up. If he just took a little nap in my bed, I'd be back soon and wake him up and help him to his own room. He wanted company. We'd started talking you know. Know I already told you once but it's important. He wasn't a nobody. You should have heard the man talk. I wanted all three of us to get to know each other better. Wanted youall to meet one another. A little family again. One that wouldn't die so quick on me. One I could love in a different way. Teach myself a different kind of love.

I think I'm getting sleepy now. Tired of hearing my own self talk. Think I've about talked myself to sleep. Are you still awake.

Here and listening.

Goodnight, baby.

Leave the phone off the hook. I'll listen to you sleep.

Don't want you eavesdropping on my sleep. Don't want you ranking on my snoring like you ranked on poor Mr. Mallory.

I'm going to hang up now sure enough, man. Thank you for listening. If I didn't love you, I couldn't have pushed the buttons on this damned machine. Wouldn't have the strength. Goodnight . . .

Call first thing when you wake up. You hear me . . . hey . . .

Her bare foot had bumped the pillow she'd kicked into Mr. Mallory's room. Who do you think you're trying to scare, old man, she thinks, drawing back her foot, remembering instantly what's soft on the floor, too soft to be a body, knew it wasn't Mr. Mallory lying in wait for her, even though the pillow belonged to him now. Why didn't she want to touch it. Why'd she kick it down the hall, the stairs. She knew better. No way to treat him or anybody. Is that why the pillow tried to scare her. She'd been ugly. Disrespected it. Disrespected him. She knew better. Knew a pillow couldn't hurt her, poor bloody choked and chewed thing, last thing he'd hugged. Searching for her, squeezing her.

Pop. A popcorn pop. Dammit. Doesn't it always happen this way. You turn on Mr. Mallory's light and *pop* the damn bulb blows. Don't matter it's her light burning all the time and his seldom on. Her light's still going strong upstairs and his snap crackle and pops off. What else did she expect on a day like this. Next thing she knows an earthquake or fire or flood. Whole god-damn city. Pop.

Shut up and just go on and find the flashlight in the kitchen where you think you left it but it won't be. Don't even bother searching for a bulb. Or try standing on the rickety rocker to screw one in the ceiling because when's the last time you bought a spare light bulb. Shit. When's the last time you saw the flashlight. Shut up and start looking.

Squishy pillow ambushing her when she steps into Mr. Mallory's room. Her pillow, his now. Booby traps everywhere in the house. Stuff waiting for you to stumble over it so it can remind you of them and break your heart. You try to spare yourself the pain of uncovering, of coming across when you least expect it, when your nerves can't handle it, something they left behind. You straighten up, tidy up, sort and bag and hide away and toss. You clean and scrub every inch of the house. Then you bathe yourself so no traces stick to your skin, so all the blood's washed off. Try as you might, you can't finish the job. Always something you miss. Some-thing you've forgotten had anything to do with one of them jumps you. She knew about that. How hard it was. Wanting somebody, feeling somebody closer than close, but nobody there. Evidence of them not only in your mind, but suddenly something up in your face you can touch, smell, hear, taste. Pillow full of somebody. You can't help making them up whole on the spot. Believing them alive again. Tripping over them, falling, breaking your neck, your heart.

She thought no, she couldn't do this alone. Even though Mr. Mallory had done most of it for her. Library books in stacks.

Magazines, newspapers, and paperbacks in shopping bags. Measly clothes in a heap on the bed. Trash in a garbage bag beside the door, behind a row of boxes. She crouches, slides one box towards her, untucks the flaps, shines in the flashlight.

She'd found two candles in a kitchen drawer, one red, the other green. Christmas colors but she had stopped that thought dead in its tracks. The red one smells like cinnamon. Green one's icy mint lost in the thick spiciness of the red. They don't throw much light but better than nothing in the dark room. Better than a goddamn bulb that does a swan dive *pop* the moment she touches the switch. Candle flicker (where's the wind coming from dancing it) and flashlight's weak beam. Batteries old or maybe the flashlight's just plain cheap and good for nothing like everything else in the kitchen, the house, up and down the block, this whole trifling neighborhood.

She'd been mean to him. Kicking the pillows. Not wanting to put her hands on them. The one Mr. Mallory hugged and spotted with his blood. Other one he probably didn't even touch. As if his head, his last breaths might do something nasty to the pillows all her nights on them didn't. And the mattress out in the alley. Not much of a mattress but perfectly good enough for another boarder. Mattresses cost money. Why did she let him drag it off the bed, down the steps, and out the door. Why hadn't she stopped him. Why had she cheered every thump of its going, said to herself, Yes, yes. Do it. Thank you. Get it out of here.

A squashed box of envelopes and writing paper on top of one of Mr. Mallory's boxes. Loose sheets covered with scribbly writing in a folder under the mashed box. Next layer a thick manila envelope stuffed with negatives. Photos under it and under those who knows. She needed help doing this, just like she'd told him. But also wanted to test what it felt like without him. Important to know she could do this alone if she had to. Figure out what she intended to do with Mr. Mallory's things. Say goodbye to him. Promise him she'd do the right thing, even though she's still unsure what it might be.

Negatives in yellow packets like you get back from the drugstore. Boxes full of them just like Mr. Mallory said. His unfinished work he'd said and made her promise to burn it. Burn everything in every box. Now not the time to decide. Let alone do it. She knew enough. One box of pictures and two of negatives and her promise already broken because she'd looked. Unfastened the flaps, peeked in with the feeble flashlight's beam.

Negatives shimmer like tar, like wet streets. Their edges are sharp enough to nick your fingers you're not careful sliding them in, out, unrolling the curled ones. Held in front of a candle, they turn its flame to a tiny sun dimmed behind a cloud. She'd wedged the flashlight upside down in the top of a box so it aimed at the ceiling. Tried to read a strip of negatives by passing it across the beam. Looked like somebody had scratched all over some of them with silvery ink. An inside-out world, glowing like the bones of Kwami's X-rayed chest that night in the emergency ward.

She snuffs both candles with her fingers. A trick she still felt powerful doing, putting her fingers in fire, magic someone had taught her and she taught her wide-eyed boys, both of them too scared to try at first, they'd been taught to fear fire before they knew its name, warned to stay away, so she took each one aside, alone, another time, and after passing her hand through the flame again, held each one's wrist, guided his small brown hand to the flame, whisked his fingers through it.

See. Didn't hurt, did it. Told you it wouldn't. You know your mama wouldn't hurt you.

In and out quick. Zoom. Wet your thumb and a finger. Just the tips. Then pinch the wick. See the little string there. Pinch it quick so it can't breathe. Quick. Like this. See. Now I'll light it again so you can try. There. Don't be a scaredy-cat now. Quick.

Last thing she does is pitch the pillows onto the pile on the bed. Her pillow, his now in the dark, Mr.-Mallory-smelling room with cinnamon breath.

PHILADELPHIA

H E SEES them first, then he'll hear them, then smell them as they surround him, curious, bumping into one another to nudge closer, to nuzzle or sniff or lick if he's in the mood and offers his hand to a rough tongue. If they've been running, their slobbery tongues loll from open jaws, ribs heave, heads bob, energy itchy in them as they mill about, the whole pack straining against a mishmash of leashes — rope, chain, leather, electric cord — anxious to go again. In the book of myths, read a thousand times when he was a boy, a picture of a god's son driving the stolen chariot of the sun. Phaeton the thief's name he finally remembers this morning. Phaeton the son's name he'd wanted to say to Dogman and couldn't recall it then but described anyway the picture from the library book somebody had borrowed, never returned.

When I saw you float by on your cloud of dogs, more dogs than I could count, John Africa, it appeared you were riding them. Couldn't see your feet, just a forest of dog legs trotting and a barechested half of you holding the reins. Now those mutts weren't galloping, snow-white stallions and you weren't a smiling young god in a chariot with a mane of yellow hair blowing behind you in the wind like the golden tails and manes of the horses and the sun wasn't even up good yet when you passed, but I thought of a picture in a book about Greek gods and goddesses, a picture of how the world started up each morning.

Of course, it was Helios owned the chariot that brought light every day but he couldn't say till this moment, and now to nobody but himself, the name of the doomed, outlaw son, *Phaeton*, in too big a hurry to be a man.

He sees the man and dogs a good distance away and he's grateful for eyes undimmed in a body ready for the junkyard. Well, maybe he saw them. Maybe he was looking for them and the little squiggle of something moving blocks away down Haverford Avenue might not be them, but that's what he saw anyway. What he's expecting to see appears in his mind, clear, bright as a drawing on a page of that tattered book of myths, even though the book probably dust now, worn out, left behind a lifetime ago and the squiggle of motion in the distance down Haverford could be anything.

Early so the Village streets are quiet. There's light but it's not quite morning and anybody out here probably out here for a good reason and if you're someone with a good enough reason to be up and out here this early regularly, you have a pretty good idea of who and what you can expect to see and not to see. You also probably have a fair idea of the reasons why other regulars are up. Except for surprises, usually not pleasant at this hour in the almost empty city streets, in this neighborhood supposed to still be sleeping.

The dog man walking or running his dogs on Haverford. Fast or slow. Can't tell the difference from here. Can't tell whether they're moving towards him or moving away either but at this hour of the day he expects he'll meet them soon, hear them, smell them, their curiosity, their panting, their wet tongues, claws impatient against the pavement, in the middle of them in just a few minutes, near the corner of 39th and Haverford. They must be coming his way, they are, unless the chariot racing across the sky's been stolen again, running on a different clock this morning.

If he continues his regular route up Haverford, he'll hear the dog man's shout and remember, just as it's broken, that there is a special kind of silence in these early morning streets of the Village that matches a silence inside him, and the dog man's voice, as much as he looks forward to hearing it and returning his greeting, is also the sound of the beginning of the end of those matching quiets that are one good reason to be out in the streets early.

When did they begin to exchange good mornings, stopping to chat or walk a ways together, and whose idea to meet later in O.D.'s diner. He should remember, but doesn't. Doesn't always remember the names of the noisy crew in the diner. Time's different now. Has been for a while. His days thinner now, slide by barely inside time. Or slightly outside. The weight of names, weight of remembering moment after moment, shaping and storing and being accountable for the weight of what's happening to him hasn't been lifted off his shoulders — free, free at last — but it's not what it once was either. A thinness now. Not hard eggshell thin but soft and sneaky-leaky thin so things slip through. A lack of recall of what happened yesterday or a minute ago he feels sometimes as loss and frustration, sometimes as a glide into different understandings. Different rhythms, different doors opening and closing.

Who he'd been, who he could be, who he is a different puzzle altogether now from the one he'd believed he'd been working on his whole life.

You fit. You didn't need to rack your brain about fitting. The bits and pieces of yourself you worried about so much, burdened yourself to keep track of, account for, the fragments you treated as your precious, unique portion, by and by come together or dissolve into just what they're supposed to be, you and not you, as they were all along. You fit. This thinner time that falls almost outside time allows you to see through endless layers, see the thick layering.

Glorious some days, a menace others. Was he learning to look at life the way Giacometti looked at his models. A head stranger, more mysterious each time the sculptor's eyes returned from a glance away. Starting over with each look, each time, each day. Failing always. Always a clean, scrubbed slate, a yawning emptiness, a chance. Clarity returned. Goodness of all things merging, blending into one. The one always many. Excitement of turning a new leaf. A shuddering blanket of buzzing, jostling insects covering the page as you flip it, threatening to rise any instant and sting out your eyes. Was he learning to see the invisible prison. Would he be inside or outside when he finally perceived it. Would it matter.

Ona Move, Mr. Mallory.

Ona Move, Mr. Africa.

You're learning, Brother Mallory. You be ready to suit up pretty soon. Put you ona Move yet.

Afraid my playing days are over, Mr. Africa. You're doing just fine without me. I'm a benchwarmer for good now.

We both know better than that. You got plenty playing days left. Plenty game too. Play a tight third base, don't you. Don't let nobody know what you're up to.

You give an old man too much credit.

Don't give credit, Mr. Mallory. This operation all cash. Cash up front, on the line. Know what I mean. Lady say, Here's my Fido. Walk him I'll pay you a quarter when you bring him back. Huh-uh. Sorry, ma'am. Lay a quarter in my sweaty palm then me and Fido have us a good ole stroll round the Village. No credit here. No turning the other cheek. Turned it once, *whack*, got no more cheeks to turn, Mr. Mallory.

Never assumed you were anything less than an astute business-man, John Africa.

Astute. I like that word. Yeah. Astute's right on. What we're all about, stone taking care of business. Ona Move. Taking care of serious business.

A fine morning.

Yes it is. Blue skies later, I bet. Blue as they get round here. And warm with not too much humility. Know it's *humidity*, Mr. Mallory. I just like the sound of *humility* better. Don't hear that word enough.

I agree.

Why they call real hot days dog days. These animals like hot, sticky weather less than people do. Don't want do nothing on hot days but cop some shade and nod off. Dogs love the kind of weather we got this morning. Little cool, little nip. They're perky. Ready to run. Look at those tails wagging, them ears pricked up listening at us. Ain't no part of them standing still. On so-called dog days feels like I'm dragging a load of dead meat around behind me. Morning like this I can hardly hold them back.

Whining dogs. Whining of film he winds in his camera. Words. Whining then howling to be free. Film sealed too long in a dark box whines like a restless animal. Scratch, tap, tap, tapping scratch of claws on the sidewalk. Ready to run again. Begging to go. If the chains fastened to their collars disappeared, would they know it. Would they run. Could they fly without their dreadlocked master, reins in hand, afloat in the middle of the pack, chanting *No woman, no cry* into the wind that flattens their ears, starches the pennants of their tails.

Your people up and at it already this morning.

Yes indeed. Every morning. You know that.

A mighty high fence you're building. To keep folks out or in, Mr. Africa.

You know how it is these days. System already got us fenced in tight as a turkey's asshole on Thanksgiving. The highest, thickest fence and they the only ones with a key. Little picket fence we putting up ain't nothing but a line in the sand.

Pretty sturdy, pretty high line.

If we going to the trouble, no point in constructing a jive fence, is there. Mize well build something solid give us a smidgen of protection. Something at least a pain in the ass when they decide to come for us and bulldoze it down. Know what I'm saying. Wouldn't want to make things too easy for the pigs, would we, Mr. Mallory.

Using good material. Brand-new, straight, thick boards.

Nightwood. You know what I mean. Kind of wood only comes out after dark. Imported. Midnight special. Piles we ain't used yet behind the fence, stacks you can't see less you go inside the compound. We'll build a barricade up on the roof when we're done down below. Build a wall around the whole neighborhood to keep out the pigs, if we could.

Going to be quite a line in the sand when you finish.

Be building with steel if we could. If we could get us some night deliveries of steel plate and some them masks and rivet guns. Build us an iron Fort Apache right out here in this Philadelphia wilderness. Ain't that what a prophet called it. Wilderness.

Come by anytime, my walking friend. Show you around. You could meet some the sisters and brothers. We need wise old heads like yours. Need our elders' guidance. C'mon round. I'm not giving up till I get you ona Move.

Your charges tugging like they want to move.

Good morning for a run. They know it better than we do. Be a better place round here if people used half the sense these animals use. Shame is we could. Got good sense inside us. Born with it just like the other beasts and birds and fish. Understanding's in our souls if we'd just go on and use it.

How long, Mr. Mallory. How long. You have a good day now, hear.

You too, John Africa.

Let's go youall. Giddyup. Ona Move.

When he'd passed the Move house earlier, the men were busy already. Through an uncompleted section of fence he could see how windows had been boarded, doors reinforced, a barricade erected in front of the porch. Two dreadlocked men were measuring and fitting a gate that leaned on its edge against one of the posts at the compound's entrance. On the roof one wearing sunglasses and a rag around his braids whistled as if to say, That old fella's going by.

Move house and Move people a constant topic of conversation at the diner whether John Africa, who the others call Dogman, part of the group or not. Either John Africa preaching about himself and his band or the others talking about him when he wasn't around.

John Africa not around when Reverend Watt said, None my business, but where they getting wood. Good wood costs plenty money and those folks ain't got two dimes to rub together. Sawed and nailed more'n my share of boards before I got called to the Lord's work and ain't stopped hammering and cutting since, so I know something bout lumber.

None my business but I ain't seen no trucks from no lumber-yards delivering to their door. Not that I spend my days nebbing on them folks. Don't really care where they get wood nor nothing else long as it ain't none mine walking away. Matter of fact if I owned me some wood, I'd give it to them, they ax nicely.

Minding my business on my porch I naturally sees most of what goes on round here. Yes I do. What be coming in. What goes out. What else I'm spozed to do, good for hardly nothing no more but praising the Lord. What else I'm gon do but look. Good Lord gimme eyes, didn't he. Musta wanted me to use them. Be plumb ungrateful not to look. Blind man wishes all his life for a look. Lord go ahead and bless you wit two good eyes and a little bit of time on the earth to use them, a sin if you don't.

Must be helping theyselves from somebody's stock. Wood don't grow on trees. Least not no trees round here. Nobody ain't come to claim it. Nobody ain't tried to snatch it back or put them folks in jail so maybe they done got away clean. Been preaching God's word and keeping God's way most my life. I'm a Christian and don't believe in taking what ain't yourn, but about time somebody round here started getting away with something. Bout time for some payback. Some pay out. Forgive me, Jesus, but hope I lives long enough to see a little more getting away clean with something round here.

Reverend Watt telling the story of a fence going up around the ramshackle house on the corner of 33rd and Powelton. How the men and women wear dreadknots in their hair. You are almost surprised when his heavy lids blink, when his lips open and words come out. His face a carved wooden mask, old as Africa, and Africa stamped in his mouth and nose, the mahogany of his skin scored by folds deep enough to poke a camera's eye in. And what would that camera see.

Yes sir. You bet. And if they'da ax me, coulda helped turn that good wood to a good fence. Square and tight and sturdy. Course they ain't hardly axin no crippled-up preacher for no help. See old three-legged Watt come shuffling and tapping, huh-uh. Long past the day and time for hammering and sawing and fence-raising is what they think.

Need me three legs now, but I'm not complaining. No siree. God's been good to Watt. Plenty folks younger than me ain't walking nor talking nor breathing no more. Plenty need wheelchairs. Plenty in them inch-along walkers. Four legs. One leg. Wheels. Many legs as a spider. Count em and be grateful for what you got. Hear what I'm saying.

Them boys too busy to stop and talk to some old-as-Methuselah fella dragging past on a cane. But that's all right. Got the Lord's business on my mind. Pray for the little children in that house. All them babies running around hair uncombed and naked as the day they born.

Some that bunch growed up here, yessir. I knew they daddies and mamas. Knew them's daddies and mamas too. I go way back. Ain't too many still walking these streets go back further. Remember some that bunch when they little-bitty chillren. Grow up fast and before you know it little ones trailing along behind them. Look like the same pack of pickaninnies always hooting and hollering and ripping round here, same hard-leg jitterbugs, same yaketty-yak flock of hens and old crusty roosters pecking in the dirt.

Neighborhood don't change. Look around and see all the spots filled up today just like yesterday. Names come and go, but it's the same spots. Some woman's belly out to here and some poor soul laid out in the funeral parlor. Name don't make no difference, somebody always filling the spot. Seem like I'm the only one got old. Ain't been standing still, been in all the spots, but seem like I been holding down this old spot more'n my share. See the mama in that one's speckled face. See his daddy's ace-of-spades nose on him. Or maybe I'm seeing his daddy. Or his daddy's daddy. Saw her mama yesterday and thought it's the daughter and today I don't know what to think. Don't matter does it, cause it's the same old thing. Keeping all the spots filled.

Young fellas ain't got the sense they born with. Cold as it was this morning, out working with no shirts on they backs. Cold just watching em. Chill up under my clothes I ain't shook yet. Must be that sap running high keeps them warm.

Look like I could almost call their names. Say who they belongs to if it wasn't for this fog on my brain. Somebody's children. Somebody I could name. Ain't nothing but children theyselves got all them kids coming along behind them whooping round nappy-headed and half-naked just like they mamas and daddies. People say they takes care they dogs better than they take care they children, but God forgive me, it's a damn, bare-faced lie. Seen with my own eyes how they treat they babies. Wit my own two eyes. People be saying that all the time, don't they. My own two eyes. Who else's eyes you spozed to see out.

I talks to them children. They little pagans sure nuff, but they cute and smart and bright-tongued. Somebody ought to take a stick to they parents but ain't the babies' fault they ain't heard God's word. Cute little devils, you ax me. And youall did, didn't you. Ax me what I seen up on that corner. Cause youall know I'm a witness every day God give me.

When Mr. Mallory passes the Move house a second time that morning it's not too early for a plainclothes cop, brown paper bag tucked in his arm, as if it's the most natural thing in the world for a white guy nobody knows to be out at dawn around here shopping for groceries. He might as well go on and wear his dress blues and polish the brass buttons and shine his tin badge, strap on his side-arm, stomp around in his storm-trooper boots. Who believes people so dumb a spy like him could tip unnoticed through the neighbor-hood, even if he wasn't wearing thick-soled police-issue shoes.

Hey, my brothers. Here come Officer Pork with some breakfast for us this morning, the one on the roof hollers down. Hide the dope and the AK-47s, comrades.

Cop tries to pretend the voice in the sky has nothing to do with him. But his neck reddens, blood flushes his cheeks, and he turns drill smartly at the corner, away from fence-building as if *away* was where he intended going all along. As if black men hammering, sawing, nailing, digging post holes, constructing a fortified bunker at a major residential intersection in West Philadelphia doesn't concern him. Just out at dawn for a loaf of bread, quart of milk, box of macaroni.

What you got in your sack, Officer Undercover. Bet he's got his mama's pussy in there. Or maybe his dick's in there. Hey Pork. Boys downtown issue you a dick this morning. You hustling it home to beat your bacon, Officer Pork.

A barnyard then. Snorts, oinks, and donkey braying hee-haws and chicken cackle and rooster cockadoo and cow moo. One of the builders must be a country boy cause he does a perfect down-home hog call, *Soo-whee, Soo-whee.* All the dreads hollering and laughing but the racket of fence-building never ceases while they hoot away the cop. You could almost feel sorry for him, pink and round and curly-tailed, slinking down 34th Street on his black, waffle-soled trotters.

These are the pictures he wants to take. Pictures of what doesn't happen as much as what does. What's heavy in this morning air. What's gone but better not forgotten. What should or might come to pass even if it doesn't. This quiet, ash-colored cityscape a thousand thousand pairs of eyes will open upon in the next few minutes and break into a million million unruly pieces no camera can put back together again.

A picture of blind Miss Gillingham on her stoop. Sightless but she knows when you go by. Knows most everybody's name. Whooing *who you* if she doesn't. She knows if you wave at her or not. Kids play a game of trying to sneak past without being caught till they're grown enough to understand it isn't funny. Understand they never win anyway. She knows. Knows and remembers.

Picture of a time when they were both children and he stuck out his tongue at the ugly little blind girl on the porch where she sat every day in a fresh, neat dress, her thick hair olive-oiled and plaited, and those dumb, white-as-snow, turned-down anklets and spotless white shoes or shiny black patent leather gleaming like mirrors. What he really wanted to do, funky and filthy from running the streets all morning with his crew, was rub mud on the frilly apron of her starched dress or yank loose a perfect braid, unravel them all so every nappy hair on her head stood up like Alfalfa's in the movies. Yes, once upon a time he'd been a scruffy brown ragamuffin boy sticking his fingers in the corners of his mouth to spread it wide open, wagging his tongue to mock the prissy little Miss Muffet sitting on her porch like a black doll baby. A picture of it he'd take and want to burn rises, shadow and light resolving on paper rinsed in baths of chemicals.

I know what you're doing and it's not nice. You're a mean, nasty boy.

While his gang watched from the middle of the street he'd stepped up on the curb, as far away from the porch as he could be and still be on sidewalk, far from the rocker she sat in all day seeing nothing, perched on the chair's edge so her baby-doll feet reached the floorboards. In the quiet after her words he considered using the fingers still stuck in his mouth to rip his face off, poke out his eyes. Instead he let his hands drop to his sides, hid them in the pockets of his dirty knickers. Let himself be caught by the most beautiful eyes he'd ever seen or will see, eyes cloudy or pus green or demon bloody red or sewed shut, dead, dead behind swollen lids that never opened, he had believed those lies about her eyes till that moment because he'd never looked, was afraid to look, or shamed to look or didn't bother because he was sure what he'd find in the holes of a blind girl's face.

After her hurt voice undressed him, the eyes melted him, spread him like warm butter over toast. He couldn't say he was sorry for sticking out his tongue. Not then, not king of the streets and anywhere else he roamed getting dirty, getting ready, getting strong with his boys. No, not with his hands on his hips now, head cocked, chin thrust out, his hard eyes faking a stare-down but fixed on the mailbox beside the green painted frame of the screen door, anywhere outside the beam of those impossible eyes. Couldn't say he was sorry because he wasn't. No. Way past sorry. Way past regretting the mistake of letting himself act mean and ugly towards this blind girl. Nothing sorry nor smart-ass he could think to say that wouldn't come back at him, hurt her again and hurt him double, so he stood a little longer on the curb's edge, as long as he could balance which wasn't very long or might have been a year, and then pitched backwards, undone by the wobble the beautiful eyes had planted in his knees. Held his ground maybe three seconds more before racing off down the street as fast as he could, as if he ran fast enough, far enough he might crash into words more ruthless, more scouring than *I'm sorry* and bring them back, all bloody with his blood, to lay at her feet.

Too early for Miss Gillingham to be on her porch, too early for the trifling little nod she offers when he waves at her. She doesn't want to give too much credit after all to somebody just because they've been raised right and act like a decent person, waving at a blind old lady trapped on her stoop who's past being surprised by anything, it's all come to her chair, to her door, who expects as she should a wave or good morning from passersby if for no other reason than she's alive and you are too so you owe each other that much at least, even if she remembers what you did one day, thinking yourself cute to make a fool of her, thinking you could get away with it, nobody a witness but your crusty-nosed, dusty-butt, burr-head buddies in the middle of the street, all of them gone now, patched into the emptiness of this hovering gray morning, this vacant porch you would make a picture of so someone couldn't hold it in their hands without wanting to peel back the edges and peek under one scene to find another.

She nods stiffly when he greets her so he can't help wondering if maybe she does remember what he remembers. But counts on her little nod, counts on it like he counts on her hearing the sound of his wave or its absence if he ever tried to play a trick on her again.

Hers the last porch, last house. If you were the Big Bad Wolf no trouble blowing it down. One good huff and puff and all the straws of Miss Gillingham's shack fly apart. Not a shack really but a wooden row house, last occupied dwelling of the last mostly boarded-up row before several blocks of nothing where no one lives in long warehouse sheds and windowless cement-block hulks inside which he's sure they store bodies, what's left after they do their dirty work and have to dump the evidence someplace no one looks.

College dormitories to the east built on top of wreckage of the same sorts of buildings containing secret waste and poisons. The city had knocked down the giant sheds and warehouses, erected cinderblock high-rise dorms that seemed to sprout up overnight, plug-ugly boxes smelling after rain like something strangled and plowed under and covered up.

O.D.'s diner on Haverford Avenue only place to sit down and eat at this hour of the morning. Always open. Used to have a red neon sign on the roof *Always Open* till one by one — it took years — the letters died. Slowly. Slowly, one after another letters giving up the ghost. He got used to letters missing. Didn't miss them in a way because he continued to read the flashing sign's message as if it were intact. *Always Open.* Surprised when for whatever reason a letter's absence would jump out at him and he'd think, Damn. Another one's gone. How long's it been out. Damn. Only one-two-three-four-five left. Like the mouths of old people old like he's getting, no teeth one day when he was sure they still had at least three or four stumps last time he noticed. One day no red letters, just juiceless tubing, grime-dull and bug-spattered atop the diner. Who had turned off the sign. Not even the big power failure that blacked out Philadelphia had bothered O.D.'s sign. After so many years burning brightly, rain or shine, night and day, why would somebody pull the plug. Took every letter missing for him to recall the sign had dwindled to nothing but half of a red *e* and that half all he'd been reading for weeks.

Excuse me, Mr. Mallory. I know you like to carry your coffee to the back before the rest of them come trooping in here yapping away like they do every morning. But wonder could you spare me a minute before you go.

Certainly, Mr. O.D. I like my quiet, but I'm a listener too.

Well, if you don't mind listening a minute to me, maybe you could hang here at the counter cause I got a kinda question for you, if I can get it in before the others start straggling in.

Mr. Mallory you ever had somebody in your family or somebody close, maybe even closer than family, in the slam, in jail I mean.

Lost my family quite a long time ago and to tell the truth, close is something I've shied away from since. But that's an old story and not what you're asking, is it. No I haven't, Mr. O.D. But you have.

Person I love most in the world.

Must admit I've heard little bits and pieces around here about your young friend and his trouble. Enough to gather something terrible happened.

People talk, Mr. Mallory. People talk but people don't know shit. Make up lies. Make up the biggest stories about the things they know nothing about. I'm a listener too, even though you hear me telling my share of lies when the lying gets good round here. I hear what people say. What they say about me and about other people and about theyselves. *Themselves* I guess I should say, right.

Anyway it don't really matter if you had somebody in the slam or not because you've been on this earth a good long while and you've seen things. It's in your eyes, if you don't mind me saying so. Noticed the first time you came in here. Could tell just by looking in your eyes you the kind of person a man could talk with.

Ready if you are.

Thank you, Mr. Mallory. Let me fix you some breakfast while I talk. Keep my hands busy while my tongue's flapping. How bout scrambled eggs. Cut up some good stuff in them. Eggs and some whole wheat toast like you and Dogman like and a glass of orange juice.

Swiveling stools line the counter, silver poles topped with red plastic cushions sealed in grooved silver rims. Every cushion split in one place at least. You can see stuffing, maybe white once, now a yellowish, dirty gray. In one or two a hole deep enough a green foam pad under the stuffing shows. The stools squeak. Some wobble. Vinyl tape binds their wounds. Hard to find red on one at the end of the row, bandaged with crisscrosses of shiny black tape. The stools sit high. A rail down near the floor you can boost up on if you're short-legged or rest your tired feet on while you sit or bang the shit out your ankle if you're not careful and forget, coming or going, it's down there. First time in O.D.'s diner he'd wanted to spin the stools. Keep them all going like a juggler spinning plates on sticks. Wanted to be a kid perched on a tall stool, licking a vanilla ice cream cone, whirling faster and faster, the whole diner a merry-go-round twirling with him, like the tigers round Little Black Sambo. Everything flashing past sizzling with speed, cold sweetness melting in his mouth and it won't end till he puts on the brakes. Hoping the look on his face that first morning gave nothing away, hoping nobody laughed at the boy, dizzy, unsteady, ice cream all over his chin when he staggers off the ride.

I kinda knew talking to you'd be easier than talking to most folks. Don't know why. Still wasn't sure I was up to bothering you till I saw you come in this morning. Appreciate your ear. I surely do.

See, Mr. Mallory, I done a bit. Crazy wild when I was coming up. Lucky in a way I got caught when I did cause my life nor nobody else's meant a damned thing to me. Trying my best to get myself killed but got caught and stuck in the slam instead. Not no short bit neither. Long enough to be sure I didn't never want to go back. Every day inside those walls is hard time, don't let nobody tell you different. Hardest for a black man, even though plenty of us in there to keep each other company. Doing time's hard enough, but I swear, if it's somebody you love inside, somebody you love like a child, like your own flesh and blood, the pain of them locked up is worse than being locked up yourself. Part of you dies every day your baby's inside.

You can't do the time for him. Would if you could, but you can't. And suffer day after day cause there's nothing you can do. He's the one with the wound, he's bleeding, it might kill him but at least he can deal with what's hurting him. He got the wound in his body. All you got is pain. No hole to plug. What's broken in you ain't no fix for. No way you can get well long as he's inside hurting. I'd take his place in a minute if I could.

O.D. scrapes the grill with his homemade grill-scraping tool, *Night man got to do better than this*, wooden backed and squarish with a cloth fixed to the top he slides his whole hand in like a glove to bear down good. Stiff metal bristles for scrubbing. One edge a kind of bulldozer blade for pushing burned sludge into a drain slot at the back of the grill. Bacon grease pops and sizzles when he spreads it with a wide, floppy paintbrush across the hot surface.

My baby would laugh in my face if I ever said to him what I said to you about trading places. I can hear him laughing that smoky laugh and saying, Ain't you a damn fool. He'd say, You must have forgot already what it's like in here. C'mon back five minutes and you'll remember real quick. You'll shut up whining. Forget all about changing places. My baby would laugh out loud at what I'm saying and I'd know what he means but what I'm telling you is true too, Mr. Mallory.

Why they call it doing time. That's another question I wanted to ask you. Do the crime, do the time. You're a smart man. Speak like an educated man. Don't everybody in the world got to do their time. How you not going to do your time. Unless you're dead. How's anybody take your time from you without killing you. Kill a man you still ain't took his time. His time's up. Man's time comes here when he's born and leaves when he dies, don't it. Nobody can take it or give it away. Time all any of us got. Little parcel of time we walk round in. Little bubble of blood and bones and heat and feelings till it busts and we're gone.

You understand what I'm saying, Mr. Mallory. Am I talking truth.

So jail ain't really about doing time or taking away time. What they do when they slam you is try and make you believe you dead. Believe your time's up. They try and make you feel you ain't nothing. Nobody. Worse than dead.

So I sit out here every day in this so-called free world knowing they're trying to kill my baby. I try to send him messages. You're still here, baby. Still in my heart, in my thoughts. With every ounce of strength in this big body, I try to push my messages through the damned walls.

Know you're there, baby. Know you're alive. Don't let them make you forget. Hold on. Hold on.

Feel like I'm mourning sometimes. Then I got to say to myself, No. Don't you dare. Don't be believing he's gone, don't be feeling sorry for yourself. No goddamn mourning. I'm his enemy if I mourn. If I give up and start believing he's gone, I'm treating him just like the devils do.

He owns his time. Devils can't take it. They can count it out in minutes and hours and days and years, counting and measuring and squeezing in as much misery as they can squeeze in every bit, but his time still belongs to him. They can lock him up in a cage, but he don't belong to them. They own the count, but they don't own him. Some days I swear I can hear their evil mouths counting down the minutes. Hear them in my sleep. Can't sleep lots of nights the counts so loud. Hear the devils pounding nails in his sweet body. I want to wrap my arms around him so the nail got to go through me first. So he don't have to take so much.

Sorry, Mr. Mallory. Don't know why I need to talk about this awful stuff first thing this morning. You come in the diner for your coffee and some peace and I start beating on your ear.

Reverend Watt tap, tap across the tile threshold of the diner, feeling his way like he's blind as Miss Gillingham. The little bell tinkles when he opens the door and tinkles again as it swings shut behind him. He blinks, twists up his rubbery face like he's come out the Valley of the Shadow, sight restored, not sure he likes what he sees.

Morning, Reverend.

Morning, Reverend Watt.

Morning, gentlemens.

Coffee, Reverend.

Yes sir, yes sir. God give us a good morning this morning, didn't he.

Amen, Reverend. Coffee and your sticky bun coming right up, soon's I finish with Mr. Mallory here.

You're going to like these eggs. Chopped some jalapeños in them. You always be sprinkling Tabasco on my eggs, thought I'd fix you some eggs make you forget about Tabasco.

Pour the reverend his coffee then I'll set these in the back for you. Appreciate your ear this morning. Breakfast on me, okay.

The bells ring again. Twice. Three times. Then it's steady tinkling, a note barely heard in the many conversations at once around the counter. O.D. hustling in his always slow, always busy fashion, never too occupied to butt in anybody's conversation.

Youall don't deserve a good cook. Way youall dump salt and pepper and ketchup on my food before you taste it makes me want to run youall out of here.

Smacking your lips and grinning at me. Talking bout Mmmmm. You sure can cook some scrambled eggs, O.D. Right. Got so much ketchup in the plate look like my poor eggs got a hemorrhage. Wouldn't know if they was cornflakes heated up in Dixie Peach behind all the mess youall be sprinkling and pouring on my eggs.

Now Mr. Mallory's different. He's a gentleman. Tastes first. Course, he's a Tabasco man. Got to have his Tabasco. And I don't mind because he tastes first. Gives my eggs the benefit of the doubt before he adds his Tabasco. Rest you clowns don't deserve good cooking.

O.D. tied his stocking cap too tight this morning.

Don't be messing with me. Not in the mood today. Bad enough I got to watch you messing with my food.

You ain't served me no food yet, Brother O.D.

Don't need to. Don't I watch you performing every morning with the salt and pepper shakers.

Anybody heard the weather.

Heard enough don't want to hear no more. Same ole shit. Rain.

Heard rain and heard clearing both.

Wish it go on and rain. Clears out the air.

Some the shit floating round in the air big as cinders. Walk around half the time with my eyes burning. Air ain't worth shit. Neither is the weather.

You born here and you gon die here. Should know by now Philadelphia got the worst weather in the world. Too hot in the summer. That bone-chilling damp cold in the winter. Tain't south. Tain't north. Worst of both.

Got that right. Stone cracker town but the crackers think they ain't crackers cause New York City just up the turnpike.

Philly always been a country town. A wannabe city. Don't care how big it gets, just an overgrown country town.

Full of mean crackers. Head-busting Bull Connor cops and Judge Lynch his nigger-hating self on the bench. Bam. Gavel brams down and Judge Lynch sends another brother off to death row. Brothers in chains be thinking, What else is new, Judge. Been on death row all my life.

Want that coffee warmed up.

Thank you. Thank you, my man. Stocking cap didn't shrink your brain much as I thought. You're a gentleman even if you can't cook a lick.

You know what you can lick.

Hey, youall. Listen up. You know where the coffee is. All three pots ready. Pour for your own selves and don't be forgetting my quarter for the first cup, while I talk to Mr. Mallory a minute. Shame he's the only one around here with good sense.

Look out, Good Sense. Here comes O.D.

I'm going to make myself sit down and write to my baby. Something tells me he needs a letter. I'm way overdue anyhow. He's on my mind, Mr. Mallory, all the time. Then I remember thinking about him ain't writing to him and it's been weeks, maybe months since I wrote. How's he spozed to know he's in my thoughts less I write. Push my messages hard every day, push till tears come to my eyes, but those prison walls are stone. Hard, thick stone and maybe a thought pushes through, maybe it don't.

Used to pray. Learned to pray from my grandmama. She's the one raised us. My mother's mother. Big Mama we called her. When I look back seems like she was always either praying or whipping our asses. I kept the praying habit even when I was an outlaw running wild in the street. Helped me get through that first bad year in the slam. Prayed hard. Real hard. Remembering Big Mama on her knees or me on my knees and her whaling my behind with a strap. Praying I'd be a better boy so she'd stop beating on me. Died in her sleep. Peaceful as a strawberry and I kept praying I'd be a better boy. Kept on flinching and praying.

One night in my cell I started in . . . Our Father who art or Sweet Jesus have mercy or whatever I used to start with and I heard somebody laughing. Shocked me right out my prayer. Mad cause I thought it must be one the loony-tune inmates awake like me in the middle of the night, but it wasn't. Quiet as a tomb. No sound except me breathing, nobody but me stirring when I stood up and opened my eyes. Forgot what I was praying about. Then the laugh again. Loud cackle cackle laugh. Is it God I'm thinking. God finally sick of my begging, sick of seeing how rotten I am through and through and still got nerve to be praying. God's going to swat me like a fly I'm thinking. He's laughing cause I been asking and asking for it and now I'm about to get his fist upside my head. Thinking foolish stuff like that in a black cell empty but for me. God laughing cause he don't believe a word I'm praying. Cause I ain't fooling him nor nobody else. A miserable, lying hypocrite on my knees. Why'd I think I got a right to ask God the time of day. Wasn't him laughing though. Was me. Me laughing at my own self. And that was the end of praying.

Except like I said I still send out thoughts to my child. Maybe I ought to be laughing at myself again. Trying to push my feelings through stone walls. Mize well try to send messages up through a million miles of empty air to heaven. What do you think, Mr. Mallory.

Can't stop myself. Hoping for a miracle just like the rest of the fools around here. Every great while somebody comes running in the diner. Hallelujah. Hot damn. Prayer been answered. They hit the numbers or some evil husband dropped dead on his job and she's got the insurance money coming. A straight flush or a cancer drying up and blowing away. Piece of good luck all it is and they think it's a miracle. Believe in miracles. Count on em. Wait for them.

Tell the truth I don't remember the last letter I wrote. Carry a letter in my mind. One long letter I'm always adding news to and erasing old news but it don't never get written, let alone sent. Be talking to him all the time but nothing goes down on paper. If I sat myself down and started writing, don't think I'd ever rise up from the chair.

Shame how they treat those boys in there. He'll be twenty-one years old the sixth of next month. Had to raise hisself from boy to man in prison. Figure out how to be a man in that hellhole where it's a crime to be a man. Where they kill you for trying. Killing the man in you what prison's all about.

You got to be a bully or a sissy in there. Thump ass or get your ass thumped. No room in between. Try to be a decent human being you get no respect from nobody. Just like out in the world. Drug games and sex games. Biggest stick rules and money rules the stick. Everything for sale. You got to know what you want and what you're willing to pay. Know all that and they still tear out your heart. Eat you alive. In a minute.

How's anybody spozed to survive. Specially somebody just a boy when they locked him up.

Why don't I visit. You making me say out loud what I been saying to myself all these years. I'm ashamed is why. I don't go to see him because I'm shamed of myself, shamed of what I am. Afraid I'd shame him in front of the other prisoners. He had to start all over inside. Make a new life. I didn't want him to have to explain me. Shit, I can't explain me to my own self.

People think I don't visit cause I'm mad at him. No, huh-uh. Ain't saying I wasn't hurt, but forgived him in a minute. No. I'm just ashamed. Hearing myself say *shame* out loud I don't like how it sounds. Sounds ugly. Sounds dumb. But it's true.

What I got to be so shamed of, Mr. Mallory. I'm fat, yellow, nappy-headed, ignorant. None that's a crime, is it. No better nor worse than most people, I guess. Struggling to make it just like everybody else. Need all the help I can get, just like everybody else. Why am I shamed and scared of the love in me. The best in me. Ain't that foolish. Shamed and scared to ride a goddamn bus to the prison and say I love you, baby. Love you with all my heart and soul.

Would he be ashamed of me. Would I bring harm on him. Big, sloppy, greasy, clumsy me showing up on visiting day with my eyes so full of love, my heart so full I couldn't help acting like a nitwit. Sit across from my baby, front of my shirt all stained, like a stupid cow leaking milk out my titties I been saving for him.

Excuse me, Mr. Mallory sir. Those fools tear my diner up I don't go back up front now. Thank you for listening. Needed you this morning. I'm closer to writing. Closer to that bus. Don't let those eggs get cold on you. Enough jalapeños they can't get but so cold, know what I mean.

Enjoy your breakfast. On me this morning.

Do you know the story of what happened at O.D.'s, John Africa.

You mean the robbery and killing.

Yes. And his young man. I'm remembering the incident, remember something ugly happening, I think, but the names didn't mean anything to me at the time. One more violent crime.

Real Wild West shoot-em-up. Everybody in the city must have

seen it or heard about it on the news. Two men gunned down in broad daylight and one of them a white cop. Headlines for days.

Bullets flying everywhere. Started in the diner. Maurice Johnson. Called him Big Tu or Tu-tu. You know, cause he was too much. Too, too much. Too big, too black, too mean, too dumb, too smart. Too evil and crazy. Tu-tu. Big Tu struts in the diner one day cool as a cucumber, don't even try to hide his face like a real bandit, just busts in O.D.'s — Give me the money. That started it and it got worse and worse. Lucky more people didn't get hurt. Bullets flying in the diner, out in the street. Getaway car had more holes than the one in *Bonnie and Clyde*.

O.D. wasn't about to let a fool like Tu-tu just stroll in and take his hard-earned money so he ducked down behind the counter, come up firing with that .38 he keeps beside the register. Tu blasting away too. O.D. got the scars on his shoulder and chest to prove he'll fight. Show them to you if you ask. And he put some lead in Tu's big ass they say because blood on the floor in front the register and the door where Tu-tu ran out.

Now comes the bad part. Part makes O.D. wish he'd just handed over those nickels and dimes in the register. Tu-tu's barreling out the diner and just about trips over a cop car. Would of been better for him if he did trip. Fall down, break some bones, and wind up with a stiff bit behind armed robbery but he might be alive today. Though being Tu-tu, I doubt it. Anyway it's been sounding like Fourth of July in the diner and here's this large spook in the middle of Haverford Avenue with a large smoking gun in his hand so the cops slam on the brakes and Tu-tu must have figured Shit, I fucked up real good this time if he's thinking at all with O.D.'s bullet or bullets in him so why not, what else he gon do, come this far he mize well go out in a blaze of glory like them big-time desperadoes. Pow. Pow. He shoots the cop car. You could call it a lucky shot cause Tu sure ain't no marksman, missed killing O.D. who wasn't but across the counter and now Tu's running and the black-and-white's behind him and he snaps off a couple rounds over his shoulder and one tears the back of a cop's head off.

Well, that's bad enough. Gets worse by the minute. Or the second, cause whole mess didn't hardly take but a couple minutes. Cop's bleeding to death in the patrol car and his partner's out and behind the front fender blasting away at Tu. Tu's down. Crawling now. Maybe O.D.'s lead slowing him up, maybe some the cop's, whatever, he's down and just about out but makes it to the getaway car.

It's the O.K. Corral for sure now. Another cop car screeches in from the other end of the block and here comes another one behind the one holding the dead cop. Seems like a pig convention all the sudden. Like a whole posse around the corner just waiting for trouble. Tu-tu's lucky shot about the only luck he had that day if you could call killing a cop lucky because must of been half a dozen pigs by the end pumping bullets into the getaway car and into Tu-tu who's laid out down in the gutter beside it. People say it was pitiful even if you know Tu the worse kind of scum, which most people knew. Neither Tu nor the getaway car going nowhere but pigs used them for target practice till they got tired of shooting or ran out of bullets. Say you could see Tu-tu's body jumping when those big police special slugs tore into him. Don't know how many folks really poking their heads up when all the shooting going on, but they say poor Tu-tu twitching when you wouldn't have thought no life left in him to twitch.

So you got one cop down and one real dead bad guy but the worst part as far as O.D.'s concerned still to come. Ceasefire finally. Smoke clearing. Tu-tu too dead to waste any more ammunition on. It's over you think. But it ain't never over, is it. Somebody's still alive in the getaway car and starts hollering, Don't shoot, don't shoot.

Miracle anybody survived. A bigger miracle the cops didn't waste him when he surrendered, one of their own with his brains splattered all over the front seat of a black-and-white. They say one or two more shots fired, then this pitiful voice again, Don't shoot. Please don't shoot. I'm unarmed. I'm hit and bleeding. Please don't shoot. Lame shit like that, you know. Somebody in the car begging and pleading. Trying to say something to keep the cops from killing him.

Like I said it's a miracle. They told him, Throw your weapon out the window and he's swearing he got no gun and they say, Come out and he's crying, I'm hit. I'm bleeding. Can't move. Back and forth like that and it's still hard to believe they didn't just blow him away, but for some reason, maybe all the people watching, the cops didn't waste the brother this time. And finally when they run up on the car and drag him out, none too gently, just like you'd expect they'd do him, him screaming like they leaving half his body parts tangled up inside the shot-up car, who is Tu's getaway driver but the boy lives with O.D., boy O.D. took in off the street and just about raised.

You know how it had to hurt O.D. He treated that boy like a son. Found him rooting in the dumpster out behind the diner. Boy didn't have nobody. Living in the street and O.D. took him in, fed him, clothed him, gave the boy a home. Been round the diner two, three years helping out O.D. Why he got to go and do what he did. That dope, you know why. Why else he sit behind the wheel of a getaway car while his partner sticks a gun in O.D.'s face and steals O.D.'s money. Money O.D. would have give the boy if the boy needed it bad.

I'm telling you, Mr. Mallory. They say people act like animals these days. If animals had lawyers, which of course they too smart to have, they ought to sue the folks who say that shit. Any jack-leg Kingfish lawyer win the case. No problem proving human beings the worst-acting animals there is. Except in a court of so-called law, you never know, do you. Ain't worth doo-doo. Lawyers, judges, courts, what the system calls law ain't nothing but a humbug to keep a few folks on top, rest of us on the bottom. Hang people and fry people and gas and shoot and poison and feel good about it cause the law say it's all right. Damnedest thing when you think on it. What other animals you ever heard of invented the electric chair. What other animals build zoos to lock up their own damned kind. What animal's strayed so far from nature it's got to look for rules of living in books.

Book of the heart's all anybody needs. All we need to know's inside us. Right here. Born with knowledge just like the other animals. It's man's law fucking up the world. No air to breathe, no water to drink. No room to run free. City's sick. People can't live like they do much longer. Change has got to come. We got to kill the system before it kills us. When you joining, my friend. We need you, Mr. M. Ona Move.

A small world he thinks, remembering John Africa on that day John Africa told him O.D.'s story. Must have been a day the same year they attacked the house in the Village, the last year he'd seen very much of John Africa. Could O.D.'s young friend have known her husband in prison. Were the two men close in age. He tries to calculate. John Africa walking dogs ten, fifteen years ago.

Wouldn't her husband be about her age, a few years plus or minus. Which would make him about how old now. He was dead now. How old was that. Died of AIDS in prison she said. How long ago. Well, the same year her two sons died. A year or so ago. But the father must have been in jail a good while before he died. Their first boy a couple years old, second on the way when the father sentenced to life so that puts it when. How old was the second boy when he was shot. And when was the firefight inside O.D.'s diner and outside on Haverford. He needs some exact dates. With a few he can estimate the rest. He remembers stories, sees scenes from them clear as snapshots, but when he's pushed for precise times and places, such details not part of what he recalls. So the smallness of the world is not about a man from one story and a man from another story meeting in prison, if it ever happened, could happen, but about how little space there always is for whatever happens, whenever or wherever. How crowded his mind is, crowded as these shacks on Cassina Way, how brutal the struggle for breathing room, no room for people's feelings, no space to be his own dying, dreamy self and also hold on to the dates and times and places and names that might help him make sense, if there were room for sense, if you didn't have to deal with John Africa's heart flying through the air with the greatest of ease in the claws of a crane while his head walks beside you telling O.D.'s tale. John Africa's head solemnly nodding, a spitty *tsk-tsk* hissing from his lips. Two cities, old man. You've got everything all mixed up, friend. Two slams in two different cities. Hundreds of miles apart. Years apart. How those guys spozed to meet.

They came for John Africa's people the first time in the heat of August. Bulldozed the stout barricade. Hot knife through butter. A policeman shot dead by somebody during the assault and all the adults — eight, nine, a dozen — living in the house put on trial and sentenced to life for murdering the cop. The way the Nazis killed a hundred hostages for every German soldier the partisans ambushed. A small world. Small lives not worth as much as big lives. That seemed to be the idea behind hostage-taking, ransom, many lives demanded for one. John Africa not captured in the raid, either he escaped or not around that day. Never had a chance to ask him which it was. Cunning or luck or both. But they caught up with John Africa a few years later when they attacked again, this time a whole army of cops shooting and dropping bombs on Osage Avenue, the entire neighborhood up in smoke, eleven men, women, and children burned up this time in exchange for the life of not even one cop. Small lives worth even less. Less room for them in a smaller world.

Did eleven even the score. Does it ever end. What were the dates. Would all the young men he saw nowadays in the city streets, the ones whose stories he'd tried to take pictures of, whose stories were his and his story theirs, so thick, so thin, piled one atop the other, would they all wind up sooner or later, *dates, dates*, in prison if they didn't wind up dead. Young men yet there seemed to be more than one generation of them tangled up in this misery. A span of years, a span of prisoners reaching backward and forward, who may or may not meet in specific places, at specific times, boys younger and older than him, yet joined to him, to each other, one arc of suffering and loss and the world too small to hold the lamentations.

The last photo he snapped before he left Philadelphia, or was it his first photo, the ruins of the house on Osage Avenue where John Africa and his people murdered. Eleven the exact total of the dead, right or wrong it's the number he carries now, couldn't forget if he wanted to, the official number even though at the time of the massacre no one could count the dead with any accuracy because bodies blown apart, incinerated, and the next day torsos chopped, bones broken, ashes ground, scattered, shoveled, bulldozed, limbs flying in buckets across the sky so who knew, who could possibly know the number of the dead, who believed the count supplied by cops who'd done the shooting and looting, the court's count, the coroner's count, the newspaper and TV counts. Who knew. Only the ones inside the Move house knew, knew who lived and perished beside them in the flames, drowned in the flooded cellar, roasted in the rooftop cave, and everyone found inside dead so who knew, who could tell the truth, who knew why he remembered eleven, eleven including John Africa and the children, or knew why he had trudged thirty blocks west from the Village to the scene of the crime and hears clanking machines digging, lifting, tossing, scattering their remains, smells the acrid smoke still stinging the air, hears them, smells them before he sees them, sees their invisible presence in the vacant space he shoots over and over, shooting and not allowing the film to advance, shooting till the film snaps off its spool and then shooting some more.

Had O.D. asked all the questions he wanted to ask. No way he could. Endless questions, no answers. O.D. knew that. More about needing to talk than expecting answers. Listening to O.D. he'd heard his own questions, the kind he never gets the chance to ask anybody. Or so it seems. In this other city, *don't worry John Africa, I know where I am, I know, I know,* he's listening again. To the clatter of spoons and knives and fork clatter. The bump and grind of O.D.'s thick-lipped cups on thick saucers. He counts the letters of the dying sign on the diner's roof. Is it trying to repair itself, turn on again. Or is it the wheeze of his asthma that sounds for a second like the hissing of bright crimson gas through filthy tubing, gas twisted into the shape of letters, gas seeping through the diner's vents, filling the space till no one can breathe.

Mother's Day. Another detail he won't forget, the police action commencing at dawn on Mother's Day. He hears the bullhorn's warning and suddenly a date flashes across a TV screen — *May 10, 1985* — clear as a bell, bright as the tingalinging of anybody leaving or entering O.D.'s diner. He can read other bits of information, numbers, facts and figures he hadn't realized he'd retained. Information in neat letters and lines prints out like he'd watched news rolling across a huge lighted billboard in Times Square on his way back from the war. Names, dates, places cluttering his thoughts, unnecessary now, unwanted, unwelcome as soon as they're available. Another city. Another time. Ten years have passed since the murders and all he needs to know, the only question mattering now, Where are you. Where are you.

The bell at the front of O.D.'s diner silent for ten years. Could it be that long. Why is he sitting here in another city waiting for its ring again, waiting for the flimsy aluminum door that never quite fit after it replaced the original which didn't fit either, even before it was strafed and pocked and ventilated by bullets they say, waiting for the silver door to open the space where an early-rising customer might appear, or the numbers runner or the mailman peeping in and hollering at everybody as they scoot past on their rounds. When the door opens, he doesn't expect to see John

Africa's body whole and alive again. He knows better than that. Then what is he waiting for. Some crossover presence tangible enough, like wind, to trick the door open, fill the space, then go on about its invisible business, leaving him with the certainty that the diner, though a dream, is real, anchored to the solid earth, a solid place and time like this one, like this room in Cassina Way where he lives, someplace real that follows the rules but can't stop the play of spirits, so lets them break rules, slip in and out, through the corner of your eye like Giacometti's people before it restores itself, restores what's solid, lasting, always.

Why is he waiting for the world to be that simple again. For the bell to ring and a ghost to enter and then be gone in the blink of an eye because in the real world there is no room for ghosts. All in his mind, isn't it. This Philly diner stage set from ten years past, a transparent layer his mind could strip away, see through, see beyond.

It's just him listening, waiting for the door to open, imagining how the space might once have contained his friend John Africa, so it's not mysterious is it, only wishful thinking after all. Nothing, no one pushes through the door. Just him fooled by his old eyes, his desire. Simple as that. A voice tells him it's simple as that. But he's listening and waiting anyway. Hears the bell. Sees the door begin to swing open.

Hears them panting, their restless paws tap, tap, scratching the asphalt, hears whining, smells the raw, rank dog funk of them shear away coffee odor, the burned-grease stink of the grill. Hears the dog man's laughing voice, though he still can't see him through the partially open door.

Hey, O.D., man. How come my dogs ain't allowed in. Thought

the sign says no dogs. Don't see nothing but hounds sitting up at your counter this morning. Bow-wow. Arf-arf.

This is my last letter. I won't be bothering you anymore, Mr. G. My picture-taking project is not going to be completed so my daydream of collaborating with you has become irrelevant.

Though it's time to end this correspondence — is *correspondence* the proper word for a conversation as one-sided as ours — I want you to understand I'm ending it with much regret. I've benefited beyond words from the example of your work and the opportunity to address certain questions to an artist of genius. However, since picture-taking was my only excuse for bothering you, and since my ambitions have been frustrated by circumstances I can't alter, this will be my final note.

One last fact about myself I must share, and then I'll write no more. I've been to your side of the ocean. To Italy, the land of your Roman ancestors. In the hills of Italy I decided to become a photographer.

When I recall the Italian countryside, I hear the sounds of war, see columns of vehicles and troops slogging on muddy roads, the blasted shells of villages, rotting bodies of men and animals in ditches, vultures circling in the sky, the black hulks of burned-out tanks and trucks in smoldering fields, packs of scavenger dogs, antlike caravans of refugees bent under boxes and bags. Fires, smoke, the moaning and groaning of the wounded, the snarl of dive-bombers scattering refugees, the thunder of big guns, single crack of a sniper's rifle that brings the worst kind of silence, that long, still moment afterwards when you're dropping to the ground, wondering if you're dead.

Yet all the war's ugliness could not hide the beauty of the

landscape, the Italy that would return after war, just as it had thrived before war. How can I say it. So much death and danger, so much unhappiness surrounding me. Then a tiny flower, a breeze, dawn on the hills. Things I didn't notice except at rare moments but I knew the small moments, the little treats and teases part of something as large as the giant horrors of war. I understood that my season in hell, whether I survived it or not, was only a season and tried to look beyond it to the far side where someone, maybe me, might find a way, an art to record the struggle, the give-and-take, the dance of light and dark I'd witnessed.

I've tried to blot the worst of the war years from my mind. My part in the killing and destruction. But I need to admit to you there are also times when I wish I could have done more to crush Europe's pride, rip the evil from Europe's heart, kill the beast that still pursues and traps and slaughters us here, as it did there, and does everywhere in the world we turn for peace.

This footnote (confession?) as good a way as any, perhaps, to close a conversation that never had a chance to begin.

Mallory, you're my main man, but admit it, brother, you are one chickenshit negro. Army has us camped out here in the middle of nowhere digging ditches every day, goddamn slave labor from can to cain't, and we owed a day off and you're scared to take it. Two fine Italian bitches I been sweet-talking for weeks ready to party and here you come hemming and hawing. So what if nobody likes seeing us with white chicks. So what these lame paddyboys eating their hearts out cause us brown bombers cop all the best pussy.

Won the bitches fair and square, didn't we. Redneck mother-fuckers lying to the women about niggers got tails, niggers stink, niggers give you woolly-headed Sambo babies just by looking under your clothes. All them bullshit lies and the women still flock to us. Yeah. Come to Daddio, sugar. Come to Daddycool. Can't lose wit the stuff I use.

Gina say there's a place up in the hills, empty cabin on a lake only a couple hours' hump from here. No way none these dumb GI Joes know nothing about it. Slip off early and rendezvous with the ladies. Get the fuck out of here for a day. Day and night if we lucky, know what I mean, green bean. Maybe the sergeant bust us for missing roll call, but so what. What's the knucklehead gon do. Put us on punishment detail. Shit. Ain't no duty harder than what we perpetrating every day out there digging fucking ditches in the hot sun. Latrine duty don't scare me. Shit's shit. Shit ain't shit. Stockade a vacation after them goddamn chain-gang pickaxes and shovels. They say we widening the road. For what. For who. You know why they got us out there digging holes. Don't want niggers wit rifles in their hands. Wouldn't have left my home sweet home in the Burg if I knew I'd wind up over here digging ditches and graves.

If the Italian girls know about this place in the hills, the Italian men will know too. And they sure don't appreciate us messing with their women. Just as bad as the paddyboys.

Fuck em. They all of the caucasian persuasion, right. So what. Since when is white boys hating niggers news. All over the world ofays speak the same goddamn language when it come to the negro menace. Fuck em. What I'm saying is some fine Italian pussy's wet and waiting. You with me or not's the question. Come dawn, I'm gone, brotherman. Tomorrow, after I do Gina, I'll be thinking about you down here playing tonk with the rest of these hard-leg chumps when I hop over and cop me some Francesca's booty. Yes or no, rabbitass negro.

Risky business, Gus. You know how tense things have been. They locked up our rifles. Put us on curfew. We got our own little war going here. They hurt Edwards real bad when they jumped him the other night.

Couple them hurt worse the next night. Uh-huh. That shit don't never cease. Enough us here to protect ourselves long as we stick together. Edwards knew better than to be walking through their part of town by hisself after dark.

You're talking about me and you traipsing off to the hills. Not exactly sticking close with the fellows, is it.

You think too much, Mallory. A day. A day and a night cause I guarantee we gon be lucky. Luck ain't even part of it. Bitches dying to drop their drawers.

For somebody who speaks about as much Italian as I speak — none — you surely do communicate well.

Sign language. Everybody in the world understands poontang talk.

Okay. Okay. Full speed ahead. Damn the torpedoes.

What damn torpedoes.

Just a saying I read in a book. Admiral Dewey or somebody when they told him he better not attack.

Damn Dewey and Louie and Huey. All those quack-quack Donald Duck nephew cracker motherfuckers. Damn Uncle Sam's navy and army and the air corps and the marines. And double goddamn them head-busting MPs. We gon win the war tomorrow, Private Mallory. We gon bring peace talks and armistice and good dick on earth for all womenkind. Amen.

C'mon. Gimme some skin, some amen, my Philly brother. Amen.

*

Mist burned off the hills early. When the air clears, the sky a pale, peeled blue. Bluer and bluer as they trek, the two girls leading the party up a forested hillside. Stubby, funny-leaved trees like broccoli with trunks crowd the slope that flattens gradually to a rolling plateau, meadowlike, full of bright wildflowers, with scattered clusters of Christmas-tree pines. Then the pines thicken until forest closes again overhead and the path's a barely visible track twisting and turning through dense clumps of prickly brush, around boulders taller than a man. At some forks the girls hesitate, chattering, gesturing, pointing, uncertain of or at least disagreeing about which trail to take. Following them, he's amazed by how different these girls have become, can't get enough of the flicking play of the hems of their short dresses, how flimsy cotton swaying unpredictably makes them more naked than if they'd been wearing nothing at all. As they picked their way through the forest their thin, bare legs moved with a briskness, a sure-footed efficiency he'd expect only from wild creatures who lived in these hills. What did these white, smooth-as-marble legs have to do with the bar girls in nylon stockings who hustled drinks and hung on GIs like the beady-eyed fox-skin wraps Philly whores draped over their shoulders.

Later, when they're all sprawled naked on a small crescent of gravel-edged beach they'd found along the lakeshore, not far from the cabin they'd set out at dawn to find, he'll notice the goldish fuzz on Gina's arms and legs, the straight black hairs lying smooth and stark against the pale flesh of Francesca's limbs. Never took his eyes off them, but the girls had changed up on him again.

They'd been waiting at a crossroads outside town. Big hugs and kisses for Gus while he stood back smiling like Gus's slave, a gunnysack full of goodies liberated from the camp mess slung over his shoulder. *Here. You got it, Mallory. I kidnaped the shit, least you can do is carry it.*

Why you hanging back, man. Don't be shy. C'mon meet the ladies. He shook their hands, they pecked at his cheeks and he pecked theirs. He'd seen them around, he's pretty sure. Hard to tell, always smoky and dark in the clubs. Recognized their names when Gus said them. Told them his, *Martin,* since Gus had only called him *my main man, Mallory.*

Gus had taken the sack, laid it on the ground. Looky what we found, ladies. For you. For you, you sweet things. As soon as they understood, they plopped down on the grass, oohing and ahing, clapping their hands, showing leg, showing drawers, greeting each item with squeaks and sputters of noise, maybe the names in their language of what they emptied from the gunny — wine, brandy, cigarettes, cheese, crackers, sausages, tins of fruit, meat, nuts, sardines, jars of jelly, a football of bread, chocolate bars, more rattling cans and bottles than he could keep track of — and then repacked it all into their straw hamper with shoulder straps. On the long walk he and Gus took turns lugging the basket, and each time his turn came he thanked the army, something he'd never done before, for all the practice humping heavy loads on his back. Enough stuff for weeks, it feels like. Damn, Gus. How long had he been squirreling away this stash. Why splurge this much on an overnight picnic.

Perfect weather for a holiday. Sweaty when the hamper's on his shoulders but a crisp breeze always finds him. By mid-morning still cool in the wood's deep shade, a warm sun when they cross open spaces. Cloudless sky, the sun continuing to oblige after they settled, gently baking their skin, throwing a dazzling sheen over the lake. It had taken a few hours to reach the cabin and lake, a half-hour or so exploring before they decided to stop on this sandy patch of beach. To the right and left of it the curving shoreline's a tangled wall of green — bushes, trees, branches overhanging the water, a rim of rocks half in, half out of the lake, forming a deep cove with their spot a golden eye sheltered at its center.

The girls shed clothes first and he tried not to gawk, play it cool, like it was an everyday thing, seeing females bare-breasted above the tacky boxer-short-looking panties that seemed to be all they wore over here under their dresses. Sporting a grin bigger than his face, Gus winked *I told you so*, and not to be outdone, stripteased, clowning and shimmying his way out of every stitch of army issue while the girls giggled, hooted, and clapped their hands. A race to the water. Everybody else naked, splashing each other before he can yank his pants off.

Easy as that and that's how everything had been on this sliver of sand, past war, past language, past clothes. Past paying too much attention to who was with whom it seemed since touching and kissing not just Gus with Gina and him with Francesca but a way of everybody being with everybody else, even Gus grappling with him, squeezing him in a bear hug after they bumped, both men on their knees, straightening up at the same time from rooting in the basket. You too light in the ass to mess with old Gus, boy. Give you a break this time, call it a tie, and they swigged brandy from the bottle Gus waved, toasting the flawless sky.

Niggers back home should see me now, head all up in this white gal's sweet cherry-pie bush. Look here man. Look at these soft, silky hairs. Let this fluffy stuff grow and grow. When it's nice and long, tell her, say, Hey baby, knit your man a pussyhair scarf and a pair of pussyhair socks.

She's smiling, ain't she. Don't understand a damn word I'm saying but she knows what I'm talking about.

Nakedness strange for a while. In this strange country, suddenly even further away from anywhere he's been. Harder in a way getting used to bare-assed Gus than the women. He didn't have to figure out how to respond to a woman's body. The girls a dream come true, weren't they. Tall Gina with flame-colored hair down to her wide hips, nice, solid pudding of extra flesh before the long glide of her slender legs. Francesca a shorter, thinner version of Gina, could be Gina's little sister, maybe two years younger, just past adolescence, her breasts just beginning to plump up, hips beginning to round like big sis's. Both of them young girls but girls whose faces are stamped by dark flesh under the eyes, worry lines at the corners of their thin lips you noticed when their features weren't busy. Girls who giggled and smiled a lot but somebody, something had tampered with the wires inside them and a wild hair switch can cut off the flashing light in their eyes instantly, freeze their faces into blank masks. He'd seen that empty look too often in the faces of kids at home, in the dirty, city rat orphans here. Kids chilled to the bone. Suddenly memoryless. A short life already way too long, too hard, too much that must not be remembered.

Lucky no rule says you have to stumble into their eyes and get ambushed. You could just enjoy watching their bodies move, the lean, firm parts stretching, the bounce and jiggle, smile at their flirting eyes measuring him. Part of getting used to Gus without clothes was the women's eyes, him wondering what they saw. Were they comparing his body to his friend's. And for a woman which differences mattered. He'd never really stared and compared. Couldn't help staring now at Gus, dark and hard-muscled from digging and hauling all day under the hot Italian sun. Gus black anyway when he got over here, lank droop of penis in his briarpatch groin the darkest skin of all. Heavy thighs, skinny calves. Stubby, thick-fingered hands. Bunioned toes, a pale trim round the bottoms, color missing the soles of his feet when the man held him by his ankles and dipped him in the vat of lifetime-guaranteed pigment.

Caught looking in someone's window how he felt when he realized he was staring at his friend. His eyes a woman's eyes checking out this unfamiliar body with Gus inside. Was Gus curious about him. Mirrors. Windows. Caught looking. A moment of awkwardness. Who was on display. Had anybody's eyes been following his. It's not about Gus, he reminds himself again. It's wondering what the ladies see when they look at me.

Because they are looking. Exchange glances, words. Are Gina and Francesca sharing little jokes, signifying in their hurry up, hurry up language that sings and rhymes. Saying to each other what they can't say or would never say to strange, baa-baa-talking black men. What do they make of our color. What do they call it. What's the word for *nigger* in Italian. Is there a word. Do they need one.

Easy to look at the girls, easier than he thought to get casual seeing them without their clothes, but still a stir, a thrill, something new he wouldn't even try to pretend wasn't there. He'd seen his wife's body how many times, but not enough, not like this. He'd memorized her body, brought a map of it across the ocean, and in the darkness, the rare quiet, he'd unroll the picture, aroused but also slightly ashamed, slightly disappointed because when they'd been alone together back home, too often it was in dark, cramped, unprivate spaces. He had to rely on that dim map when he imagined her now. Wanted more of her now. Wanted bright snapshots of her smiling, at ease in her naked body as she walks across a room, sits in a chair reading a book. Why hadn't there been more sunlight. More laughing. More naked time to touch her, learn her, explore her body in the full glow of day, on a long, lazy afternoon beside the sparkling water of a mountain lake. He'd drawn the map of her as they thrashed and shuddered and held their breath, his love creating her shape from the blackness beneath him, the form molded to his. And that plunge, needing her but not knowing, not seeing, merged them, paired them, and seemed more than enough, everything. He'd yearned for her, for the plunge, the meeting, for what they stole pressed together in darkness. Hadn't he missed her, her voice, her heartbeat, every day of this terrible, distancing war.

And yearned for this day too, though he'd not been aware till now on a tiny half-moon of sand on the far side of the world what was missing when they loved together in the dark. Was it why he cheated on her. Why he peeked in other people's windows. Had he been searching even before he could guess why or give it a name, a name for this bright day, this space, this time to study her, free her, for her to study him, teaching each other what couldn't be seen or said in the dark. Had they lost their chance to make new maps.

He sees her. The snapshot of her he wears next to his heart. Her on the back steps of the crooked house in D.C., faded housedress stretched between her knees, the razor-sharp shinbones, hidden eyes, the boundless mystery of her shrouded under the tent of old-lady dress. A picture of her he wore in an invisible locket around his neck, so real he hears it on the end of its gold chain he made up too, *ping ping* striking his dog tags.

The others are playing in the water. Gus the shark dives, attacks. The girls jump and shriek, chop at the water, fight the biting, pinching devil fish. Gina swims for her life, windmilling strokes splashing rooster tails of white spray. Francesca reaches shallow water, dashes for shore. Takes his breath away when she bounds onto the sand, wild-eyed, glistening, sun behind her, eating away the edges of her body. Plastered to her skull, streaming past her shoulders, the black shiny mass of her hair some squirming, live creature from the lake's bottom she wears like a crown.

Her thighs icy against his warm leg. He hollers when she drips, then drags her cold, drenched hair across his belly. Grabs her, pulls the whole loud, wet, chilling shock of her down on top of himself.

Propped on one elbow he can scan the huge sky or lower his gaze and travel close-up across the terrain of Francesca's body — freckles, pimples, a scar, one wild black hair in the reddish, pitted halo of skin around a nipple, the bump of her groin, how the hairs there live anchored in tiny holes, how they curl and cling and mat. A patchwork of shades, textures, mounds and hollows, blemish and irregularity that equal the nearly perfect sum of her. Her child's scratched, moist skin, a pearl of sweat in the well of her navel.

Proportion. The parts of her trim body arranged just so, so they fit neatly together. Just so. In balance. Harmony. Nothing big if small's enough. Never less than needed. *Proportion.* He loved words. Their science and silliness. Collected them from his reading. Tried to learn a new word daily from the raggedy chunk of pocketbook dictionary, L–W, he found and carried everywhere. Loved the way words fooled you into believing you could say the very thing you mean.

A huge, purplish cloud had settled over a portion of the lake, dividing the sky, one side fair, the other uncertain weather. The cloud dyed water underneath it inky blue-black, curtained the far shore with a bank of gray mist that creeps closer an inch at a time. Further down the lake, at the dark cloud's edge, between its shadowy bottom and the water, he thought he could see a skirt of slanting rain, yes, probably raining a few miles away. Tight, choppy waves rushing from that direction slapped against rocks at the cove's mouth. Nearer, across the dark cloud's face, a few smaller, pale clouds float, outlined and veined with bright white lines, a surprise because he can't figure out how sunlight reaches them.

In front of him, to the right of the looming cloud, the lake is shining and quiet. He watches a long, shimmering reef stripe the water near the opposite bank and then widen, a field of light driven slowly by the breeze, spreading, gliding over miles of water till it slips through the cove's entrance and breaks up in starbursts of glitter just yards away. He can see a dark wall of trees lining the far shore, and rising behind them a lighter green ridge of treetops and behind them more and more till a final, faint silhouette fades into blue distance. No shadow on the water, no gloom, no threat of rain in this travel poster view. High above the last screen of hills a few thin, snowy clouds. Calm stretching miles and miles as if bad weather hasn't been invented.

If he had a camera he could aim it in different directions and the snapshots would look as if he'd been here on different days at different times with different weather. A whole album, each picture a different story he could send to convince her to join him, to say take a chance, anything can happen here, change happens here, right in front of your eyes, Love. A beautiful island, many islands in one. Wish you were here he'd write on the back of one photo. Please come on another. Yours forever the last words on them all before his scrawled initials.

He's flat on his back on the hot sand, eyes closed, drowsy. Pops up to swat the dive-bombing bug that's after his leg. It's not a hungry bug, it's Francesca's finger teasing the inside of his thigh. Lazy circles tracing his kinky hairs, circles shrinking in tighter and tighter swirls.

Their eyes lock softly on each other but both see the one-eyed dragon's head swelling, rising. She gasps in fake terror. He grins. Knows what she's going to do next, what he wants, what he wants her to want. He drops back on the gritty sand. Feels her fingers close round the bobbing stem of him, steadying it, wetting it with her tongue, then her mouth slides up and down to the butter-smooth, lazy rhythm of a Big Bill Bronzy blues *been so lonesome/just on account of you* and he wonders how she knows the song, how it crossed the sea to this faraway place and found a home.

Water's something, man. Bee-you-tee-full. A hot fudge sundae. Lay here and get all sticky, syrupy hot, then boom. Hit the water and you cool as a dip of vanilla ice cream. Cleanest, clearest damn water I ever seen.

You ever wonder what it's like in a submarine. Like traveling to Mars, I bet.

Couldn't pay me to go in one now. No, no. Not with no goddamn war going on. Motherfuckers riding those subs now got to be out their minds.

When he'd stood motionless, knee deep, staring down into the lake, it was sure enough clean and clear as Gus said, said to him but speaking to the girls too, as if after a few hours here they understood his baa-baa-black-sheep language. The lake's bed a desert of hard sand rippled like a washboard, studded with sleeping rocks and pebbles, wiggling golden patches where sunlight passing through the water's restless skin dances on the sand. Could you learn the lake's history down there, is the bottom where it all starts. Another world underwater. Was it older, cleaner. And if you got down in it, where would this one go.

You coming in. I got to hit it one more time.

Know what, Gus. I can't swim. Like to paddle around and duck under and float, but if the water's over my head, man, I'm in trouble. Wish I could swim, but never learned. No place to learn. Pools in Philly for whites. One city pool where black could go so crowded and filthy you wouldn't want your dog to swim in it.

Same way when I was coming up in the Burg, but shit, man, we just swam in the river. Big guys throw your ass in, you better learn real quick. Nasty Allegheny not real water like this, though. How far you think it is across.

You considering swimming to the other side.

Hell no. Just wondering. Might be another country over there. This a whole lotta water, ain't it. Most water I've seen except the ocean.

First time I saw the ocean was on the troopship that brought me over here. Ocean all around Philadelphia, it's a port city, but I never saw ocean. Ready to see it again. Sooner the better. On my way back to the States. While I'm still in one piece. Tomorrow wouldn't be too soon.

What you talking about, man. What's your hurry. We ain't

hardly seeing no more combat. We the cleanup crew. Mops and pails, shovels and brooms and body bags. Army don't want niggers to get used to shooting white boys. Anyway, where you think you gonna find anything better back home. You got women like this at home. You got all this clean water and blue sky and trees. What's wrong, brother. You miss the motherfucking white man hollering, *Niggers keep out. All the good shit's mine.*

Look at these pretty white women, man. They love us. All they thinking about is making us happy. Been off peeing in the woods and now ain't nothing on their minds but what's on our minds. Tuning up those damp little fuzzy-wuzzies between their legs. And you talking about going home. Shit. Thought you was an intelligent guy, Mallory. What's your big hurry. What you got or ever gon get tomorrow cross the pond compare to this.

Don't care if I ever go back. Never's soon enough for me. Matter of fact I might just decide to stay right here. Fuck the water. Gina. Yeah you, baby. Bring that sloppy booty over here, girl.

Hey, my friend. Don't mind if I borrow Francesca for a few shorts, do you, man. C'mon, c'mon to Poppa-do. Both you gorgeous wenches. Uh-huh. That's right. You too, lil black-head darling. Gus got something for both youall.

Good gracious. My-oh-my. Bloods on the corner ought to see ole Gus now. Shit. What I'm talking about. Ain't no bloods on the corner. All over here slaving in the Man's war.

> *Ladybug, ladybug, fly away home*
> *Your house is on fire and your children are burning*

Does he really want to see her in this place. What would she understand if she arrived. Naked bodies in the bright sun. What would she think if he mailed her a snapshot. Would she believe he's saving a place for her, that he's waiting in his fashion for her to join him and make the island real, this island not an island but he can't help thinking of it that way, the lapping water, the breeze, sand, an island past war, past clothes and language, past her hidden in his arms in the dark. Yes. I'm yearning for you, trying to move closer, return, start again. Would she understand those words written on the back of a picture postcard with a stamp from another country.

He glances over his shoulder, up at Gina's sleek back, the pinch of her high waist, the crease above each hip. She's riding high in the saddle, buckety-buck, her behind splatting against Gus's thighs. Giddyup, girl. Hi-ho, Silver. She bounces, her cakes shuddering, spreading on each stroke. Crack of her hairy ass flying above the pale, sandy soles of Gus's feet, his rubbery toes. Francesca's kneeling, the upper half of her hidden by Gina's back, doing something he can't see to the top of Gus he can't see either.

He tries to picture her again, here, transported across the sea by his wish. Light, bright, almost white. Whiter than these Italian girls. Her stiff, pomaded hair red under the blazing sun. Possesses no snapshot of her that fits. He needs to take one. Many. Her sprawled naked with a girlfriend and two colored soldiers. Her and a pal with two German soldiers who paid the girls to lead them to this perfect spot and fuck on the sand a couple of months ago when the Nazis were winning the war.

Gus outdoors in the black, starless night peeing must have seen needles of light shuttling through the woods. Off-on, off-on, on-off, a code he instantly broke *We're coming to get you, coming to get you.* Or maybe he heard the metallic clink of dogs being chained or unchained, carried miles in the still, pure air.

Wake up, wake up. A husky, urgent whisper in his ear. Is it Francesca's tongue again. Has she learned to speak English in her dreams. He smells lake on her, the smear of their juices. Prickle of light hairs he brushes with his lips as he lifts the dead weight of her arm to scoot out from under it to the floor.

Shhhh. Shhhh. Don't make a sound. Motherfuckers coming for us. Close. Damn close. Git your shit and move. Out the back door. Go. Go. Go. Let the girls sleep. They coming for us, not them.

Years later when he sees Emmett Till's mutilated face in *Jet* magazine he'll recall Medusa, but this moment too, the black cabin, frightened whispering. How close.

Crouching beside the door Gus pantomimes a wide loop, splitting them up, bringing them together in a place far below and beyond the lights he must have seen or the dogs he must have heard in the woods.

Then it's scrambling solo in utter darkness, tripping, stumbling over rough ground, lunging downhill, out of breath after a few dozen steps, blind until he looks up and sees above the treetops a faint luminous fringe he follows. He's fifty yards from the cabin, a hundred before the *pop pop pop* of rifles in the direction Gus had taken. He stops stock-still. Spins around. Running back to help his friend crosses his mind just long enough to freeze him in his tracks and that dumb thought, that bad idea probably what saved him. Bullets whiz through the air. Close enough to stick out his tongue and taste. Thunk into a tree inches away, stinging his face with a shower of bark.

Automatic weapons begin to rake the cabin. All the trains in the yards below 30th Street Station full speed ahead, jumping the tracks, crashing into each other. He wanted to shout, No, no, we're not in there, but who would hear him over the racheting gunfire clack-clack-clacking, too fast to follow, hundreds of thirty-caliber slugs splintering the log wall, raising the building from the ground, tossing the riddled bodies inside like rag dolls.

Tracers. Salvos of bullets like thunder, like axes hacking chunks out of the cabin. Did he hear flames crackling. Screams. They weren't here to arrest them, haul them to the brig. It was open season on niggers. They'd come to kill and kill anybody, anything that got in the way.

More rounds probe the dark surrounding him. He's down, hugging the earth, breathes in the unexpected sweetness of pine sap.

No one's seen him he guesses. Hopes. Shit. They're just filling the woods with lead. Trying to get lucky. SOP. Our trigger-happy, ammo-spoiled troops, blasting away at anything that moves, that might have moved. Bang bang bang. You're dead. Everything's dead. Bullets chopping down the trees.

Beams of light flicker, skitter, stab the black slope. He's crawling, the snap and crackle and crunch of pine needles too fucking loud, impossible for anybody nearby not to hear, hear above the machine gun's rattle, even though he's inching along, holding his breath. If he breathes it will be louder than the crackling needles, louder than the giveaway thumping of his heart.

He draws his leg forward to propel himself another inch from the firestorm engulfing the cabin and feels an incredible weight, the drag of quicksand, of an iron boot. Then every scared numb nerve end fires at once. Pain rips from leg to jaw. His jaw clamps shut. He thinks he's bitten off his tongue. Mouth's full of blood, full of the knowledge he's been hit.

Bullets and lights sweeping the trees, moving up and away from where he sits. Dogs bark. He thinks of tearing a strip from the tail of his shirt to bandage his wound. Remembers how sound carries, snakes the shirt over his head, wraps it whole around the wet mess of his thigh. A hunk of flesh gone. Or turned to hot soup. That's what he thinks, wincing when he jerks his hand back.

Then he's crawling on his belly again, pushes up to all fours to go faster, tests weight on his leg, hunkering low to the ground for a step, then the bloody leg howls, gives way, and he tumbles sideways, can't stop himself as he flies headfirst through a slick wash of pine spill that starts him skidding downhill towards a hospital in Philadelphia. He plunges through roots and bushes and punishing stones, down the steep embankment whose abrupt lip he never saw coming, down a slippery muddy slope that ends in the soaking black shock of her hair, dream and nightmare and miracle saving him, landing him on his back, no bones broken, in the roar and rush of a swollen stream he now recognizes as what he's been hearing all day, an ever-present sound he'd thought was wind sighing through the cove, but it had been this water, chilling him now, almost drowning him, planting the pneumonia in his chest he'll never shake, but also eating his scent to throw off tracking dogs. Water restoring his wits, cleansing his wound, dulling cuts and knocks of the battering fall.

When he rights himself he remembers runaway slaves he'd heard about and keeps to the water for painful miles, teeth chattering, wound a hot iron branding his leg, the leg he won't ever be able to depend upon again, source of misery and a lifetime pension. He splashes upstream, the wrong way, away from help but away from danger till he can't move another inch. Tries to rest, drifts in and out of consciousness, teeth chattering, too tired to fall asleep, to care anymore whether anybody's waiting to kill him or not, so he reverses direction, starts back the right way, towards the war.

Not his night to die. Somehow he hobbles and crawls back to the road where his gang is working and his homeboys truck him to base and blame a sneaky fucking Nazi sniper. Neat enough lie to get everybody off the hook he tells John Africa. You know. Something like enemy activity reported at blah-blah hour in Sector blah-blah. In separate incidents one U.S. soldier KIA, one wounded, two civilians dead from enemy fire, blah, blah, blah.

Four dead in O-hi-o. First time he heard the song he thought the brothers sang *All dead in O-hi-o.* Couldn't help changing the line, singing it silently to himself, *All dead in It-a-ly.* Not funny, but he couldn't help it. Not funny, but true. True and funny. *All dead in It-a-ly. All dead on O-sage-Ave.* Same dying. Same lies to cover it up. Same clean slate. So true it's past true, past time, place, and color. So far past you have to laugh to keep from crying. Walked around for days with the singsong chant in his brain. You have to sing along. Sing to wear it out, sing to survive the all-dead. The all-clear.

In a makeshift recording studio around the time of his birth, Bessie Smith, Empress of the Blues, is vamping a last run-through of "Backwater Blues," *Ima shoot em if he stands still/Cut em if he run,* when the producer, a white guy in a folding chair beside the piano bench, interrupts. Don't you mean, *Cut em if he stands still/shoot em if he runs.* A female companion of Bessie's leaning in a corner of the studio, glass of gin in hand, cuts her eyes at the man and

hollers, Shut up, fool. Let Bessie kill the no-good nigger any way
she want to.

> Good morning, blues, blues how do you do
> Good morning, blues, say how do you do
> My name's Martin Mallory, what do folks call you.

PITTSBURGH

S HE'D SENT IT to the dry cleaners last time, the black dress
with its mean-to-iron, calming pleats, and it hangs on the
back of the closet door, dull in a plastic bag, lucky it's not
ashes because she'd promised herself it would burn after the last
funeral, the dress had outlived enough lives and she needed it
gone, gone out of sight, out of mind, the ashes of it scattered with
the ashes of the lives she'd mourned wearing it, her good black
dress purchased for fine restaurants and fine gentlemen at a time
when she believed she might find time for such things.

The pile of odds and ends she planned to throw in the flames
grew daily. Mr. Mallory's things. Her pillows. The dress. This
house on Cassina Way. When she really set her mind to it, not idle
daydreaming but making serious lists of what to keep, what to
discard, it sometimes saddened her, sometimes she smiled at the
very little she'd have left once she lit the bonfire and started pitch-
ing.

Mr. Mallory's boxes and bags. His ancient camera. His clothes
which would all fit in the army overcoat if you made a sack of it, if
you could work his shape out of it and bend and twist and tie the
arms of the old stiff wool coat into a sack. He was an old, old man

and those boxes and bags, that sackful all he had left behind, all that he'd gathered and needed and kept after living long as he did on earth. Why should she have more. How many things did anyone need to begin a life, to live one, to finish one. One moment you're here breathing, believing you need shoes, boxes, a black dress, then you're gone and what you've saved to keep you company nothing, smoke drifting away like you drift away, just a nuisance, smoke getting in somebody else's nose and eyes who has to clean up behind you.

And if you're left behind by somebody you love, a mother, sons, a man like she'd found or who found her that night dancing in Edgar's, you can't stack them here in the keep pile or there to throw away because they stay with you whether you want them to or not and how long does anyone need to stay locked up with another person loved and lost. You can't own them like things, but they own you. They'd probably say no, say you're wrong, say it's the other way round, I love you and I'd do anything for you baby, and might mean it too, but when the time comes they can't stay alive, can't leave you alone either, no matter which pile, keep or toss, you think you need to put them in.

The radio man this morning happy about something, all smiles and jive bullshit and perky time of day and lots of great stuff to give away and sell and tons of jams nonstop with no commercials this hour and how finger-popping good or dope or righteous or butter or foot-stomping flat-out righteous or whatever words he's shouting she forgets the moment she hears them, the words that mean this batch coming up is soul-shaking or boogie-down get-down number-one top-of-the-chart bad and it will start your hips shaking or heart breaking or whatever. His excited, happy voice after the news he must not have been listening to while he read it, hearing even less than she did, her mind barely paying enough attention to learn the news bad as usual and as usual at the tail end some young black man or boy had hurt another somebody like him. Didn't seem possible really, how you could hear the same news day after day after day and still have anyone left alive in a city this size who was black, male, and under twenty-five. She didn't understand. Didn't want to know so she halfway or half-ass paid attention. No need anymore to listen heart in her throat every morning for the names of the dead and hurt and the names when they're caught of the ones did the killing and hurting. Nothing the same once she knew the list would not contain the names of her sons. After she'd heard one son's name a day late and never any mention of the other, even though she knew he was shot down and gone too. She wondered if her boys had listened. For their friends' names. Their own names starring in the tail end of the morning news clips. Wondered about this smiley-voiced black man or white man speaking black as some of them did pretty convincingly if you were white or only halfway, half-ass listening, greeting you, pleased with the world, pleased with hisself, pleased with the music he's deejaying for you, pleased with you for tuning in and listening after a news flash featuring King Death boogying through the streets of Radioland.

If she were the deejay's mother she'd go upside his silly, empty head with a board, knock some sense into him, some respect for the dead, but she's not a mother, she lost her sons, and his mother probably a nice light-skinned lady sitting somewhere in a nice part of town in a decent house on a nice sofa proud as can be of her son who's doing real well she tells the other ladies at church, her fine boy who's escaped the killing and tries to help people have a good time even with all the bad news.

She tells herself, Leave the man and his mama alone. She doesn't want to be bitter. What bitter means exactly she's not sure but works hard to avoid it ever since Mr. Mallory said to her one day, one of the worst days till he said it, What I admire most about you is you're not bitter. Every right to be bitter, if anybody ever has the right to be bitter, but you're not, and I can't tell you how unusual a person that makes you. You're not permitting something terrible that happened to your family crush you, rob you of dignity. You're not allowing what's outside your control to set up shop inside you and run you. You're quite a strong person, miss. I can't express how much I admire and respect the way you carry yourself, the strength you find to do what you must do.

She'd thought a bitter person meant you went around always whining inside, mad because you believed you deserved to be in somebody else's shoes, somebody whose situation's better than the one you found yourself in. Mr. Mallory said that was a good way of putting it, part of what he meant, and he'd look up the word for both of them since what she said made him think more about what he'd meant so he'd look up *bitter* in his dictionary and write down on a piece of paper for her what it said about the word. That's okay, she said, I can look it up. I have a dictionary. No trouble, he said. It's for me too. But he never did or maybe he wrote a definition on a piece of paper and forgot to give it to her or changed his mind or died first.

Those words about bitter, the other talks with Mr. Mallory, definitely helped. She was sure, even if she wasn't sure how or why or how much they'd actually talked when so much of that hard time after her boys dead was going backwards and forwards in her own mind over things she never shared out loud with anyone, things real and hurting and hard, storming through her mind while a conversation may or may not have been taking place because the feelings ran so deep she couldn't keep it straight — the here and now from before and after, none of it safe, none of it settled or separate so she could make sense and get past it.

She hoists the big book in its shreds of black cover from the top of one of Mr. Mallory's boxes. Opens it towards the beginning, the first cut-out finger place in pages thin like the pages of her Bible. Leafs forward from the *ba*'s to the *bi*'s, finds *bitter* marked with a length of string she'd ignored when she picked up the book but couldn't pretend any longer wasn't there, left for her to find.

Many meanings. The first about food or drink, *Having or being a taste that is sharp, acrid, and unpleasant.* She skips to (3) *difficult or distasteful to accept, admit, bear.* Backs up to (2), where her eyes had noticed *painful . . . stinging . . . harsh.* The numbered meaning she finally chooses to copy the way he said he wrote down definitions to help himself not only learn but remember words is (6) *marked by resentment or cynicism* (she'd look up that *c* word later).

Six must be the bitter Mr. Mallory meant, *He was already a bitter, elderly man with a gray face (John Dos Passos)*, it was the one that scared her, sent a shiver through her, a mirror in which she saw her face staring back at her, a dull mask, her features and Mr. Mallory's blended, white-haired like him, skin dry and wrinkled like his, faded to ashy gray like him dead in her bed.

It must be Mr. Mallory's pencil scrawl at the bottom of the page. She stares and stares. Unprepared for this fresh sign of him, this sudden proof of his presence and absence in his room. She can make out the words *love* and *bitter* and *sweet* in a scribble-scrabble thicket of what might be those words repeated again and again, darkly scoring, nearly scratching a hole in the paper, the three words over and over, one atop the other, a briarpatch, tarbaby pit of jagged strokes and swirls like the trap the foolish, flop-eared rabbit she'd read stories about to her boys got tricked into and couldn't escape from until he tricked the trickster.

They both stand looking down at the closed wooden casket Mr. Mallory had picked and paid for. He'd requested it this way, closed so no busybody will stare at me when I can't stare back he said in one of their conversations. She was surprised how much he must have talked about his dying. How else could she go straight to the drawer and his papers — a paid-up burial policy, deed to a plot in Allegheny Cemetery, the will leaving her seventy-nine dollars — how else would she know so many details of what he wanted done after he was gone.

Surprised because the conversations she remembered were about life, about the facts of his long life, the unexpected twists and turnings of it his way of urging her to carry on with hers. Yet he'd prepared her step by step for his dying, she could look back and see now. His guiding hand in everything that had happened so far since his death and it was strange to think of that same invisible hand steering her through what must be done next.

The viewing parlor empty except for the two of them and what remained of Mr. Martin Mallory in a no-frills wood box. They are the first and last so far to sign the visitors' book on its stand under a silky-haired, smiling Jesus with pale, open arms. Why wasn't Mr. Mallory's name anywhere in Wardens, on the front door, in the lobby, nowhere. How would anyone find him. With no children, grandchildren, or great-grandchildren around, a person old as Mr. Mallory, a man who kept as much to himself as Mr. Mallory did, what does she expect. The pair of them may be the only mourners.

He had called in a death notice to the newspaper, a notice every time the person on the other end of the line asked a question, he had to make up as he went along. Who would know Mr. Mallory by name anyway, who would connect the name in the paper with the strange old guy who appeared one day and soon stopped being a stranger because you'd see him everywhere, a tall, straight-backed old fella, going around wrapped in a big army overcoat winter summer spring fall.

When I dropped off the box of pictures the lady up front said she couldn't post names and rooms in the usual place outside by the front door. Somebody smashed the glass door of the outside case, took away all those little white letters from inside it. She said she didn't intend to put up names anyway. A gangbanger's laid out in one the other rooms. He shot some big chief of a rival gang and they shot him but it's not over, big chief's people not satisfied. Want more blood. So it's not over, it's never over. Bo-coo trouble brewing is the word on the street. Killing each other, one for one, tit for tat's not good enough. Dead's not enough. Go after one another in the funeral parlors. Bother the families. Disrespect the damned dead bodies. Want more blood. Why am I telling you this. You know more about this craziness than any one person ever needs to know. I'm sorry. Point is no names posted. As if that's going to keep the peace. Jesus. She told me she sure didn't want to but she's burying the boy because she knew his family since before he was born. Bury him but sure wasn't advertising the funeral. She's Mrs. Betts, Wardens's widow's sister, I think. A nice woman. Manages the place since Reba Wardens been sick. Poor woman's in a no-win situation. Said she called and asked the police for a guard. They told her she'd have to hire a rent-a-cop, not police policy to provide protection for funerals. She asked if they knew a gang war was about to break loose and they said, Don't worry, we'll have the beat officer keep an eye out.

Keep an eye out. Now here you have a small army of hoodlums armed to the teeth with better weapons people say than the police, and some peckerwood idiot behind a desk downtown telling me the sorry-assed, don't-give-a-damn cops who patrol around here will *keep an eye out.* Which means after the shooting's over they'll screech up, sirens and lights flashing, with a meat wagon and an evil attitude to scrape up the bodies and steal anything not tied down.

We pay taxes. Run a legitimate business. Been at this location serving the community since Skippy was a pup. Ask the police for protection and you discover real quick you're in the wrong part of town to be asking for anything. Don't care who you are. Don't matter I've known that white-hat lieutenant supposed to be in charge of this precinct since he was a snotty-nose brat running around here.

I understand just what you're talking about, Mrs. Betts. Makes my blood boil too, the way the city does things, way it does nothing in this community. At least there was a cop car up on the corner of Homewood Avenue. Noticed it when we drove past. The car just being there might help.

Those two thieves. Hummph. I know who's in that black-and-white and just why it's sitting there. Know exactly what business they carry on out of that particular car on that particular corner every day. You can forget getting help from them. If shooting starts, you won't find them anywhere near it. Those crooks have other fish to fry.

Anyway, no names posted she said. Visitors will have to stop at the office for information. Better that way she said because she can keep track of traffic. Only letting in a few of the young crowd at a time and only between five and six. Just a single hour for them and that's hard, I think, because the kids are grieving too. The dead boy's one of them, after all. But she's on edge. Real upset with the cops. Has a right to be. So like I said, as far as Mr. Mallory's concerned, if anybody wants to pay their respects, they'll have to ask up front which room he's in.

Makes me feel bad for him. Hidden away again like he was his whole life.

Didn't he want it that way.

Nobody really wants it that way, do they. Much as I was determined to hide from people, I know now I was waiting for someone to come looking for me, maybe nobody but my own dumb self looking, if that was the best I could get.

Do you want to sit down or go or what.

I hate this place. Hurts me to walk through the door. But now I'm in here, let's sit a while. We're the closest thing to family. I don't want to be in a hurry now I'm here. Don't want him to think I think I need to hurry.

Old Mr. Mallory past worrying about what other people are thinking.

You think so. Maybe I do too. But how would anybody really ever know.

Certain as I need to be. As a matter of fact, I depend on it. I'm sure in no hurry to find out firsthand, but the idea of peace and rest, nobody bothering me, me not bothering them, ain't all bad. Hope that's where Mr. Mallory is now. Hope I get some peace like that a couple hundred years from now when it's my time to go. You willing to put up with me for that long.

Not very long is it. However many years you get. He must of

lived the better part of a hundred years, didn't he, but being around him, even the little bit I was really around him, you know, not counting the time we was just living in the same house before we started talking, just being in the same house I started to understand all the years he lived didn't make him all that different from me. In some ways, I mean. I mean in the first place he wasn't just old. Had lots of ages in him. Like me. No name for how old I felt after my sons gone. Like that. It's how you feel inside. Age ain't nothing but a number, like people say.

Looking down at the lid of that skimpy-ass box he's in I thought about Mr. Mallory old and thought about him young like he was in some the stories he told me. Wondered what he'd be if I could see him now, see past the wood. I've heard old age melts off some people's faces when they die. You ever heard that.

I've seen dead faces that looked younger than they ever looked alive. On the other hand some people rot real quick. Start rotting and stinking no matter what the undertakers do. Don't ask me where I've heard that. But I do believe it happens that way too. People will be what they got to be, living or dead.

Did you think about your death when we were up at the coffin. I did. Mine, not yours, I mean. Maybe a little of yours too. Same thing I was saying before. Life's short, no matter how many years you get. Didn't understand how short till I lost my boys.

I don't know if a man old and sick like Mr. Mallory feels life is short. Getting older and sicker by the day. I wonder if he'd say life's short.

Made me cry sometimes. Seeing him dragging his stiff leg. Hearing him cough up his lungs the way he did some nights. Lying there choking to death. Gasping for breath. A terrible sound. I know all that was getting to him but it wasn't him. Told me once he liked me because I wasn't bitter. He's the one should get the prize for not being bitter. Told you about him taking my picture, didn't I.

You did.

You say that like you don't want to hear any more about it. You're not jealous of him taking my picture, are you.

Who? Me? Why should I be.

Course you shouldn't. Or maybe you should. Just a little.

Well, I'm not begrudging an old man, especially a freshly dead old man just a few feet from me who you say was your friend, the pleasure of taking a pretty woman's picture. But I'm interested in any reason you think maybe I should be even a little jealous, if you care to share it.

If I picked up a taste for older men, you're to blame, you know. And maybe he wasn't so old, so different after all, if you been listening to what I been trying to tell you. Maybe he moved slower and slurred his words some when he got tired, but mostly little things, not amounting to much. Specially if you looked inside and let his outside alone.

Don't get me wrong now. Not saying I was ready to hop up in bed with Mr. Mallory or nothing even close to that kind of carrying on. On the other hand, you never know, some of these older men will fool you. Ended up in bed with you, didn't I.

He flirted. I told you how he flirted with me, didn't I. Winking his eye at me. Not dead yet, he said, so I can't help flirting with a beautiful lady like you. My, my. Not an invitation or nothing. Just teasing. Having fun back and forth and neither of us needing it to go no further. Wish we'd done more of it. Good for both of us. You weren't around. I missed smiling and fun and just being silly with a man. I wonder. You never know do you. Who's to say it couldn't go no further. Mr. Mallory pretty feeble with that leg and asthma and pretty wrinkled up I guess but he still had some surprises in him, I bet. Sparkle in his eye. What do you think. Those older fellows can fool you, can't they.

You're still flirting, aren't you. I know he wishes he could hear you.

Maybe he does.

Are we disrespecting him.

Nothing even close to disrespect in my mind. Or my heart. I'm just playing with the idea of him being more than meets the eye. Way, way more. Because he was. I wish there'd been time to get to know him better. You saw the pictures. Not just anybody could take those pictures. Beautiful pictures. Something sad too. Not weepy sad. More like now you see it and now you don't. Like pictures of something you'd always wanted and have it in your hand a minute, then gone. They were beautiful, weren't they.

They are.

Right. They are. Not gone nowhere yet, are they. Still alive as the day he took them. Never seen pictures like them. Not just anybody could take pictures of how people feel inside. He was a special man. And I was just getting to know him. Just beginning.

Amen to everything you say. A shame those pictures won't go any further than the two of us. People should see them, especially people around here because he caught us dead to rights, no doubt about it. No hiding from his camera. Snap. Mr. Mallory got the goods on you. Caught you red-handed. Like those boys in the post office.

Now you see why I'm so upset, so tore up. One side says don't you dare harm those pictures. Other side says you made a promise to a dying man, no way you can break it. Would be awful to go back on my word. Kinda scares me to think I might. He trusted me. How am I supposed to live with myself if I disrespect his trust. How's anybody supposed to die in peace if there's no one you can count on to carry out your last wishes.

I understand it's a burden. What I can't understand is why he'd want to put it on you.

I wasn't supposed to look. Just burn everything after he died. He said he started working on something many years ago but never finished and it would do more harm than good for anybody to see what he was working on before he got it just the way he wanted. I cheated and looked. Let you look. Already broke one promise. That's why I got this hard choice now. Damned if I do, damned if I don't.

I wonder why he printed the pictures he did and not the rest.

Checked out the rest before you came over. Rest as far as I could tell couldn't be printed. Nothing on the negatives. Every one I looked at, and I looked at lots from each box, just blank. All grayed out. He must of ruined them. Accidentally or on purpose. Who knows. Told me he took pictures on top of pictures. Don't make sense to me. I never used a camera much and sure don't understand nothing about them but you take one picture then you have to wind the film, right. Well, he said he fixed his camera so he could take a dozen, a hundred without turning the film. Said every picture was there on the film and one day he would or somebody would figure out a way so everything he was photographing could be printed for people to see. All I could see when I held the film up to light was gray, gray, gray. Gray close to white in some and some closer to black and some with silver veins running through or maybe some different shades of gray.

Sad to think what's lost. Wonder what Mr. Mallory had in mind. What's in the negatives nobody is ever going to see. If the grayed-out and whited-out ones anything like the box of pictures I saw . . . it's a damned shame.

Hey. His camera, baby. His film. His time he spent doing whatever he called himself doing. Had the right to take pictures and spoil them or burn them, whatever he pleased.

Huh-uh. Pictures of us so they belong to us too in a way, don't they. Think of it from that side and people around here got a right to see their own pictures even if he's the one took them.

You need to get off the fence, whatever. Let me fix it so you don't have to keep going back and forth. Just close your eyes and turn your back a minute and I'll slip back out front, snatch that box of pictures, and stash it in my trunk. You won't have to worry about box or pictures again. You can say I stole them if somebody asks, and who's going to ask. Then it has nothing to do with you. You brought the box this far, just like you promised. I asked Mrs. Betts to burn it when they cremate his body, just like you said he asked. His other stuff's gone. You got rid of it like you promised. You did what he asked you to do so you're off the hook. Not your fault if somebody steals the last box of pictures. Just turn your back. I'll take care of the rest. Let the burden of breaking a promise to a dead man be on me.

Who am I supposed to be doing all this lying to. He can't hear me, can he. And if he could, don't you think a dead man, of all people, be the first to know a lie when he heard one.

Nothing needs to happen one way or the other till the funeral. You have a little more time to think about it. With him a couple feet away this is the last place we need to be discussing what to do.

You're right. But what you said about shutting my eyes and turning my back, no way nothing like that's right.

Tell me some more about the picture-taking of you. Didn't see your shining face in the batch I looked at. Why didn't you say you were in there.

One big envelope of negatives not spoiled like the others. They were in with the pictures. I saved them. Wasn't going to say anything about them till I made up my mind what I'm going to do, but I'm in them. Pretty sure it's me, anyway. Me inside out. You know. White where I'm supposed to be black the way negatives are. Those negatives looked to be okay, you could tell they had pictures on them. Left them where I found them. Didn't know if I was saving Mr. Mallory's pictures or not but figured the good negatives ought to stay with them. If his pictures burn when he does, I want something of me to go with them. Want to be there in his pictures if they get saved. Either way. Both ways. Whatever. Some of me's with him in his pictures and that's where I want to be, where I should be.

Let me throw on something quick besides this ratty old house-dress, Mr. Mallory. Makes me look like somebody's grandma. Wanna look good for your camera. Take me just a minute to throw on something nice and comb my hair.

You shaking your head no. No, huh. Well, I guess it don't bother me if it don't bother you. Maybe you just doing my face. Maybe that's all you want and what I'm wearing don't matter. Run a comb through these naps won't take me a second. No. Huh-uh. Why you smiling. What you thinking, Mr. Mallory. Like me just as I am, maybe. I guess you do, way you're looking at me. What kind of picture of me you after, Mr. Mallory.

Shy aren't you. Cat got your tongue this morning. I bet I can figure it out anyway. Look at you. Grinning ear to ear. Haven't seen a grin like that since my boys in the house. It hurts, Mr. Mallory. You take me back and it hurts, but it's okay too. Been too long since I let their smiles back in this house. Loved to see them happy. Loved their smiles. Best thing in the world when your little ones look up at you and you know they think they seeing the best, prettiest, smartest, kindest person ever on earth. Lucky it don't take much to make a child happy sometimes. No better feeling than when one of them lets you know you got it. Got everything. Just being who you are is everything in the world that little smiling face needs.

What kind of picture, Mr. Mallory. Bet I know. You want me without this rag, don't you. You want just me. Head to toe, just me. Nothing else. If that's what you want that's what you get. It's okay with me. I don't mind. I'm not ashamed. Nothing to be ashamed of. Nothing wrong with it. Just us two grown people here. Nobody's business. I trust you, Mr. Mallory.

Here. Is this better now. And this mess off too. Okay. Now, you want me standing or sitting. Whatever you want's okay. Here, on the bed, sitting. Sure. I'll just lean back on the pillows and think about those smiles I'm missing, the smiles I'm going to open my door for again. Let Kwami and Marcus come and go a little bit, if they please. Don't worry. I'm not afraid, I'm not unhappy. Do me a world of good to see my boys smile again.

I'm glad you asked. Real glad I can do this little something for you. It's just me. Just skin and bone and hair and I'm happy if it makes you happy to take my picture.

Should I look straight at the camera. You don't care. Then I will. Peekaboo. Where are you. You can't hide. I know you're in there, Mr. Mallory. Ain't I a silly thing. Lounging here butt naked at my age playing peekaboo with the birdy.

He can't imagine how she feels being back here in Wardens. Should he ask her. Would talking about it do any good. She's the one said they had to bury Mr. Mallory out of Wardens. Wardens probably buried both sons. One son for sure, the first one, because she'd talked about Wardens, about walking outside to meet the prison van when they heard it drive up on the gravel lot out back, the two burly sheriff's deputies escorting her chained husband to view his dead son, how either burly deputy could have lifted and carried him under one armpit, chains and all, shrunken up as he was. Said they led her husband, hobbling in leg irons, wrists shackled, chain connected to a thick belt around his waist so they could pull him along like a dog through the rear door where they deliver the bodies to be embalmed. How dark it is even in mid-afternoon on the landing under its little aluminum awning where you could go up or down, either up a couple steps into the viewing rooms and office or downstairs to the basement lab, the stink of which hit you, gagged you even though you tried to pretend it wasn't there, tried to believe you didn't know what they do downstairs, what the bad smell had to be. Said they let him stand no more than ten minutes alone over the casket before they closed in on him and hustled him back to prison. Twenty minutes total all he was allowed inside Wardens. Said she had to pay to rent the van, pay for the cops' time and other fees they sprung on her when she went to the courthouse and begged permission for her husband to see his son one last time. She didn't begrudge her husband the money she had to borrow or the hassle, she said. But it was a crying shame, she said. Ten minutes, much as they cost, too late, not worth a damn thing, too, too late for the son and she couldn't help asking herself what could it mean to the father, thin as a stick, skin burned black with disease, almost dead himself he knows, chained like a wild animal, this last look, too late, cheated down to ten of the shortest, longest minutes she ever watched pass in her life. The rules the cops said. By the book the one with the skinny blond mustache who let himself be a human being for twenty seconds said. By the book because it's too difficult for everybody otherwise. Too emotional otherwise. No control. It could get out of hand. So it has to be quick. Quick. Sorry, ma'am. You have my sympathies. You understand, I hope, ma'am. I'd let him stay longer if it were up to me, but it's not.

A strong, strong sister. How else could she step in Wardens' door again. Sit on these rickety folding chairs. Smell the stale perfume of air freshener. Listen to piped-in organ music he wanted to strangle and put out its misery. He loved her strength. Loved the soft core her strength guarded. Core of what. Not soft. Core of giving. Core of pain. Core of worry. Of caring. Core of longing for a world she could live in without the hard shell she grew speck by speck till it covered her. Core he learned to see down through all the dark layers of strength, see it and love it but not understand it even though he could name things there, no word for the core but the word for what was inside him, his core of what . . . what he'd be nothing without.

You know something, my friend. Or rather how would you know, my friend, unless I decide to tell you, which I'm just about to do — I'm the best blues singer in the known universe. As long as I don't open my mouth. My secret talent. Didn't know that fact, did you.

No kidding, Mr. Mallory. No, I have to admit what you're telling me comes as a big surprise. Never heard so much as note the first from you.

Of course you haven't. And won't because I intend to keep my chops shut tight as far as blues-singing goes.

Oh well.

That's the trick. Keeping it to myself. I write blues, accompany myself on guitar, piano, harp, a whole gut-bucket juke-joint band if I need one. All in my head of course. And it's perfect as long as I keep it all inside.

You mean like folks singing in the shower.

Not exactly. Somebody might overhear me singing in the shower. Even if no one else did, I'd hear myself. No, no. My blues-singing can't be out loud. Has to play inside my mind. Where it's perfect.

Nothing wrong with that. Sorta like how everybody thinks they own shit don't stink. No offense, Mr. Mallory. You know. Some folks even kinda likes the stink of they own caca.

Exactly. Singing the blues to myself's just like a dog sniffing its own turds.

Hey. I didn't say that.

Yes you did. And it needed to be said. You hit the nail right on the head. As you often do, John Africa. Right on.

I tell myself I want to be a photographer, to take pictures, but the way I go at it is like singing the blues inside my head. Act like I'm the camera, not a photographer. Worried the picture on the film won't be the picture in my mind. Know damn well no way it could be. Why can't I just snap, snap, snap. Turn the pictures loose.

I'm following you but you're moving kinda fast for a slow dog-strolling man this morning. Tell the truth I didn't know till this minute you cared that much about blues-singing or picture-taking. Seldom seen you pull your camera out your bag.

And that's the problem. Not yours, mine. I'm scared, John Africa.

Person can be their own worst enemy. I'm a witness.

Speaking of enemies, your fence is about finished, isn't it.

More work on the roof, but the rest's pretty tight.

Do you still believe the police are coming after you.

They got to come. We'll remind them, if they forget their duty. Confrontation's the only way things are going to start changing for the better. Our job's about making people see what they don't want to see. What's right in front their eyes. We got to be such a royal pain in the ass nobody can ignore us. And we will be. Oh yeah. Cops are coming, all right. And we'll be ready.

How can you be ready for the manpower and firepower they'll throw at you if they decide to take you down.

Beauty is, we don't have to win. That's why we can't lose. Just got to let people know a war's on. Gotta let folks in the Village, the whole city see for themselves what we're all up against. System wants invisible war. System don't want you to know who your real enemies are. It wants you scared and ignorant and confused so it can keep kicking your ass daily. So you don't make no progress, so you stay up in each other's faces fussing and doping and shooting and stealing and crying the blues and letting your kids kill each other. All that dumb shit instead of taking care of business. That's why we ona Move. Doing the right thing, moving out, moving on. People see us and see the cops trying to stop us. War ain't invisible no more. Time to get busy. Time to choose sides.

*

Did you know he was a soldier in World War II.

Always wore that big old army surplus coat, all's I know.

He traveled cross the country. Went to college till he ran out of money. Didn't like school much anyway, he said. Said he was self-taught. Best kind of education he said, slow but it sticks. He took pictures of dead bodies in a hospital. When they autopsy people, his job photographing the body parts. Hearts, livers, lungs. Got wounded in the war. Did you see how his leg was hurt.

Withered and scarred. Wondered about it when he was in your bed. Wondered how he stood so straight and walked with hardly a limp.

Mr. Mallory married and had children. Left them. Never went back to his family after the war. Just up and joined the army one day. Never said he was going away. Just up and left. Said he was wrong to do what he did. Wrong and sorry ever after but said he had no choice. No choice about going away. Just a question of when. He was a teacher once and in a hospital a long time. Bits and pieces all I know of his story but he tried lots of jobs, went lots of places. Funny, these little bits I know about him, more than I know about you and here I am loving you, getting all tangled up with you and know less about you than I know about Mr. Mallory.

Ain't that peculiar. And just as peculiar is the fact I ain't asked and you ain't offered more about yourself. You a close-mouthed somebody, aren't you.

About some things.

About yourself, I'd say.

Not much to tell, really. And I admit I'm out of the habit of telling. Not much anybody'd be interested in, anyway.

A black man don't get to be fifty something and have nothing much to tell. He just ain't telling. What about family. You ever been married.

Oh yes. Once. Very married.

And . . .

She's gone.

Gone. That all you have to say. All you'll have to say about me one day. Gone.

I can say it still hurts. I lost a woman I loved and it didn't happen just yesterday and it still hurts very much. But I never met anybody who's grown and hasn't lost someone. Sometimes I believe it's what grown means. Means you been hurt bad at least once. So I'm plenty grown. A grownup man. Dues-paying grown. Is that enough about me.

Do for now. Enough to keep me civil towards you for now. I'll let you know when I need more. By the way, knowing a bunch of facts about you wouldn't make me love you more. Nor less.

You sure about that. If you are, I'm happy cause it means we're starting at a real good place. Even. A damned good place to start.

Way past starting, ain't we, sugar.

Only two she had said. Only two deceased in her care at the moment. Thank goodness she said. I can put that boy in Room A, closest to the front where I can sort of keep an eye on what goes on. Your Mr. Mallory in D, room down the hall furthest away from the Truesdale boy. Your Mr. Mallory an unusual man the way he arranged his affairs, came in and picked out what he wanted, settled with me, long before he passed.

Unusual or not, seemed as if nobody yet had arrived to pay their respects to him. No names in his book, and he wouldn't be surprised if no visitors ever turned up. Less than a day till the funeral. Mr. Mallory so old. No family here, she said. He came to Pittsburgh late in life. Walked everywhere but a kind of hermit on top of everything else. Commotion coming from up front sure wasn't folks lining up for Mr. Mallory, had to be kids crowding in to view the dead boy. Who was he. Didn't know any Truesdales. He hated the idea of any boy dead. Intended to peek in at him. More than a peek. In his way a mourner. He mourned all the young men killed and crippled in the streets, mourned for the killers, for the survivors who will show up at the funeral parlor today to mourn, the ones who will come to grieve and find themselves shut out again, their grief mocked, crammed into a narrow hour, raked over by Mrs. Betts's sharp tongue and sharp, suspicious eye. She probably wished she owned a metal detector. Or a room to the side for strip-searching the kids. She would if she could. And she had a right, maybe. The dead boy's people had a right to feel safe, to be comforted and put at ease during these last hours when the child they'd scuffled and scrimped to raise slipped once and for all the last slow inch from their hands. He was going to make it a point to go in Room A and tell the young man how he felt. How those tears that burn but don't fall filled his eyes at unexpected moments when he thought of everything a young person had to live for and how little those boys struck down so early would receive of their portion.

Who owed them their portion. Who owed kids the chance he'd been granted, chance he'd grabbed and squeezed to make a life. Who cared if this new crowd of kids got their chance. Not the white people who run things. Not the black people who have a little something and say, Fuck those niggers too dumb to get something for themselves. Nothing's guaranteed. Nothing's written in stone. He knew that. And knew worse things in the world than dying young. But not too many. He understood that too.

He'd see a boy in the street and wonder is he the one, will this one be struck down tomorrow or will this boy be one who pulls the trigger. Will this kid die for nothing, gunned down by bullets meant for somebody else. Bleeding to death on this sidewalk they share, on this neighborhood street the boy struts down like he owns it. Would he die for that strut, that wish to own. Blue or red not the colors they die for. They die for the color of their skin, the color that is his color. The color he stamps them. Color keeping them here, passing each other on these streets. Is this kid headed for the park, for the post office where he'll saunter in and insult everybody and find himself staring down the barrel of a pistol whipped out from a big coat faster than he can draw his.

Since the young men had started dying like flies, the newspaper pushed their stories to the back pages, but one killed in a drive-by last week got some serious ink because he was only nine. Pitiful. Easy to cry over that one. Too easy. Everybody, including the people don't give a damn, get a good cry over a nine-year-old boy cut down by bullets in front of his own house, but what about the ones ten, eleven, twelve, thirteen, the sixteen- and twenty-year-olds. Not about one, about many. Something terrible happening to everybody every day in Homewood.

Reading the nine-year-old kid's story he'd flashed back on Emmett Till. Just a couple years younger than Emmett Till when Till murdered and maybe that's why he was scared shitless first time he came across Till's dead face in *Jet* magazine. Black boys like Emmett Till, like him, could die. Die suddenly, no hope, no mercy. Faces ripped off. Bodies dumped in the river. He couldn't really look at the photograph in *Jet*. Read the story squinting, eyes narrowed to avoid Till's crumbled face.

He'd peeked once. Peeked at the picture and run away. But never forgot. A few months ago he'd seen Emmett Till's mother in a TV documentary pointing her finger down into her son's open coffin. *I want the world to see what they did to my baby.* Shouldn't somebody, him, every soul in Homewood be standing beside the casket in Room A, shouting what she shouted. Never happen here, would it.

He mourned them. Needed to spend some time with the boy in Room A. Remind himself how angered he was by the waste. Angry and hurt and beyond these feelings, harder, more important than these emotions that come and go, remind himself how much more he owed these boys, the debt that had always been more than he was ready to admit. Couldn't admit most of the time because in his heart he knew he was allowing the killing to happen. Doing nothing to stop it. Party to the slaughter. Victim. Her sons. His. He was the one. He owed them more life than they were getting and in the quiet, alone in Room A, perhaps he'd begin to find a way to speak of some of this, this business so unspeakable. Begin to deal with it, to promise more.

Noise and confusion in the lobby. Mrs. Betts's office blocked. Can't see her through the loud, boiling mob of young people. Only a few dressed for mourning. Wardens could be a park, a picnic given the clothes people wearing. How the fuck you supposed to dress for funerals when funerals an everyday thing. So it's everyday stuff people have on. Bright colors. Jeans. Sweatshirts. He's the one different. Not fitting in with his double-breasted blue blazer, tie and shirt, pressed pants, shined shoes. Must be a dinosaur to the kids. A clown. A Tom. He's probably nothing to them.

Somebody they look at and see right through and go on about more important business. It's what he feels anyway, out of place, out of time, dressed like they dress the dead in the coffins, invisible in the swirl of young faces, young eyes, young clothes.

Red's everywhere. Their red colors. Someone's tacked a red scarf across the top of the doorway of Room A. Red ribbons dangle from the casket.

Young man in a red shirt unbuttoned to his navel with a gun tucked in his belt. Red silk undershirt frames the pistol's silver grip.

A crush at the front door. It's flung open and a crowd streaming out. Others behind them caught in Room A, stuck in the lobby pushing to get out too. Nowhere to move. In the way, out of the way. Some of the young guys, one or two older men dressed in monkey clothes like him, are trying to usher their children, their girls and women through the helter-skelter. Shouts back and forth. Guns drawn now, waved in the air. People covering their heads with their hands. People trying to duck, to squeeze into corners. Panicked eyes. Scared eyes. Warrior eyes looking for trouble, for targets, for someone to protect, someone to blast. A scream. A louder scream trying to quiet a girl's hysterical sobs. Wardens emptying and filling up at once it seems. Traffic of frightened bodies swelling. The lobby ready to explode.

We're out of here. C'mon. The back door. Stone craziness up front. Couldn't even see Mrs. Betts. I don't know exactly what's happening, but none of it good. World War III maybe, but we don't need to stick around and find out.

Oh no. No.

Take it easy. We're just going to scoot on out of here. Fast and easy out the back.

Please. The pictures. We can't leave Mr. Mallory's pictures. We have to get his pictures.

Don't know if I can get to the box now. Set it in a corner of her office. Couldn't even see the office door so much confusion out there.

We have to try, please. I'll go. I should be the one going to get them.

You go on out back to the car. Here, take the keys. I'll get the box some way.

No. No. No. I'll go with you. I'm not staying here while you take your life in your hands up front. You start the car. I'll get the pictures. Nobody will bother me.

How you know that, girl. It's insane out there. A mob. Who knows what anybody might do. I'll go.

We'll go together then. Because you're not leaving me behind and I'm not leaving you and we can't leave without the pictures.

A shot. Outside, inside. More screams. Glass breaking. Heavy stuff slamming down. Is Wardens' front door still on its hinges. Is the mob busting through windows, walls. Stampeding to get in or to get out.

He'd pushed her down, thrown himself on top of her. Her heart pounding. Fists digging. Is she fighting to get up or to get on top. Wrestling, then motionless, gripping each other tighter. Sprawled out on the floor like teenagers trying to sneak a little quickie in this room for viewing the dead. Yes, he thinks that a moment, flesh of her cheek pressed to his, her soft hair, warm breath, her racing heart and urgent hands. Smell of her perfume he knows will stay in his clothes.

Wardens coming apart. Dozens of bodies battering the small space only a few at a time can squeeze through. In minutes like hours it's over. A sudden stillness in the building. Feeling foolish on the floor. Scrambling up. Time out. Step away, step back. Like boxers staggering for a neutral corner. Time the fuck out.

She's smoothing her black dress, her hair. Figures he better try the same, give himself something ordinary to do. Then a shot outside and the crowd's driven in one more wild wave against Wardens, hammering, knocking, breaking shit, as if everybody wants back inside. Then silence again. Mrs. Betts's voice. Help. Help. Jesus Lord, won't somebody please help me.

Her chair's on top the desk. Lying on its side, the gray swivel post of it looking like the spine of some broken animal poking from its guts. File cabinets overturned. Broken glass, framed pictures and certificates, paper, coffee cups, pencils and pens litter the floor. Long-stemmed yellow flowers spill from a blue vase shattered on the desktop. Water drips. Mrs. Betts under the desk. Was the chair stacked for more protection.

You all right, Mrs. Betts. It's us, Mrs. Betts. Mr. Mallory's people. It's okay. Everybody's gone. You can come out from under there now.

No. They're coming back. Coming for the Truesdale boy. That's what started it. One came running in here hollering *Blue coming. Blue coming.* And God help us, Blue rules. Rules us all. Said they're coming and nobody better be here in their way.

Lock up what you can fast and c'mon with us, Mrs. Betts. We came for the box I gave you. Over in the corner. I'll grab it and we're out of here. C'mon, Mrs. Betts. Forget about locking up.

Nothing to lock. Somebody wants in they're coming in. Where the damned cops when you need them.

Where's the cops. I called the police. I spoke to them yesterday. Begged them to come a half-hour ago. Half-hour ago when I saw this mess starting up. Little hoodlums come in carrying guns. How am I supposed to stop them. I try to help. Do my best to help the families. Bury half them out of my own pocket and look. Look around. See what they've done. Forty years in this building. My God. My God. What's happening to us.

Please, Mrs. Betts. Take my hand. Let's go.

Help her, babe. I'll bring the box.

Sweet Lord Jesus. Look what they done. Look at us. Running from our own children.

Before I had the pleasure of making your acquaintance, John Africa, I did a lot of walking alone. Strange habit for a one-lunged, one-legged man, but walking improved my spirits, perhaps even strengthened my bad leg. Trekked all over the city. One day I found myself on a pleasant street, big elm trees, well-kept homes set back from the sidewalk, each with its green lawn, the kind of street that causes you to doubt a little bleeding corner of the city like ours exists just blocks away. I glanced down and saw a dark something crushed and dead in the grass border along the curb. Could have been a bird or small rodent; whatever it once was, it was well on its way to being something else. The instant I saw it I knew I'd seen it before, that I'd been on the street before and had noticed the dark shapeless shape before and had asked myself some of the same questions I was asking again — how and why and what had the carcass been before it wound up as a blot in the grass. But none of those questions the most interesting one for me.

What I really wanted to know was, did I remember and then see or see and then remember. Had I remembered the dead thing was there and my memory of it caused me to look for it and find it or had I noticed by chance a dark shape passing through the corner of my eye and seeing it brought back the memory of seeing it before.

On my long, solitary walks I would worry questions like that for hours. Even though thinking about them never got me closer to an answer. Even though I knew an answer wouldn't matter very much if I found one, would it.

Know just what you mean, Mr. Mallory. It happens to me. A question sneaks in my head and takes over. Says, Hey, figure me out. Not giving you no peace, sucker, till you do. Lotta times ain't no big question. Not nothing worth spending my time puzzling over. But it gets me. Like a dumb little piece of music I can't stop humming to myself. Stuck going back and forth with it knowing I ain't never getting to the end.

On the other hand, remember what you told me about blues-singing and picture-taking. You know. Holding something locked up in your mind to keep it the way you want it. You being the baddest blues singer in the world long as you don't open your mouth. I thought and thought about what you said and all that thinking wasn't a waste of time. Come to me that the system . . . okay, not the system, I know you don't approve of that word, so it come to me that white people, okay, okay . . . there you go shaking your head . . . the *mostly* white people then who own this city and run it got an idea in their heads about us, us African people and people like us who ain't white and don't own shit nor run shit. The whites got an idea about us and won't let the idea go. Can't let it go. Scared to let it go.

See what I mean. I come to that conclusion thinking about what you said. They got a picture of African people locked up in their minds and nothing's gon change it. Cause they don't want to change it. Sitting pretty believing what they want to believe. Why they gon change. Sitting pretty's a helluva lot easier than dealing with what's out here. Easier than dealing with us.

Am I making any sense to you, my friend. Hope I am cause you the one started me thinking this way. Thinking how people go in circles. Lock themselves up and swallow the key. Ones on top think they the best people in the world and everything all right, just the way it's spozed to be. Sad thing is how many of us on the bottom believe that shit. Shame is how many of us still sitting at the system's table and starving. Or busting a gut to get there. Shame is we're sitting here exactly the way they got it fixed up in their minds. Shame on us. We just as sick as they are, staying put where they put us. Forgot we got minds of our own. Forgot we don't have to think what they think.

Move's about not standing still. Move's about biting the damned hand calls itself feeding us.

Hope I'm around to see the day.

Hold on, my friend. Won't be long now. Everybody's way past disgusted with everybody else's foolishness so something's got to give. War about to break out on these streets. Not no slow smothering invisible war, neither. People will have to take sides. I been knowing it since that traitor Wilson started coming around. I ever tell you about him. Got a quick minute. He's a pistol. A regular pistol.

First time I seen Wilson I knew he was going to betray us. Maybe in a minute, maybe a couple years down the line. Just a matter of time. Knew he wasn't trustworthy cause ain't nothing inside him. Say he want to help black people. Damn. How he gon help people in the village when he can't help his own pitiful self, coming round here in holey blue jeans and a ratty T-shirt looking like death warmed over and nothing inside the boy but bad breath.

If this trifling dude the kind of person the system sending through college and turning out of goddamn graduate school, no less, to rule the world, shit. Wasn't a matter of *when* the system gonna fall, the motherfucker's already on its rotten back, all four legs stiff and this white boy one the maggots crawling out.

I wonder sometimes if he really started out thinking he could help. And who did he believe he was helping. Didn't like his own kind. Turned on them, but found out he didn't like black no better. Problem was he hated his own self. Maybe he dreamed up some idea African people better. Maybe he hoped we'd like him more than his own people liked him. Treat him better. Figured he could be a big fish over here in this little pond with us grateful little fishes. Whatever on his mind, when he start coming round, you sure knew better than to trust him. Grinning up in your face. A glass man. You could see right through him. Skittery kind of guy subject to break up in pieces you holler *Boo* real loud.

Tall, skinny guy, soft hands, a smirk on his lips, light hair, flat eyes, cold eyes don't change no matter what the rest his face doing. Eyes running over you with that cold, flat look like he's a clerk checking numbers on boxes and don't care if pieces of his mama're in the boxes.

Trying to jive me. Tell me I'm someone special. Said the world needed to hear my message. Like I'm some prize ho he's turning out to make us both rich. I never trusted him a minute, but I let him believe he was using me, lapped up the honey he spread round, followed it right to the ambush I knew he was setting up. Even if he caught me, knew he couldn't hold me.

Said he wanted to make my words into a book. We'd sit for hours, me talking, him asking questions and writing down, so he said, my every word. Book got fatter and fatter. He'd say wonderful. Terrific. Profound, truly profound. Say he never heard nothing like that from his professors over at the university. Nothing like this in the textbooks. Bullshit like that, you know. Called me a genius. A savior. But them same cold, flat eyes no matter what's coming out his mouth.

Come down to him wanting to suck my dick is what I figured at first. Got to be some reason he hangs around, keeps coming back. Wasn't pussy. I can tell pretty quick from my days in the street when a guy's not interested in women. Definitely not women for this joker and not men neither I realized after a while. To this day I don't know what turned him on. Unless it was lying to people kept him going day to day.

We'd sit in his apartment, second floor in one of those big houses at the edge of the Village where college students live. Sit till two and three in the morning, a candle on the table between us, jug of red wine on the floor for me, him like some god-damn owl behind his thick glasses. Me talking trash, him scratch-scratching, supposed to be writing down my every word. Every now and then a car blaring loud music rips down the street, maybe a drunk gang of students hollering and giggling pass under the window, fridge cutting on and off, a radio in the building pumped up for somebody's favorite song, but mostly I remember quiet, a long, empty quiet like a cemetery at night and you the only live soul in there and wind's howling but it's quiet too, quiet past quiet to something quieter. Felt like I could spill my guts. Tell all my ugly secrets and sweet secrets, tell it all because nobody's listening. Nobody cares. Everything I'd say just a little bit of noise the quiet eats up. A time to say I'm sorry to everybody I ever hurt. Time to forgive them that hurt me. Time to promise to do better.

Course I didn't say nothing like that. Just told the fool what he wanted to hear.

How'd I know what he wanted to hear. It was easy. Told you he was a glass man. He wanted to hear anything. Everything. Anything better than that bunch of nothing inside him. Told you he was one empty-gutted white boy. So I just shoveled shit. Old shit, new shit, whatever came into my mind. Some of it wasn't all that dumb, you know. I mean in the dark, getting close to daylight, a nice buzz and I'd get on a roll. Spout stuff I didn't even know I knew. Stuff sounding pretty hip to me at the time. Trying to entertain my own self, you know. Way-out shit. Not for his benefit cause I knew what I said didn't mean nothing to him, one way or the other. Just words. Just crazy nigger talk to put in a book and sell.

He was hungry, hungry, starving for whatever I fed him. Wanted to feel something inside but he didn't know how. Too scared. Scared of what might happen to him if he woke up one morning and had to deal with flesh-and-blood people. Not words, not books. Deal with you and me.

He was smart enough to know books wouldn't fill the hole in him. But here he was trying to turn me into a book. The Philosophy and Opinions of John Africa. Now what kind of sense does that make. Maybe he did want to suck my dick. Maybe I liked the idea of him on his knees in the dark begging me to turn him on. He thought he was slick, flattering me, making me feel good about running my mouth all hours of the night. Had me halfway believing I might be some kinda prophet, some kind of wise man or holy man. Brought me presents. Let me crash on his couch when I didn't have nowhere else to sleep. For a while I think he just might have talked hisself into believing I was Jesus or John the Baptist. Like if he listened hard he might hear the truth. Just might walk away with his belly full.

Bound to betray me, betray the Movement, if I gave him what he wanted or not. Because he wouldn't know the real thing, couldn't tell life from death if life jumped up and bit him. Too empty. Couldn't handle the real deal. A fucking ghost in his jeans and nasty T-shirts. Ghost with b.o.

He was working for the police long before they scared him into dropping a dime on us. Boy born working for the pigs. A natural-born traitor and informer. System breeds them by the ton. And it just takes one to fuck things up. He's the reason people afraid to talk truth to one another. Always got to worry there's one like him in the crowd. Listening in. Ready to carry your business just ex-actly where you don't want it to be. Might be him you pour out your heart to. Might be him hears you curse the system. Him eavesdropping, taking down your confession in his notebook. Him always in the way so you don't say shit. Him inside your head so you can't talk to yourself in private. Can't say you're sorry. Can't say what you truly feel. Everybody walking around with their lips and hearts sealed tight. System's bullshit drowning everybody.

She's puttering around the room in the house on Cassina Way in the half-light thinking if this were a storybook and storybook end-ings could come true this is as good a place as any to end it. With the promise of new life in me and me thinking about how nice it would be to read a story with a happy ending to a child. A story that would make a new little Robert or Roberta, a new Martin or Martina smile. No new little ones inside me. No. No. No. New life in me can't be babies now. Not babies growing inside me, anyway. Maybe one day a baby we can give a name to and raise. Too early now for names, for new life so small and light to carry the weight of a name when it doesn't even have feet yet. Or arms or eyes. When we get down to serious deciding about a whole lot of things, then maybe we can start picturing names, listening to how they sound, my name for instance I bet he'll say, changed for a boy *Kassim* or my name period *Kassima* for a girl baby but it's too soon except for seeing how names might sound said inside. Names with their weight and noise too much for a little one's shoulders who doesn't even have shoulders yet. Fins and gills first they say. Inside of you you thought sometimes a fish, sometimes a bird, swimming or flying, you can't tell which, both, bird or fish depending on how you look at the pattern of brown and black and tan painted on the African gourd he gave me for my birthday.

Thirty-five years old and in less than a year a husband dead in prison and two sons killed in the killing streets but here I am where I am, in a place I would have promised, would have sworn, I'd never be, loving a man and carrying the chance of more life inside me.

No way it was going to happen. No way could I have known because that afternoon in Wardens sounded like the end of the world. We'd got that lady Betty or Betts whoever she was, poor woman, into her car and she'd drove off and we were about to be gone too, had got to the end of the gravelly alley runs along Wardens from the parking lot behind the building to Homewood Avenue. Got right there to the corner at the homemade SLOW sign where the alley meets the street and here they come stopping traffic, blocking the intersection, a whole troop of boys marching down the middle of Homewood. Blue everywhere. All wearing blue. A blue wave in front of where we were stopped. Couldn't move the car except backwards. Couldn't do anything except watch these boys come flying over the sidewalk, up the steps into Wardens.

Scared me, I'm not ashamed to say. They were hollering. You could see guns. Scared me and turned me ice-cold too. Cold and if somebody could have grabbed down inside me and pulled out my heart it would have burned off their fingers. Those wild blue boys mize well be dragging my sons by the heels behind them. That's what I saw when they tore into Wardens. Mad enough to jump out the car and fight them all.

They run everybody off. Run off Red even though it was a Red in Wardens and they stick by their own. Blue coming down in full force what the jungle telegraph said and sure enough, here they come decked out in their colors, blue, blue, blue. Had the nerve to call her on the phone, that Mrs. Betts, and tell her they was coming. Peewee runners spread the word on the street. Blue coming. A holiday, you'd think. Street full of young people following the blue parade.

Red boys didn't want to die that day. Everybody knows when it comes to who's boss around here it's not the grown people, not the cops, not God. It's Blue. Red a fly Blue swats when Blue gets tired of Red buzzing round. And that day Blue out to make a point. Teach a lesson nobody would soon forget. In a swatting mood. Marching then flying down the street shoulder to shoulder like an army won the war. No Reds in sight. No cops. Blue's day. Blue rules.

They came for the dead boy in Wardens. He shot the wrong person. No rest in peace for him. Could see it happening right out the car window. Like on TV or the movies.

They sweep into Wardens, sweep out carrying a casket. Lift it high. Lots of arms lifting. Crush it on the asphalt. Another casket right behind the first one and bust it wide open too.

People say some spit and peed on the dead boy. Somebody said one dropped his baggy trousers and shit, but I didn't believe that. Say the leader shot the boy some more. I did hear shots. Big, gaping holes in the casket like cardboard ripped up people say. Tearing up what was left of that poor child's face. How could anybody be so mean. So full of hate and nastiness. I couldn't see much after the caskets broken in the street and Blue closing round doing all the nastiness they could think to do. Couldn't help but remember them kicking my boy when he was dead on the floor. Couldn't help thinking of them gathering round me saying how much they loved my sons, soft-soaping me with a lie about Kwami shooting hisself playing Russian roulette with a loaded gun when I knew damned well it wasn't true. Calling me Mom and doing hand signals over Marcus's coffin.

I'm so worked up and sick inside and mad jammed up in a car with so much bad stuff flashing back, so much bad right in front of my eyes, I'm losing track of what's out there and what's just in my head, just cold and trembling and pictures in my mind taking me back, way back, deep back in my sorrow and anger and pain. Took me a minute to wipe the tears out my eyes, blow my nose on one his Kleenexes before I stop shaking and realize they got Mr. Mallory out there in the street.

Had to be. Who else it gon be. One in A. One in D, he said.

I said, Bring the pictures. Don't know why I said it, but I did.

Bring the box of pictures and he sure heard me and heard what was in my voice and we're out that car in a hurry headed for the center of the trouble out there on Homewood Avenue.

I knew some of them. Some had been to my house. Others must have known who I was. Knew what happened to my boys, to me. Some of them anyhow. They remember their own and they'd seen me at Wardens for my boys' funerals. Spoke to me. Tried to help. Comfort me. Patted my hand. Mom. I'm sorry, Mom. We loved him, Mom. We ain't letting them get away with this. Don't worry, somebody gonna pay, Mom. They knew what they'd done to me twice, knew my little fame for losing double so they moved out my way. Some did. Others I had to keep walking up on them in my black dress, their mother, big sis, wife, cousin, aunt till something had to give, me or them, and I made it clear in my eyes, in my walk, straight and hard and in a hurry, it wasn't me giving way that day heading straight for Mr. Mallory's coffin. Some moving aside so we could pass and me walking and talking softly *thank you* and *excuse me* or louder *move out the way, please* and him with the box of pictures in his arms behind me.

Stop. Stop, goddammit. Stop. I'm yelling now at the top of my lungs at the few around the sideshow of Mr. Mallory. Move back, move away. Don't you know who he is. Stand back youall. Don't you dare touch him. Leave him and that coffin be. You ought to be ashamed of yourselves. Bothering that old man. Don't you see who he is. Don't you see yourselves.

He's beside me again and we're staring down at Mr. Mallory again, not through the wood lid of a box this time but down on his gray, wrinkled face, his face not younger, old, older than he'd ever been, older than anybody needed to be, because his casket cracked wide open and the light of day streaming in and him lying there, part in, part out, his bad leg draped over one edge like he tried to crawl out but couldn't, the bad leg too weak to make it over the split-up side. Him naked as the day he was born because they don't waste a suit unless you ask and pay extra and guess he didn't, all he got a shroud, a plain old bed sheet really all it was, I could see now that's all you got for decency's sake since the coffin supposed to stay closed anyway like he asked for and thought he'd get. Him laying naked, half in the busted coffin, half in the street, him way past caring I hoped and me without the slightest idea what to do.

I look over at him with the box in his arms and tears almost in his eyes too. What we gonna do. What the fuck we spozed to do.

And they say I reached over and snatched the box and stood taller than anyone would expect a shortish person like myself to stand and raised the box which wasn't light and dumped the pictures at Mr. Mallory's feet. They say the pictures floated down like snow beside the coffin. I think I shook and poured to get them all out fast but I can't really say for sure. Don't remember much else. They say I started shouting again when the pictures falling.

Look. Look what you've done to him. Look what you done to yourselves. Look. Look.

I remember grabbing up the yellow envelope of negatives. Don't remember much else.

They say I talked, preached they say but I don't remember any words, what I remember is kneeling down beside him, kissing his rough, icy cheek and hunching my body over the smelly coffin so no one could hurt Mr. Mallory and him dropping down, holding me and a voice whispering to me don't worry, everything's going to be all right.

Guess I probably did preach. From my anger. My hurt. My love for those boys. For him and Mr. Mallory and I don't know what else. Don't remember much of what I said but remember once I got started I couldn't stop and wore myself out saying it. Then some of them started coming up, looking at us beside the coffin, looking at the pictures all over the ground, picking up pictures, looking at them, looking at each other, handing them around, talking, walking off with pictures in their hands. Who knows what they were seeing. What they said. Who knows what they thought. And that was the beginning of the end of the worst part of that day.

Zugunruhe: A Postscript

(One last snapshot somebody shot of the back of Mr. Mallory's head underground in the bus terminal beneath center city to answer the question: Why at his advanced age did he leave Philadelphia for Pittsburgh . . .)

         a city, built on hills like Rome, in the crisscross groin of three rivers, Allegheny, Ohio, Monongahela. At his age, why not. What's to lose. Uncle Sam's check works everywhere. One city as good or bad as another. Or no city. A patch of wilderness where he can lay his old body down. Bop-bop-a-loo-bop. *Been so lonesome/just on account of you.* Why can't you just crawl inside a song when your time comes. Bundle up in a song top to bottom, ride to sleep in it, a bother to no one, instead of ending up under some bridge or over a grate or in a cardboard packing crate. Nobody never even knowing you're in the song of your choice when they sing it.

Pittsburgh a city where he knew somebody dead. And that's another good reason. Gives him a history there. He wouldn't be a stranger, not a newcomer or johnny-come-lately. Hey, Gus. You come lately. How you doing, soul.

Well, I'll be. If it ain't Private First-Class Martin Mallory. Didn't think I knew your first name, did you. Could be General Mallory, long as it's been since I seen you last. A coon's age. A peckerwood's age. Gimme some skin, some amen, General Private.

And Gus carries him to Jazz at the Crawford Grill, Seagrams boilermakers with Iron City nips in Birdy Dunlap's Hurricane and they slide by to holler for the Homestead Grays featuring Josh Gibson and Cool Papa Bell playing the best baseball in the world and party after-hours at the Loendi Club on the Hill and dance Sunday in the heat of the Barn in South Park, and swoop in gangster clean to break Gus (no relation) Greenlee's bank and afternoon tea with the light, bright, siddity Frogs, all those sweet things Gus lied about in Italy during the war that wasn't true either, except, except if you were there, you know what I mean, you had to be there didn't you and then it's too true, too sweet and deadly and always too true, too, too, too, too Tootsy goodbye, too too Tootsy don't cry I'm on my way Gus, save one for me, be there soon's this Greyhound puffs over the mountains through the holes cut in the hills. Home again, home again. Jiggedy-jig.

Sunday, August 10, 1997 — Naples, Maine